Sexy Beast VI

Also by Kate Douglas:

Wolf Tales

"Chanku Rising" in *Sexy Beast*

Wolf Tales II

"Camille's Dawn" in *Wild Nights*

Wolf Tales III

"Chanku Fallen" in *Sexy Beast II*

Wolf Tales IV

"Chanku Journey" in *Sexy Beast III*

Wolf Tales V

"Chanku Destiny" in *Sexy Beast IV*

Wolf Tales VI

"Chanku Wild" in Sexy *Beast V*

Wolf Tales VII

Also by Lydia Parks:

Addicted

Devour Me

Also by Anya Howard:

Submissive

Sexy Beast VI

KATE DOUGLAS
ANYA HOWARD
LYDIA PARKS

APHRODISIA

KENSINGTON BOOKS
http://www.kensingtonbooks.com

APHRODISIA BOOKS are published by

Kensington Publishing Corp.
850 Third Avenue
New York, NY 10022

All Kensington titles, imprints, and distributed lines are available at special quantity discounts for bulk purchases for sales promotion, premiums, fund-raising, and educational or institutional use.

Special book excerpts or customized printings can also be created to fit specific needs. For details, write or phone the office of the Kensington Special Sales Manager: Kensington Publishing Corp., 850 Third Avenue, New York, NY 10022, Attn: Special Sales Department. Phone: 1-800-221-2647.

Aphrodisia and the A logo Reg. U.S. Pat. & TM Off.

ISBN-13: 978-0-7582-2869-7
ISBN-10: 0-7582-2869-4

First Kensington Trade Paperback Printing: April 2009
10 9 8 7 6 5 4 3 2 1

Printed in the United States of America

CONTENTS

Chanku Honor

Kate Douglas

Foreword

They live among us, often unaware of their true birthright as they try to exist in a world that, in many ways, forces them to abide by laws and customs contrary to their nature. Ruled by a powerful libido, by an innate sense of honor and a loyalty to their own kind that is so deeply ingrained it cannot be denied, they often live lives of quiet desperation until their feral nature is finally, often explosively, unleashed.

Descendants of an ancient race born upon the Tibetan steppe, they are more than human—they are shapeshifters.

They are Chanku.

1

San Francisco, California

"Hey, Jazzy. What's up?"

"Yo, Deacon. Nuttin'. Just enjoying the sunshine." Jazzy Blue stepped over her buddy's long, bony frame, rapped his head with her knuckles, and flopped down on the ground. She lay back in the warm grass beside him and flung her arm over her eyes to block the glare—as well as any further conversation. It was better this way, when all she wanted to do was think about the dreams.

She felt the ripples of arousal between her legs and wished that particular feeling would go away. That and the itchy skin. At least she could scratch her arms. She couldn't very well sit out here in the park and rub her clit. Sex with the johns hadn't done it for her.

It never had, not since she was a little kid and her pimp had her out working the streets, but that wasn't unusual. Not for a kid who whored to stay alive. Sex was work, not pleasure, but damn it all, she really could use some pleasure about now.

Even Deacon was starting to look good.

She lifted her arm and glanced his way. He'd always felt more like a big brother than a potential lover, but beggars couldn't very well be choosers. It was getting worse, that sense that if she didn't have an orgasm *right now* she'd explode.

The odd thing was, the sexy feelings and all the weirdness seemed to be tied into the strange dreams she'd been having.

Really weird stuff about wolves and tall trees and the sound of animals huffing and growling beside and behind her. She'd been waking up scared half to death, waiting for something wild to pounce.

Of course, camping under a bush on the fringes of Golden Gate Park wasn't necessarily conducive to a good night's sleep, but it was the only place she had after trying to kill the man who'd kept her all these years. The corner of Jazzy's mouth curved up in a grin. It had definitely been one powerful moment, when she'd finally cut loose and attacked the bastard.

Of course, that had been the end of a roof over her head. One does not try to gut one's pimp with a serrated kitchen knife. Made for bad working relations. Crap. She was well rid of him.

All she knew about him was that he'd bought her from a slaver when she was about six and set her to whoring right away. No actual intercourse until she was ten or so, but the pedophiles who wanted to play out their sick fantasies would always disgust her. She'd rather not think about her not-so-pleasant childhood . . . as if she'd ever had a chance to be a kid. Thank goodness she'd always had an active fantasy life. It had given her a way out, even if it was just in her mind.

Jazzy stretched her arms over her head and closed her eyes against the glare. Red flashed through her eyelids and she flopped her arm across her face once more. Images from the dream she'd had last night slipped uninvited into her mind. She felt again the bunch and stretch in her muscles as she'd leapt over a woodland creek in a futile attempt to run down a rabbit.

On four legs. She'd had big paws, a long, bushy tail, and she'd awakened exhausted, as if it had all been true. She wished she could ask the rest of the guys about their dreams, whether they ever had nights like hers, but they'd probably think she was nuts.

Amend that. More nuts than usual. Of course, that's what friends were for, wasn't it? To tell you when you were headed over the edge?

Either that or hold your hand and take the leap with you. *Sanity's overrated, anyhow.* Jazzy heard footsteps and the rustle of clothing. She lifted her elbow from her eyes enough to see who all was wandering by. Matt flopped down on the grass next to Nicky and Beth. It looked like the rest of the guys were hanging out as usual, down here at the memorial garden instead of their old turf over on Stanyan.

The crowd there was just too edgy, always looking for trouble. She used to fit in with them. Not anymore. Now she preferred hanging with the pack: Deacon, Matt, Nicky, and Beth.

And Logan. She couldn't forget Logan.

They fit together almost like family. Like a pack. Logan was the one who started it when he called them a mangy pack of wolves, said they had a feral kind of connection. Jazzy liked that. She could handle being called mangy as long as she got the feeling of being connected to someone.

It was a long time coming.

Maybe that's why she'd been dreaming of wolves and sex. Face it, anything that had to do with Logan was enough to make her horny.

She sat up and yawned, leaned over and picked a long strand of the grayish green grass that grew in clumps around the memorial garden. She ran it between her fingers and popped the thick stalk between her teeth. It was such a beautiful day. Perfect for hanging with her buds, nibbling on sweet grass, and watching the jet trails in the clear, blue sky.

She slanted another look toward Logan. He leaned against one of the slabs of granite that made up the heart of the memorial garden. With his face and all its sharp angles and planes lifted to the warming rays of the sun, he almost looked like a part of the stone. Damn, she could watch him all day. That long, lean body of his moved with a rhythm all its own. He gave her a hot, liquid tingle deep in her gut. Logan was way special.

He was tough, too. And really strong. Older than the rest of them. Kind of scary sometimes, with his head shaved halfway and all the tats. His body was a veritable canvas, covered in some absolutely rad artwork.

Nicky'd said even Logan's cock was covered in tattoos. Now that was something she'd like to see.

Sometime.

Of course, Matt had whispered to her one day that Nicky had studs in his dick, something he called a Jacob's Ladder. Little barbells running from the tip to his balls. She couldn't care less about Nicky's dick, but she couldn't help but wonder about the tats on Logan's.

Was he hard when the guy did it? How much did it hurt? She had a little tat of a flower on her ankle and it hurt like hell to get that one. She couldn't imagine sitting still while some guy stuck needles and dye *there*!

What was it with guys and their parts?

Jazzy turned away from Logan, flopped back down in the grass, and closed her eyes. She scratched at her itchy arms and wished she could just eat Logan up—after she got a look at his dick, of course. That wasn't going to happen. He didn't like it when anyone tried to get close, and checking out those tats would mean she'd gotten way too up close and personal.

"Jazzy? You got any of that cream?"

She blinked and there was Nicky, kneeling so close he blocked out her sunlight. "Your skin itching again?" She sat up and dug into her jeans pocket for the tube of skin cream she'd gotten a couple days ago.

"Feels like I'm ready to crawl right out of it. Just pop myself free of this bod and turn into"—he bared his teeth and growled—"a wolf!" He laughed and took the tube, squeezed a little lotion into his palm. "Sounds good in theory."

Nicky was such a sweetheart. Tall and slim, yet so gentle and quiet with dark eyes and olive skin. She wondered if he might be Indian, or maybe even Middle Eastern. His skin was almost as dark as hers, but right now his arms were covered with red streaks where he'd scratched himself raw.

Just like hers.

Nicky sighed as he slapped the lotion over his long arms. "I feel like a dork using your girly stuff."

Beth flopped down on the grass next to Jazzy and laughed. "That's because you are a dork." She swung her dark hair back over her shoulder and tilted her chin. Nicky snorted and jabbed her with his shoulder. She bumped him back and took the tube from Nicky's outstretched hand. "I need it, too."

Jazzy noticed Beth didn't really look Nicky in the eye. If she did, he'd know for sure how much she loved him. Jazzy knew, but only because she'd guessed. Beth never said a word about her feelings. She was afraid to, Jazzy was sure of that. Beth was really shy, not anything like Jazzy. She kept her chin tucked close to her chest and squeezed a thick spurt of white cream into her hand. Then she handed the tube back to Jazzy. "I wonder if we're allergic to something around here? Your arms are all red, too."

Jazzy chewed at the stalk of grass. She shrugged her shoulders. "Nothing here but grass and trees."

"Hey."

Jazzy swung around at the sound of Logan's deep voice. "Holy shit. Check this out."

When she looked in the direction he nodded, Jazzy felt her skin go cold. Beside her, Nicky went very still but he radiated an almost palpable tension. Jazzy grabbed his forearm. He shrugged her away. She turned him loose and watched the drama unfold.

Montana was nice, but it really felt good to be back in the city. Tala picked up her pace as she headed down Stanyan to Haight, where she planned to cut through the park to check on Keisha's memorial garden. She'd promised, after all.

As if she'd had a choice?

That thought alone was enough to make her smile.

Are the plants doing okay? Is the rock work still in place? Please, don't let there be graffiti . . . like that's all Keisha had to worry about. Still, Keisha had won a national prize and the chance to design the garden, and it was lovely. Planted entirely with grasses native to the Himalayan steppe . . . amazing, the varieties she'd chosen.

The same mix of grasses the Chanku needed to shift.

Only Keisha hadn't yet known of her Chanku heritage. That alone had made her choices special.

Tala reached the corner of Haight and Stanyan. The usual group of homeless youth whistled and made lewd comments. No big deal. She smiled and waved when she walked past the half dozen young men lounging around the street corner.

At another time, she might have been terrified by the suggestive leers and off-color comments, given her small stature and female gender. Since she'd become Chanku, it took an awful lot to frighten her.

Still, it never hurt to be cautious. She held her head up and kept walking. The sun passed behind a small wisp of fog. Tala shivered. Moments later, as she drew near Keisha's garden, she caught the sound of footsteps behind her. Memories of the recent attack here in the park were way too fresh to ignore. Luc, the leader of the San Francisco pack, had assured all of them that the wanted posters were off the Internet and for the moment, at least, no one seemed to be hunting Chanku, but . . .

Tala risked a look back. Two of the young men she'd passed had broken off from the group and now followed her toward the memorial garden. Dressed in black, lips, noses, and eyebrows pierced with metal studs, they both had the glittery-eyed look of chronic drug users.

Rather than risk a surprise attack, Tala turned and faced them. She sent out a mental call for help and hoped like hell Mik or AJ heard.

The larger of the two kept coming until he was well within her personal space. He reached out to touch her hair, but Tala twisted away.

She wasn't afraid, but she wasn't stupid, either. Just very, very pissed off. She raised her chin and glared at the jerk. "Keep your hands to yourself."

"Bitch. Think you're too good?"

Tala heard something moving behind her, but who? She'd only noticed these two and her senses rarely failed her. She heard a low growl, sensed Chanku power—a wolven presence.

An unfamiliar wolven presence.

The kid groping her had his eyes glued to her breast. He grabbed her right arm with one hand, her left breast with the other.

Tala let her legs go limp, using her body weight to help her twist free, but his fingers tightened around both her breast and her arm.

Pain twisted through her body. She screamed in anger.

His friend screamed in fear and took off running.

A flash of gray knocked Tala to the ground. Her head hit the pavement, hard. Lights flashed behind briefly closed lids. She opened her eyes to a dark shape, spinning, snarling. Flashes of red, the coppery taint of blood. Nausea welled up with a rolling wave of vertigo when she tried to raise herself on one elbow.

More snarling and growling, a choked scream.

Another scream, behind her. A woman crying out, "Ohmygod, Nicky! Ohmygodohmygod . . ."

Tala blinked. She was too close to focus. Her nostrils twitched with the thick smell of blood. Lots of blood, and bits of gray still spinning, a kaleidoscope of life and death and horrible sounds that seemed to go on forever.

Sounds that ended in a heartbeat, leaving only silence.

Harsh sobs broke the momentary hush, the cries of the dark-skinned woman who knelt beside her. Who put her hand out and touched the shoulder of a slender young man lying naked on the path in front of Tala.

All around them were pools of blood, and the torn, lifeless body of the punk who had grabbed her. One of the guys knelt beside the body and touched the chest, the side of his neck, the pulse point at his wrist. His movements appeared surprisingly competent, as if he'd done similar examinations before. He raised his head and frowned at Tala. "He's bled out already." His deep voice showed no emotion. "Nicky got both his jugular vein and carotid artery. The kid didn't have a chance."

Tala raised up on one elbow. She shook her head and caught her breath; waited for her vision to clear. "Who?"

"The wolf or this kid?" He stood up. "I don't know who he is, the one who grabbed you. The wolf was . . . is Nicky, our friend."

The young woman kneeling beside her looked totally traumatized. She raised her head and stared at Tala. "He just changed," she said. "He joked about it, but I thought he was only kidding. I didn't believe him. Nicky saw that guy grab you, and he ripped off his clothes and changed." She shoved her knuckles into her mouth and closed off a sob.

Another young woman ran up and wrapped her arms around

the first girl. Two more young men appeared, both of them dressed in black, lips, noses, and eyebrows pierced, arms and hands tattooed, heads shaved in strange patterns. They knelt beside the unconscious youth lying in the trail. The first punk, the one who'd examined the body, stood off to one side, apart from the others, but Tala knew he was one of them.

They'd all come from the direction of Keisha's garden.

The garden where the Tibetan grasses grew.

Suddenly Mik was there, and AJ beside him, and Tala's head was still spinning, though not nearly as badly. The three guys pulled back, cautious, obviously intimidated by the two large men.

All but the first young woman who stayed beside her comatose friend.

"Are you okay? What happened?" Mik touched Tala's shoulder, but his eyes were on the naked young man lying next to her on the ground. He was alive, his chest barely rising and falling with each breath.

"Do you have the car?" Tala glanced up at AJ.

He nodded. "I do."

She held out her hand. AJ grabbed it and helped Tala sit up. She bowed her head a moment against her bent knees while the world spun. Then she looked up at AJ. "We need to take them with us. All of them. Now." Tala touched the shoulder of the young woman kneeling beside her on the path. "I want you and your friends to come with us. We can help you, but not if the police get here first. Mik, can you carry him?"

Mik nodded. The girl nodded as well, but it was nothing more than an automatic response. Her black hair swung like a silken curtain; her eyes still looked glazed.

Her amber eyes.

Mik carefully picked up the unconscious youth and cradled his lanky, naked body gently in his arms. The others watched him, each with a feral gleam in eyes the color of dark amber. All of them shared the same look: the tall, lean bodies, the golden eyes with flecks of green. Tala took the hand of the young woman who'd cried out and gestured to the other girl, who'd walked back toward the garden, still obviously dazed. "Come with us. We'll keep you safe. We'll take care of your friend."

"Why?"

It was the one who'd been playing doctor, a tall, lean man. He appeared to be a bit older than the others, but he wore the same kind of silver studs in his eyebrows, nose, and ears. The same dark, heavy clothing. The left side of his head was completely shaved while hair hung in long tangles from the right. His face and hands, all that showed outside his black shirt and pants and heavy, knee-length coat, were covered in tattoos. He stared at Tala a moment longer. "Why do you want to help us?"

"Because your friend helped me," Tala said, slowly rising to her feet. "And because we"—she gestured at AJ and Mik, and then herself—"we are just like you."

2

_____

Jazzy shook her head to clear the weird sensation of having done way too many drugs, something she'd actually avoided most of her life. Her ears buzzed, her body trembled. She looked around and saw Beth coming back from the garden. Jazzy held out her hand. Beth grabbed it and pulled her to her feet.

Beth had Nicky's pants and boots under her arm. She kept her eyes away from Nicky, and Jazzy wondered if she'd ever seen him naked before now. Even unconscious, curled like a child in the big man's arms, he was surprisingly well built. She'd never have expected a package like that on such a quiet guy like him. She looked closer, but didn't see the studs she'd heard about. His penis lay nestled in its bed of dark, curling hair, unadorned and flaccid.

Jazzy's skin went hot and cold and hot again. She knew she was blushing. Why was she even looking? Now certainly wasn't the time. But her body was still aroused in spite of her fear, and her clit rode stiffly against her jeans. This was all just too weird.

Beth glanced back at the garden where Nicky had changed.

Where all their lives had changed. "Shouldn't we get the rest of Nicky's stuff?"

"Yeah. He'll want it." Jazzy looked at the tiny woman beside the two men, and then she made eye contact with the one carrying Nicky as if he weighed nothing at all. "Be careful with our friend."

The man, an oversized vision of Hispanic and Native American male perfection, merely nodded. He carefully stepped over the bloody and torn clothing and disappeared into the bushes with Nicky's limp body in his arms.

Jazzy grabbed the rest of Nicky's torn and tangled clothing and Beth found a bunch of the studs and rings that had somehow fallen from his pierced flesh. Jazzy straightened up and glanced at the strange woman, who was looking more impatient by the second.

"Okay. I've got everything. I sure hope you can explain what happened." Jazzy hadn't meant to sound so confrontational. These people were here to help them, for whatever reason.

Logan grabbed her elbow, as if he were escorting her to the Oscars instead of the big SUV parked on the other side of a copse of bushes and flowering plants. He didn't say a word, but Jazzy soaked up the sense of his strength and took some comfort in his closeness.

Her head buzzed again, like the sound of bees inside her skull. Nerves. Must be a delayed reaction to what she'd seen. She glanced back, once, at the mangled body lying near the garden. Then she looked up at Logan. His jaw was set, his eyes narrowed. He'd looked so different when he was checking out the guy on the ground. Like he knew exactly what he was doing. Sort of like a doctor examining a sick person.

"What were you doing with that guy . . . the dead guy?"

Logan's head jerked around and his fingers tightened on her elbow. "What do you mean? I didn't do anything."

"You were touching his neck and checking his injuries. You looked like a doctor."

"Someone had to check and see if he was still alive. No one seems to care that a guy's lying dead on the ground back there."

Jazzy frowned. "We all care, Logan. But maybe we care more about Nicky than some fucking punk who tried to molest a woman in the park. Sorry, but he doesn't get any sympathy from me."

"Pretty heavy price to pay for coppin' a feel."

"Not heavy enough, as far as I'm concerned." She tugged her arm free of Logan's grasp. The dead guy deserved what he got and then some. She'd had more than her share of punks trying to cop a feel and way too many had succeeded and gotten away with it.

Sirens screamed in the distance. "Sounds like they're getting closer," she said, to no one in particular.

"Hurry." The woman held the doors open on the SUV. She seemed surprisingly calm, considering the circumstances. The big guy had Nicky laid out in the backseat. He threw a towel over Nicky's midsection to cover up his nakedness while the rest of them packed in as best they could. Deacon, being such a big guy, took shotgun next to the really gorgeous dude; Jazzy got into the second seat that was designed for two passengers, and squeezed in with Beth, Logan, and Matt.

The woman climbed into the third seat in the back near the still unconscious Nicky. She sort of scrunched down on the floor. Then she poked her head around the edge of Jazzy's seat as the one she called AJ slowly drove the car away from the curb. "A couple of you guys, duck down so the cops don't pull us over for not having enough seatbelts. That's the last thing we need. We're just a couple blocks from home."

Beth and Jazzy hit the deck in a tangle of legs. "Oh shit." Jazzy slapped her hand over her mouth, but she still got the giggles. Crap . . . that always happened when she got nervous. Beth just looked totally shell shocked, but she had it bad for Nicky, not that he'd ever noticed her. She had to be worried sick right now.

They drove for no more than a couple minutes when it suddenly turned dark. Jazzy poked her head up and realized they were pulling into a garage. "You weren't kidding. We got here fast."

"Your friend's coming around. Let's get him inside." The lady turned to Jazzy. "I'm Tala, by the way. The big guy with your buddy is Mik, and the cover model behind the wheel is AJ."

AJ flashed her a wide smile. "Cover model? That's a new one."

"Ah, you know you're gorgeous, sweetie." Tala opened the back door and helped hold the towel around Nicky's waist. He was definitely coming around now. Wide-eyed and scared, he jerked his head from side to side.

When he spotted Beth, his eyes closed for a moment. "Beth? What happened?"

"Wait until we get inside. I'll help you." Mik had Nicky in his powerful arms before Nicky even had a chance to protest. Beth followed quietly. Tala led them all up the stairs from the garage, into a surprisingly large, sunshine-bright hallway.

Mik kept going. Jazzy and the rest trailed along behind him. AJ passed them in the hallway and opened a door into what looked like a separate apartment. "Let's put them in the rooms we had for Adam and Eve. I doubt they'll be back anytime soon."

Jazzy nudged Logan in the ribs with her elbow. "Adam and Eve?" she whispered, grinning. He just looked at her and frowned. She ducked her head. He made her feel so damn small sometimes.

"Good idea." Ignoring her stupid comment, Mik carried Nicky through the door, across a large living room, and into a larger bedroom. Tala fluffed up a couple of big pillows and leaned them against the iron headboard. Mik set Nicky carefully on the king-sized bed.

Nicky shook his head, confused, looked down at the towel that had slipped away from his waist, and quickly covered himself. He frowned and glared at Mik. "Is anyone going to tell me what the fuck happened?"

Before anyone could answer, he lifted the towel and stared underneath, then slammed it back in place. "Where's my studs an' rings? There were studs and rings in my dick." He lifted the blanket again, flopped it back down and looked at his chest and then his arms, frowning. "I had a nipple ring. The hole's still there. My tats are all gone!"

Beth stepped forward. She unclenched her fist. Inside were half a dozen metal studs and rings. "These were on the ground after you . . ."

Logan turned toward Mik. "After he what? What the hell happened to Nicky?"

Mik shrugged his big shoulders and grinned. "He shifted. Turned into a wolf. Piercings, tattoos, anything foreign to the body . . . it doesn't make it through the shift." He turned to Nicky. "Your tats are just dust in the dirt now. The ink flaked off when your skin changed. The studs and rings fell out. If you want to put them back, the holes might still be there, for a while, anyway."

AJ started laughing. "When you know Tala better, you'll have to ask her what she lost during her first shift."

Tala elbowed him in the ribs.

"Oomph! What'd ya do that for?"

She rolled her eyes and smiled at Jazzy. "My IUD fell out on the ground. So much for birth control."

"That's all a bunch of crap. People can't turn into wolves. It's physically impossible. Nicky just, he just . . ." Logan took a long, shaky breath.

Jazzy actually felt sorry for him. She wasn't sure why, but for some reason everything Mik was saying made perfect sense to her. Why couldn't Logan accept it? They'd both seen Nicky change. Watched him tear that guy to shreds.

It even helped explain the dreams she'd been having, as if anything could.

Mik glanced at AJ and shrugged. AJ grinned, and suddenly he was taking off his shirt. Jazzy's mouth hung open. The guy really was gorgeous, and he wasn't stopping at his shirt. Before anyone could say a word, he'd kicked off his sandals and slipped out of his jeans.

Okay, so AJ went commando. Jazzy heard Logan's quick intake of breath behind her and wondered if he was reacting to the guy's package or just circumstances in general. Beth moaned, but it was a sound of fear, not desire. Jazzy grabbed Beth's hand and hung on tight, but she didn't take her eyes off AJ.

"What the . . . ?" Matt's voice clipped off when AJ turned and smiled at all of them, and disappeared.

Just like that.

"Fuck." Logan grabbed Jazzy's other hand. Beth fainted and almost pulled Jazzy down with her. Deacon and Matt stood perfectly still. Tala quickly knelt beside Beth.

Jazzy slowly released Beth's limp fingers. Her heart was pounding in her throat. She heard a weird buzzing in her ears and wondered if she was going to throw up or join Beth on the floor. She glanced down at Beth, who was awake now and blinking owlishly, then back at Nicky. Anywhere but at the big wolf sitting calmly on the floor in front of them.

Right where AJ had been. Then suddenly AJ was standing up and slipping his jeans on over his long legs. "It's easier to show someone than to try and explain," he said, as if he'd done nothing special at all.

Beth sat up and shook her head like she was trying to clear it, but she didn't get off the ground. Jazzy reached over and took her hand again. She really wanted Beth to know she understood how she felt.

"You just turned into a fucking wolf." Logan's voice actually shook. Jazzy jerked her head around to see if he looked as scared as he sounded.

Yep. His face was white as chalk.

"So did your friend. And I want to thank you, Nicky." Tala smiled at Nicky as she stood up. "You got me out of a really ugly situation. I couldn't shift without giving our species away, but I doubt either one of those punks actually saw you shift. I imagine the police report will come out that there's a wild wolf on the loose or a vicious dog or something like that, so we'll have to be really careful about running in the park, but because of you, I'm safe and our secret is safe."

"Nicky, do you think you could do it again? Can you shift now?" Mik gazed steadily at him.

Nicky shook his head. "I don't know how it happened. I've been having these weird dreams, you know—running in the woods, chasing rabbits and stuff—so I was joking about being a wolf." He held his hands out in a helpless gesture. "Just now, when AJ shifted, I tried to do it, too. Nothing happened."

Mik nodded. "Probably the adrenaline rush. When you saw that punk grab Tala, it kicked in and instinct took over. It's happened before. To Tala, for instance."

"We don't need to go there," she said. "But don't worry, Nicky. Once you start taking the pills we've got with the nutrients you need to shift, it's going to be a snap."

"I hope so. I want to do it again." He grinned sheepishly. "But this time, without ripping some dude's throat out."

"There is that." AJ finished buttoning his shirt. "One thing we all have to learn is to control our animal instincts. There are times when it would feel so good to just tear into some jerk. You can't do it." He laughed and winked at Nicky. "At least not every time."

"You guys are fucking nuts. He killed a dude and no one cares!" Logan took an aggressive step forward.

What the hell was he thinking? Jazzy reached out to stop him, but Tala wrapped her fingers around his arm and gently halted his forward movement.

Jazzy buzzed with a frisson of awareness that felt suspiciously like jealousy.

"Hey, bro . . ." AJ raised his arms up and stretched, but it was obvious he was doing a little alpha male display for Logan's benefit. "It's cool. We don't treat death lightly. Honest, we really don't, but we do value our packmates a lot higher than some scumbag out to do us harm. As far as me shifting without warning, well, I'm sorry if I shook anyone up, but it's easier to show something like that than try and explain it. I know I about shit the first time I saw Ulrich Mason shift. Without warning, I might add."

Mik, the big guy, laughed. "You and me both. I think it's like a Chanku rite of passage. Scare the crap out of the newbies. Here . . ." He pulled a couple of chairs away from the walls. "Sit. We'll explain."

Tala dropped Logan's arm. If Jazzy'd had hackles, they would have very slowly gone down. She couldn't believe how territorial she felt over him. Logan sat on the edge of the bed beside Nicky. He looked so confused, Jazzy almost felt sorry for him. Tala moved closer to Mik, but she remained standing. As tiny as she was, she barely came to Mik's shoulder, even with him sitting. "It was the memorial garden," she said. "The grasses. They're what drew you to that spot, what helped Nicky shift. You've been nibbling on the stems, haven't you?"

Jazzy glanced at Beth and they both nodded. They all loved the taste of the sweet grass.

"I thought so. We—all of you and all of us—share a genetic identity, one that doesn't manifest itself without certain nutrients. Those nutrients are in the grasses you've been eating. You were probably attracted to the garden by your body's needs for the chemicals in the grass. Your instincts, latent though they are before your first shift, led you to the foods your body needs. They activated a small gland at the base of your brain near the hypothalamus. That's what controls your nature and gives you the ability to shift. You'll also be able to read each other's thoughts."

"That's a bunch of crap." Logan shook his head. "Nutrients in grasses changing our brains? People turning into animals? Mind reading? It's impossible. It's some kind of group hypnosis. I'm not falling for it. I think you people are fucking nuts." He stood up and towered over Tala. AJ and Mik immediately rose to their feet. Logan blinked rapidly and took a quick step back. His legs clipped the edge of the mattress and he sat down whether he'd planned to or not.

Jazzy figured he might be rethinking his stupid moves. He was probably trying to figure out how to get out of this one alive.

Tala just laughed. "No need for a pissing contest, boys. It is what it is. If you want to put a name to your new reality, we are all Chanku. Shapeshifters with a common genetic background that appears to have evolved somewhere in Tibet, on the Himalayan steppe. Hence, the Tibetan grasses giving all of you a kick start."

She turned and grabbed the door handle, then flashed a smile right at Jazzy. "I know it seems weird now, but trust me. You are going to love your new life. It's an adjustment, finding out you're not really human, but if I can do it, so can you."

She winked, and Jazzy immediately felt herself relax. *Not really human? Chanku.* She liked the sound of that. There was a name for what they were. What she was.

She'd never fit in with regular people before, but this . . .

"I'll see if I can round up some clean clothes for Nicky," Tala said. She appeared to be in charge of both the guys. For some reason that struck Jazzy as absolutely hysterical, that tiny little woman bossing two big hunks around.

"Mik, you and AJ find out what you can about our new roomies and what they need. I imagine we're going to have a long list. We have a lot of extra stuff here, but I'll plan to make a run to the store after dinner for anything else if I have to. This apartment has two bedrooms and two bathrooms. There are extra rollaway beds in the closets. You'll find new toothbrushes and other stuff in the bathroom drawers. Condoms in the bedside tables . . ." She grinned. "You guys comfortable bunking together?"

Jazzy nodded, but she couldn't bring herself to look at the bed, or at Logan or any of the others. It suddenly clicked that she was sleeping here tonight. This was all just way too weird.

Last night she'd slept under a bush in the park. She glanced at the bed where Nicky still looked lost and scared, and ran her hand over the smooth spread. She couldn't remember when she'd last slept in a bed with real sheets.

And she'd never, not once, slept with Logan.

Of course, watching the way he'd handled himself with Mik and AJ, she wasn't so sure she wanted to anymore.

He'd played at being the alpha in their little pack. Here, up against Tala's men, he wasn't much more than a mangy mutt.

A very sexy mangy mutt, but a mutt just the same.

Mik interrupted her rambling thoughts. "Okay, you know we're Mik and AJ. Miguel Fuentes and Andrew Jackson Temple, to be more specific. And you are?" He looked directly at Jazzy with those gorgeous eyes of his, and smiled.

And she forgot entirely about Logan. "Jazzy Blue," she said.

"That a real name?" AJ laughed.

"It's the only one I've got." She wasn't about to tell him her very first john had named her. She'd long ago forgotten the name she was born with. It was too foreign sounding and difficult to pronounce. Her pimp liked to keep things simple.

"I'm Chris March. They call me Deacon." Chris shook hands with both AJ and Mik. Jazzy thought that was pretty classy.

"Nicholas Barden." Nicky shrugged. "Just Nicky." He dipped his head, but didn't offer his hand.

"I'm Matt. Matthew Rodgers." Matt sort of scuffed his feet and smiled. Typical. He was even more shy than Beth.

"I'm Elizabeth Garner. Beth." She blushed and chewed her lower lip.

"It's nice to meet you, Beth." AJ held out his hand and she grasped his fingers very briefly, but Jazzy had the feeling she'd rather be far, far away instead of touching the hand of a strange man.

Mik leaned against the door and counted off names. "Okay, we've got Jazzy, Matt, Deacon, Nicky, and Beth." He looked directly at Logan. "What's your name?"

Logan glared at Mik for a minute too long. Jazzy wanted to kick him. "His name's Logan," she said, sensing the rising tension between the two men. "He's really good at acting like a jerk."

AJ laughed. Mik merely folded his arms across his chest. "Got a last name, Logan, or is that it?"

"That's the only name I've got."

"Works for me." Mik sort of dipped his head in acknowledgment. "I think we've got enough clothes and stuff here for you guys to wear. Closets are full and so are the drawers. Everything's clean. Just take what you need that fits. We'll make a run to the store later and add in whatever's missing, and we'll get rooms straightened out for you as soon as we can. For now, take an hour to rest and get your bearings, feel free to explore the place. This is an old mansion we've renovated. Three stories, lots of small apartments like this, though in most of them the beds aren't made up or the closets stocked with clean clothes. We'll have dinner in the main dining room around six. It's another floor up. Stairs at the end of the hall."

With that, he smiled at Jazzy again, spun around, and left the room with AJ.

Jazzy watched the two of them go, and wondered what the hell was coming next.

The door shut with a soft *click*. Logan stood up and immediately began pacing. Nicky raised the blanket again and stared at his crotch. Beth turned around to say something, realized what he was doing, and blushed ten shades of red.

Deacon leaned against the door; Matt sat on the bed beside Nicky and bumped shoulders. "I'd help you put them back, bro, but no way am I touching your dick."

"I'll do it."

Jazzy almost slipped her neck out of joint, turning around at the sound of Beth's offer. "You'd put his studs back in his . . . his . . . whatever?"

Beth nodded, but her usually dark olive skin blushed brick red.

"You'd do that for me, Beth?"

She nodded again.

"I've got a JL, a Jacob's Ladder. At least I had one. That's why you found so many of 'em after I shifted. I used to have barbells running the length of my dick." Nicky stood up and tightened the towel around his hips. He grabbed Beth's hand, scooped up the little pile of silver barbells she'd left lying on the spread, and tugged Beth along behind him. "We'll be in the other bedroom."

Jazzy stared at the door Nicky closed behind him. "Who'd of thought Nicky had a JL?"

Deacon just shook his head and laughed. "Who'd have thought quiet little Beth would offer to put those suckers back in? Especially when they'll just fall out again next time he shifts."

"What do you mean, next time he shifts?" Once again Logan was pacing like an alpha dog on meth. Jazzy realized she was finding him less and less attractive.

"Tala said we're all shapeshifters." She stood up and glared at Logan. "I, for one, believe her. Haven't any of you been having the dreams?"

Logan blinked and looked away. Matt slowly nodded agreement and Deacon gave her a high five. "You, too? And here I thought I was the only one flipping out."

Jazzy nodded. "Yep. Me, too. Dark forests, the sense of running, hunting wild game. It's like some sort of freaky feral memory." She wrapped her arms around her waist and shivered. "I can't wait to do it for real, if you want the truth."

3

Beth followed Nicky into the second bedroom. It was as big as the first one, the colors all dark browns and greens and pale blues. Colors that suited both of them with their not-so-white skin, dark amber eyes, and darker hair.

Nicky sat on the edge of the bed. The towel still covered his nakedness, but he was obviously aroused and there was no way the terry cloth could hide anything that noticeable.

Beth stood in front of him, not quite between his knees but still close enough to touch him if she wanted. She couldn't believe what she'd offered to do for him. Her hands shook so badly she was afraid even to try picking up one of the little silver barbells. No way in hell would she be able to touch him there and actually stick something into a hole in his skin. The whole idea grossed her out. . . .

Turned her on.

Made her wet.

"Are you sure you want to . . . ?"

"Are you sure you want me to . . . ?"

They both laughed. Nicky hung his head. "I couldn't say anything out there but there's something weird going on with me."

"You mean besides turning into a wolf?" She cocked one hip and tried to play it cool, but her whole body trembled.

Nicky shook his head. "Yeah, besides that. I feel like I could crawl out of my skin, like if I don't shoot my load right now I'll explode. Beth, I have never felt so horny in my life. Never, but ever since I . . ." He raised his head and stared directly into her eyes. No way could Beth turn away from the need she saw on his face.

He raised one hand, as if to touch her face, then let it fall to his lap. "Fuck. I'll live if I don't get off, but I did it, Beth. I've been dreaming about running on four legs for so long now that when it happened it felt right. It *was* right. It was me, who I am. Who I should be."

"Did it hurt? I mean, your bones changed and everything, and . . ."

Nicky shook his head. "No. Not at all. It was fucking fantastic!"

"You killed that kid, Nicky. You ripped his throat out, but no one's saying anything about that part of you changing at all. Those people act like it didn't happen. AJ just brushed it off when Logan called him on it."

"I saw that punk grab her breast and everything went dark." He turned away and gazed out the window. "I sort of understand their feelings, though. It's like . . ." He took a deep breath. "That guy threatened a member of their pack and I protected her. They understand that. It's why they got us out of there so fast, so I wouldn't get busted. It's hard to explain, but I see things differently since I shifted. I feel differently about stuff."

He took Beth's hand in his. His fingers were warm and strong. Protective. She felt safe with Nicky. Felt as if she understood him better than the others.

"You do, Beth."

"What?"

"That's another thing that's really weird. I can see what you're thinking. You just thought about how you understand me better. You do."

A cold chill ran down her spine. What other things had she been thinking over the past few minutes? Beth put her hands on her hips and struck what even she considered a defensive pose. "Do you really want me to put those studs back in, Nicky?"

He shook his head and grinned for the first time since he'd changed. "No. They'll just come out again next time I shift."

"I want to watch when you do it. Do you really think I'll be able to shift, too? Tala said we're all able to turn into wolves if we just eat more of that grass. I really want to . . ."

Nicky put his fingers over her lips and smiled. "What I really want you to do is get naked with me." He raised his head and cocked one eyebrow.

Beth burst out laughing. It took her a minute, but she got herself under control and really looked at Nicky. Nicholas Robert Barden. She liked the sound of his name almost as much as the way he looked. Tall and slim with his dark hair and smooth, dark skin, he could be anything from Native American to Middle Eastern. He looked different now, without the studs in his eyebrows and the tattoos that had covered his arms and chest.

Quiet and introspective, he was usually reading a book when he wasn't working. He'd been the first of them to find the garden in the park. The first to chew the thick stems of that weird Tibetan grass.

The first of them to become a wolf.

He'd also been the first and only male she'd ever considered choosing to have sex with. It wasn't like she was a virgin or anything. Her stepfather had seen to that, and life on the streets wasn't always the safest place for a young woman, but she'd never willingly had sex before.

Well, that was about to change. She was twenty-one years old and it was time. Slowly she began unbuttoning her shirt. Nicky's eyes went wide and he pulled the towel tighter around his waist.

"I was . . . I didn't . . . Beth, I was teasing."

She shook her head as she slipped her blouse over her arms and felt her long hair brush her naked shoulders. "I'm not. I've wanted to get naked with you for weeks now, but you never paid me any attention. Whether it's the grasses or the changes in my body . . . or just you, I don't know, but I've never felt so needy in my life. I'm not going to pass up this chance."

Nicky dipped his chin almost to his chest. "You weren't watching very closely if you think I haven't been paying attention."

Beth paused with both hands on the snap of her jeans. She raised her head and he raised his, and once again she found herself falling into Nicky's amber-eyed gaze. "You were?"

He nodded. "I was. Most definitely."

"Oh."

"I don't have any rubbers."

"That I bet I can fix." Leaving her jeans on but unsnapped, Beth leaned over and opened the drawer on the bedside table. It was filled with packages of prophylactics in all sizes and styles. "Tala said we should find everything we needed."

Nicky reached for one of the condoms, but Beth grabbed his wrist. "No. This is my job."

She heard him swallow, saw the tent in the front of the towel twitch as his cock surged in expectation, and her own nervousness fled. Slipping out of her jeans, Beth walked slowly across the room in her bra and panties and turned the lock on the bedroom door. When she turned around, Nicky was pulling back the bedcovers.

Beth shook her head. "I slept in the shelter last night, but I didn't get to use the showers. You might have been a wolf, but you still killed a guy with your teeth. We're taking a shower before we do anything else."

He laughed and held out his hand. When she tugged him to his feet, he let the towel fall away from his hips. She stood dead still and just stared at him. Damn but she wanted to touch him. Wanted to run her fingers along the swollen length of his cock and rub the tip of her thumb over the smooth glans where a tiny drop of white fluid clung to the narrow slit. He'd feel like silk beneath her fingers. Silk and steel.

She held herself back, though. If she started anything at all with Nicky, she'd have to finish.

She really wanted that shower.

Tugging on his hand, she dragged him into the bathroom. It was bright and clean and the shower was huge, with two showerheads and seats built in at both ends. Nicky turned the water on while Beth slipped out of her bra and panties. She wasn't at all nervous, which was absolutely weird. She should be scared to death, getting into a shower with a guy who was as aroused as Nicky. As aroused as she felt.

She stepped beneath the warm spray, and it was pure heaven the way the water pounded over her head and shoulders. She hadn't had a good shower in a nice bathroom since she'd run away from home, and that had been at least four—no, five—years ago.

As if she could forget the night she'd lost her virginity. She shuddered as memories flowed unbidden into her mind, how just three days after her mother's death from breast cancer, the night before the funeral, her stepfather had shown up in her bedroom and demanded that she *service* him.

The word still made her stomach lurch. No matter how hard she'd tried to fight him off, he'd been stronger, and he'd taken her. Violently. Brutally, without any concern for her age or inexperience. Without a care for her grief over her mother's death. Beth always felt as if her soul died that night. Now she existed merely as a wraith among the living, a soulless being without an anchor, without form or substance.

"Beth? Are you okay?"

Blinking, Beth dragged herself out of the old and oft-repeated nightmare. She nodded. "I'm fine. Just got hit with an old memory. You didn't see what I was thinking, did you?"

"No. Too busy looking at your gorgeous body." Nicky smiled and rubbed soap into a thick washcloth. "Why? Old boyfriend?"

She shook her head violently. "No. No, nothing like that. I was thinking of my mother. Of when she died." But she wasn't, not really, and she tried to shove the image of her stepfather's leering gaze as he'd ripped her cotton nightgown off her body and pushed her down on the bed. The pressure of his callused hand between her breasts, holding her prisoner while she fought him. The scrape of steel teeth after he fumbled with his zipper with his free hand and finally ripped it open.

And the pain. The searing, ripping pain of his huge penis forcing entry through tight, dry, virginal tissues until she'd screamed and thrashed and tried to . . .

"Beth!" Nicky's palms held her cheeks and she wasn't sure if he kissed away tears or the water from the shower, but his lips were on her face and his soft words were in her ears. "Why didn't you tell me? I wouldn't have asked you for sex if I'd known."

She raised her head, mortified he'd seen her memories.

"Don't." He shook his head and looked away for a moment. Then he used the washcloth to scrub gently at her arms and shoulders. "It wasn't your fault. You were a kid and he was an adult and an abuser. Don't ever feel guilty, not about something so awful and so totally not your fault. He was dead wrong."

He kissed her again, aiming for her cheek, only this time she turned her head. Her lips met his and suddenly things were so much better. The old memories faded and new ones took root.

Her hips swayed gently toward Nicky's and she felt the hot sweep of the silky tip of his penis against her belly. She clung to him then, cried a little, kissed him again. They washed themselves, turned off the water, and dried with big, fluffy towels.

And then they stood there, staring at one another. Beth was glad, then, that Nicky could see her thoughts. Glad she didn't have to explain how she wanted him but was afraid, how her body needed his touch but didn't know how to ask.

She watched the slow spread of his smile as he reached out and took her hand. His long fingers wrapped around her smaller ones and he tugged lightly. She followed where he led, out of the bathroom and into the bedroom. He had her sit on the edge of the bed, and then he knelt at her feet and gazed up at her.

Suddenly Beth understood the saying, the one about how his heart was in his eyes. That described Nicky at this moment. She saw real love in his amber eyes, felt it in her heart and suddenly, surprisingly, heard it in her mind. Nicky's words, in his voice, but in her head, not her ears.

I love you, Beth. I've loved you since the first time I saw you. I wish I wasn't such a wuss. I wish I had the courage to say how I feel.

You just did. You're not a wuss. I love you, too.

"You do?" Nicky wrapped his big hands around her thighs and stared at her with frightening intensity.

Beth nodded and then she lost it. The tears flowed down her cheeks, dripped onto her breasts, onto the backs of Nicky's hands. She couldn't stop crying, and she couldn't have spoken a word if she'd wanted to.

He moved slowly, sliding up her body until he stood between her legs and towered over her. He was so tall. His young man's body was lean and strong with the promise of more muscle in a few years, but right now he was perfect for her. The perfect lover to bring her back into the world of the living.

* * *

Nick wondered how well she read his thoughts. All of this was so new, so unexpected. This morning he'd wondered what he'd be doing all day, wondered if Beth would be at the garden, if the other guys would hang there, too, where he'd sleep tonight.

Everything had changed. Was changing. Beth's skin felt like silk beneath his hands, still warm and damp from her shower. Her body trembled. He absorbed her desire, her need for him, and turned it back to her, touching her breasts, her shoulders, the firm line of her jaw.

He settled back at her breasts. They were small and firm and so beautiful he wanted to kiss them. Instead, he rolled one of her nipples between his thumb and forefinger, tugging lightly, pinching with just a bit more pressure. Beth groaned. The sound of her need, of her desire for him, sent shivers up his spine and made his dick swell even bigger.

It was so good, this sense of connection. Today when he shifted, his entire world had blown apart. When he killed, it was as if another creature had taken over. The scary thing about it was . . . another creature *had* taken over.

Only it wasn't separate. It was still a part of him. He'd never in his wildest nightmares imagined himself a killer.

Nick gave in to his strongest desire, lowered his mouth to her left breast and sucked her nipple between his lips. Deeper, until he caught it between his tongue and the roof of his mouth and all his confusion melted away. Her nipple peaked immediately, drawing up into a tight bud against his tongue, holding him in the here and now. He kept rolling her right nipple between his fingers and suckling the left, increasing the pressure, sucking harder, concentrating on Beth's taste and texture, thinking only of Beth. Her heart thundered beneath his lips and her blood pulsed fast and hard.

He'd never been aware of the sound of a heart beating, of blood racing through veins and arteries, never experienced the rush of sensation as he felt it now. It had to be from his new reality, his changed existence from human to Chanku, but whatever the cause, Nick loved it, accepted it, welcomed each alteration of perception, each new sensation and experience.

There was so much that was good in this new reality.

Beth lay back against the bedspread and reached for him. He leaned over her so that she could touch him, and she didn't disappoint. She cradled his aching balls in her warm palms and stroked his cock. Gently she teased the smooth glans, ran one soft fingertip over the slit, smoothed the drops of pre-cum and stretched the rib of foreskin with the tip of one finger. It felt so good he wanted to weep, but he raised his head and arched his back, sliding his erection between her fingers.

She slowly rolled a condom down over his straining cock, and smoothed the latex along his shaft. He'd never felt anything so exquisite as the gentle touch of her fingers when she stroked the thin film along his full length. When everything was in place, she smiled up at him and lay back with her legs hanging over the edge of the bed.

She was the perfect height. All he had to do was lean forward and the tip of his cock brushed the fine dark curls between her legs. Her sex pouted, dark pink and shining with her fluids. He touched her softly with the tips of his fingers, spread the swollen lips enough to rest his cock at her entrance.

"Are you sure?" He knew if she said no he'd die, but Beth smiled and nodded. Nick took a deep breath, closed his eyes, and slowly pushed forward.

Damn, she was so tight he worried that the condom might tear, but she was slick with her own natural juices. The soft ripples of her inner muscles pulled him in deeper, until he filled her completely. His balls pressed against the soft curve of her buttocks and he wriggled his hips back and forth for deeper penetration.

He sighed. She whimpered and raised her hips, forcing him even deeper. Nick lifted her legs and rested her thighs over his forearms, thrusting now, rolling his hips and moving in a slow, steady rhythm that quickly increased in tempo.

She thrashed beneath him, twisting her hips this way and that until he raised her legs against his chest with her heels hooked over his shoulders. In this position he felt the hard mouth of her cervix on every downward thrust and knew he filled her completely.

Beth caught his rhythm. Her eyes closed but her smile never wavered. She whimpered softly with the rise and fall of her hips, the steady thrusts as Nick rolled his hips in tune with Beth's silent music.

He shifted his feet then and plunged deep and hard, upping the pace, watching the thick length of his cock disappear between Beth's pink nether lips on every forward thrust. Her dark curls were bathed in moisture and the tendrils clutched at his cock on each outward pull. Her lips had grown puffy and slick, and her clit protruded now, poking up out of the fleshy hood protecting it.

He reached down and found it with the pad of his thumb. She jerked her hips and her clitoris slipped beneath his touch. He spun circles over the entire surface, pressing just enough to make her tremble with each gentle pass.

Shivers raced along his spine and a coil of heat built in his back and balls. His control eroded with each powerful thrust, his heart pounded in his chest. Flashes of light sparked behind closed lids.

He held on, groaning in an agony of desire. The slick walls of her sex rippled and tightened around his cock and for a moment he missed the row of studs that should have given Beth even more pleasure. He'd only had his piercings for a few months, and he'd been celibate all that time.

Waiting for this. Waiting for Beth.

His thumb swirled over her clit and he felt the tightening in her muscles, knew her climax grew close.

Suddenly, she was there. In his mind, in his heart . . . and he was Beth and the thick length of his latex covered cock was bringing her unbelievable pleasure, taking her to unimagined heights. Showing her exactly what she'd missed before.

He thrust forward and felt the clench of his own vagina grasping the hot length of erect cock; he rolled her nipple between his fingertips, and his own nipples peaked.

Building, expanding layer upon layer of sensation, Nick to Beth and back again until he felt the coil of energy strike from balls to cock, felt the convulsive pressure of orgasm as if he were Beth even as he was Nick, plunging deep inside her wet heat.

There was an exquisite moment of pure connection, a moment out of time when he somehow became Beth. When he knew her feelings, her thoughts, her needs, and her fears.

A momentary melding of all he was, of all she was. Before he could fully explore the sensation, the full force of their shared orgasm wiped out all conscious thought. The moment passed and he cried out with the rush of his seed into the condom. Groaned as his legs shivered and quaked.

Gasping, heart pounding, lungs billowing in and out with each tortured breath, Nick slowly eased Beth's legs down along his chest and let them hang loosely over the side of the bed. His legs shook, and he leaned forward before they gave out entirely. Resting his weight on his elbows, he rubbed his bare chest over Beth's taut nipples.

She groaned and arched against him, wriggling her hips.

"Oh, God. Be careful." He laughed, but it was a choked-off, wimpy sound of utter and complete depletion.

"I'm trying to make you big again." Beth giggled. "I had no idea it could feel that good, or I would have been after you before now. Good lord, Nick. That was amazing."

He raised up on his elbows, but thrust his hips forward, sinking back inside her slick channel. "I like that. You calling me Nick instead of Nicky."

She smiled, a slow, secretive woman's smile, and ran one finger down his chest. Then, in a most seductive voice, she said, "Nicky's a child's name. I think we've just proved you're no child."

Laughing, he leaned over and kissed her hard on the mouth. She grabbed him by the back of the head and held him close for a deep, tongue-twisting kiss.

Gasping for air, he pulled away and laughed even harder. "I need to get rid of the rubber before we can do this again."

"Okay, but I'm holding you to that."

Shaking his head, Nick carefully disengaged from Beth's warmth. He was headed for the bathroom to dispose of the condom when someone pounded on the bedroom door.

4

"Ya think they're gettin' it on?" Deacon sat on the floor with his back against the bed.

Jazzy looked up from the magazine she'd been staring at and laughed. "Nicky and Beth? Not if it's up to them. They're both pretty shy."

"Nicky didn't look all that shy tearing out that dude's throat." Logan's soft comment brought Jazzy up short.

"That was so freaky," she said. Her head filled with images she'd been trying to forget. The fear in the kid's eyes. The disbelief. The deadly and utter silence of Nicky's attack, then the snarl and those deep throaty growls . . . and all that blood.

"Well, it's something to think about," Matt said from his perch on the bed near Logan. "Be sure you don't piss Nicky off or he might want another wolf sandwich."

"Nicky? He's our friend." Jazzy leaned her chair back against the wall, going for nonchalant. Inside, her stomach felt like it was tying itself into knots.

"Nicky might be, but what about the wolf?" Logan sat Indian fashion on the foot of the bed. "When you shift, do you think like a person or an animal?"

A loud knock on the door interrupted the silence following Logan's question. Jazzy opened the door and smiled at AJ. "When you're a wolf," she asked, "do you think like a wolf or a man?"

AJ shrugged. "Depends. When we're out running or we've got a task at hand, we're fairly rational. Throw a fat doe or a juicy rabbit into the mix—or a female in heat—and all bets are off. C'mon. Dinner's on. Your friends Nick and Beth will be there in a few minutes."

"Nick? Not Nicky?" Deacon laughed. "I told you. They're gettin' it on."

They climbed the stairs behind AJ and followed him into a huge kitchen–dining room combination with a long table at one end that could have seated at least twenty people. It was set for nine.

Tala and Mik were both in the kitchen. Tala sat on the counter with a glass of wine in her hand while Mik tossed a huge bowl of salad. He wore a shirt and jeans with a white chef's apron and looked totally domestic. For some reason, Jazzy found it hysterical.

The scent of something spicy and Italian filled the air. "I hope you like lasagna," Tala said. "It was the one thing I had enough ingredients for without a huge shopping trip."

"There they are." AJ waved as Nicky and Beth wandered into the kitchen. The two of them held hands.

Deacon jabbed Jazzy with his elbow. "Wish I'd bet cash on that one."

"Shhh." Jazzy bit back a giggle. She hoped like hell she never got that lovesick look on her face. Nicky and Beth looked absolutely sappy.

Within a few minutes Mik had cleared off a long section of

the kitchen counter and Tala set up tons of food and stuff to drink, for everyone to help themselves.

Jazzy loaded her plate with thick slices of sourdough bread, a pile of salad, and a big square of lasagna. Everyone took a seat and started eating right away. No one talked about Nicky's attack, though midway through dinner, Mik glanced at the clock over the sink and turned on a small television for the six o'clock news.

The dead kid in the park was the lead story, blamed, of course, on rival gang activity and dangerous dogs out of control. Tala breathed an obvious sigh of relief. She smiled at Nicky. "Looks like we're all in the clear on this one, but we can't risk another incident like this."

Mik stood up and reached for a big jar of pills on the kitchen counter. "I want you guys to start taking one of these every day. They contain the same nutrients as you've been getting from the grasses in Keisha's garden, just compressed. I expect the rest of you will be making your first shift within a day or two."

"We made some calls," AJ said. "The property I was hoping to take you to up near Mount Lassen is unavailable to us, but I checked with friends and they said we can use their place in the redwoods. It's out of the way, very rugged and wild, a perfect location to make your shift without risk of an unwanted audience. I'm going to talk to Anton, our friend, later tonight and find out what all we'll need to take up there."

"We'll leave early in the morning." Tala took one of the big pills from Mik and swallowed it down with a sip of wine. "Is there anyone who might be worried about any of you? Family or friends?"

Logan carefully set his fork down on his plate. Jazzy noticed that his table manners were impeccable. She'd been really nervous, watching to see how Tala and the guys ate, copying their every move. Logan seemed naturally comfortable at a nice table. Once again she wondered where he came from, who he was.

"We don't know a thing about you," he said. At least he wasn't being confrontational. Jazzy breathed a sigh of relief.

"You're right." Tala smiled. There was absolutely nothing threatening about her, unlike the big Indian guy who hovered beside her.

"Let's see . . . Mik and AJ were cellmates at Folsom when Ulrich Mason, the head of Pack Dynamics, found them and realized they were Chanku. He managed to get their sentences commuted and got them out of prison. They were lovers behind bars and still are. In our society, they are also bonded, which means they are a mated pair."

"It's like being married," Mik said. He got up and stood behind AJ, rubbing his shoulders in a gentle caress. "One thing you'll learn once you make your first shift is that your libido sort of takes over afterward."

"As in, you really, really want to get laid." AJ smiled. He reached up and touched Mik's hand on his shoulder.

"What about you?" Jazzy frowned when she looked at Tala. "I thought you were with one of these guys."

Tala laughed. "I am. I'm with both of them."

Jazzy blinked. "Wow. I'm impressed."

"I was working the streets," Tala said. "It was a crappy little town in New Mexico when my pimp finally got a bit too rough. I stowed away in Mik and AJ's SUV to get away." She gazed at both men with the same sappy look Jazzy had seen on Beth's face. Then she laughed out loud. "They were both so hot, I couldn't make up my mind, so I kept the two of them."

"Actually, she was like a little stray puppy tagging along. We felt sorry for her." AJ's sexy, loving smile spoke volumes, and when Mik leaned over and kissed Tala's cheek, Jazzy felt her eyes well up with tears. To have someone love her like that . . . she blinked away the moisture and smiled.

"What's Pack Dynamics?" Logan stood up and began clearing plates from the table, much to Jazzy's surprise. No one else seemed to notice how out of character that seemed.

But then, she didn't really know his *character*, or anything about him.

"It's an investigative agency founded by Ulrich Mason. He's retired now and living in Colorado, but all of us, including Mason, are Chanku. His daughter and son-in-law run the business. They're the ones using the property up near Lassen. Tia's pregnant and I think Luc wanted to get her away to himself before the babies take over their lives."

"Babies? As in plural?" Beth had a huge smile on her face. Deacon was right. She and Nicky had definitely been having sex if she was smiling about babies.

"They're not positive," Tala said, "but Ulrich's convinced she's carrying twins. Tia's not so thrilled about even a hint there might be a twofer."

"If it was me, I think I'd rather shoot myself." Matt rolled his eyes. "My parents had twin daughters after they adopted me. They were little monsters."

When the laughter died down, Tala said, "Well, Tia would never have horrible babies. She's just the sweetest thing. You'll meet her and Luc before long. Tinker and Lisa, too. Lisa's my sister, Tink's her mate. They've moved over to the main house to be with Luc and Tia."

"They're all Chanku?" For some reason, it made Jazzy feel better, knowing how many of them there were.

Tala nodded. "There are a bunch of us that I know of. Two bonded pairs in Maine, four bonded pairs in Montana—two of them have babies—and a pair in Colorado, the three of us here, and two pairs at the house over on Marina, here in the city. That's twenty-one adults. And of course, now the six of you, which tells me there must be a lot more around."

Mik agreed. "Probably a lot more than we realize. Our goal

is to find as many as we can. One thing we know is that we get our Chanku heritage through the females."

Tala shrugged. "Of course you do. Evolution would obviously pick the smartest and best of a species." She flashed a grin at Mik.

He growled and everyone else cracked up.

"Mik's right," Tala said. "All the offspring from a woman carrying the Chanku genes will be capable of becoming shapeshifters, even if their mother never developed her potential. Whether the father is Chanku or not doesn't seem to matter. It's sad, really, because those that never find out what they are lead such sad lives, always wondering what's missing, why they're never totally happy."

"Horny all the time and never really knowing why." AJ raised his head and looked at all six of the younger ones. "I would venture to say that most of you have had sex when you didn't even like the person, or you've not cared what your partner's gender was, or if you even liked them."

The guys all looked guiltily at one another. Jazzy glanced at Beth and both girls shook their heads.

"I've always hated sex," Beth said. "I was raped by my stepfather and it's never been good for me. Until now." She smiled shyly at Nick. He grabbed her hand and held on.

Jazzy nodded. "I was brought into this country as part of the sex trade." She'd never admitted this to anyone before, not even her friends, but for the first time in her life she felt no shame about her past. If Tala could admit to being a prostitute . . .

"I was six years old when I came here," she added. "At first there were just pictures and lots of touching by disgusting old men, but by the time I was ten I was an experienced whore. I might have been little, but I was old enough to know I didn't like what they did to me. At least I survived. A lot of the other girls died of AIDS."

"You're all lucky to be alive," Tala said. There was no laughter in her voice now. "Thank your Chanku heritage. For whatever reason, we appear to be impervious to human illness. AIDS and other STDs don't touch us. I haven't had a cold since I started on the nutrients, and rarely before. You might have been HIV positive before, but once you started nibbling on those grasses, once the changes started to happen in your bodies, any virus in your system would have been removed by a whole new set of antibodies."

It was quiet around the table. Jazzy felt a new sense of family, even stronger than it had been before, when she'd been part of the group they called the wolf pack.

There'd been no condemnation, not a single negative comment about her and Beth. She glanced at Tala and got a big smile in return.

"For now," Tala said, "we need to see if there's enough stuff around here for you guys to wear. I see Nick found some clothes. That's good. Nothing worse than a naked guy at the table."

Mik patted Tala on the knee. "We do have our standards. Tala happens to think they're too low."

Laughing, Tala hushed him. "We're leaving early in the morning for Anton's place up north. I'm tired. I'd love to skip that trip to the store."

They finished their dinner, talking about the trip north. What it would finally feel like to run on four legs through the towering forests of their dreams.

Somehow, Logan and Jazzy ended up doing dishes while the others went in search of extra clothing. Since his earlier posturing, Logan had grown quietly introspective.

Jazzy liked him a lot more this way.

"You gonna go with them?" Logan started rinsing dishes and adding them to the dishwasher.

"Aren't you?" Jazzy slid the leftover lasagna into a smaller dish and covered it with plastic wrap.

He shook his head. "I don't know. It's all happening pretty fast. We don't know them."

Jazzy stared at Logan. "I don't know you."

"Huh?" Logan straightened up and frowned at her. "You've known me for almost a year. What the hell is that supposed to mean?"

"Just what I said. I know your name is Logan. I know you showed up one day when we were all hanging out on Stanyan. I know you followed us when we moved to the garden in the park, and I know you like to be in charge. That's it, Logan. And by the way . . . is Logan your first name or your last?"

His broad shoulders slumped and he looked away from her. Jazzy's instincts suddenly went on high alert. "Logan? What's wrong?"

"I don't know."

She frowned. "You don't know what's wrong?"

"Don't know my name. Don't know how old I am. Who I am."

"But . . . you're Logan. I don't get it. Isn't that your name?"

He shook his head. "I woke up in the hospital a little over a year ago. I found out later that someone found me unconscious near Glide Memorial Church and called an ambulance. I've got some memories, but they're all screwed up with TV shows and fictional stuff, so I can't tell what's true."

Jazzy wrapped her fingers around his forearm. This time he didn't pull away. Instead he looked directly into her eyes. It felt as if he was trying to talk to her, but without words. She jerked her head and the buzzing in her brain stopped, but she didn't look away. "Your name *is* Logan, right?"

He sighed and shook his head. "I don't think so. It was the name I remembered on the ID tag one of my nurses wore. I needed a name. I took his, but to this day I don't know if it was his first or last name or if I noticed it because it was familiar. When I got better, they discharged me. One of the doctors said my memories should come back at some time, but they haven't. Not yet, anyway."

"Do any of the guys know . . . ?"

He shook his head again. "No, and I don't want you to tell them."

"Why'd you tell me?" Jazzy raised her chin. He trapped her once more, holding her prisoner with the feral intensity of his gaze. The harsh sound of his voice was urgent, insistent.

"Because you're different, Jaz. Because you matter."

Then he blinked, and Jazzy watched him disappear once again into his cocky, all-knowing, and irritating persona. He tugged his arm free of her grasp and went back to rinsing the plates from dinner.

Somehow, she'd ended up in the same big SUV they'd ridden in before, but this time it was just with Mik, Beth, Nicky—who, now that he'd gotten laid, wanted to be called Nick—and Logan. Tala, AJ, Deacon, and Matt were in Tala's smaller vehicle, and they were all headed somewhere into the redwoods of Humboldt County in northern California.

Last night they'd called some guy everyone talked about in hushed voices. He'd told them his cabin would be stocked with fresh food and clean linens, so they didn't have to take much of anything. Jazzy wasn't sure who Anton Cheval was, but he must be someone important to these people. Even Mik seemed to hold him in awe.

Jazzy sat by herself in the middle seat, scratched at her itchy, tingly arms, and stewed most of the way north. Beth and Nick had the backseat to themselves and spent an inordinate amount of time staring into each other's eyes. Made her sort of nauseous, to be honest.

Logan was up front with Mik. They were getting along fa-
mously, now that Logan had dropped his cocky bastard attitude.
In fact, she'd never heard him quite as animated as he'd been
over the past hours while Mik drove north. They'd talked about
the Chanku, the history of their kind. The fact they were so
heavily controlled by their overactive libidos that sex sometimes got in the way of smart thinking.

So what else is new? Jazzy slumped down in her seat and
stared sightlessly out the window. Wasn't that usually the way
things worked? Of course, on the other hand, she'd really been
hoping for something to happen last night, once she knew they'd
have beds and a roof over their heads. She wasn't sure exactly
what, but sleeping on a rollaway in the bedroom with three snor-
ing, farting guys hadn't been it.

She'd sort of had some strange idea of sharing the bed with
Logan, especially since that little window he'd opened into the
real man, but they'd all flipped a coin for the big bed and Deacon and Matt got it—with a row of pillows jammed between
them. She knew Matt swung both ways, so the pillows had to
be Deacon's idea. Like Matt was going to make a move on him
with both Jazzy and Logan in the room?

"Logan? You mind getting that gate? Here's the key."

Jazzy blinked herself awake when she heard Mik's voice. She
must have fallen asleep miles ago, because the scenery sure had
changed and she really had to pee. Logan grabbed the key ring
Mik handed to him and climbed out of the car. He stretched
and then walked around the front and opened the gate. Mik drove
through, followed by Tala's vehicle. Logan closed and locked
the gate and got back in the car.

Jazzy took a good look around her and realized that while
she'd been stewing and napping, they'd left the dry foothills and
entered a thick forest of unbelievably huge trees and monster-
sized ferns like something out of a movie. The air was damp
and foggy, the ground smelled like wet dirt and mushrooms.

A chill ran along her spine when she realized she recognized the smells, the trees, the very essence of this place. "I've been dreaming about this forest. I recognize the way it smells, but how could I? I've never been here before." She rolled her window down and took another deep breath.

Mik glanced back over the seat and grinned broadly before he answered her. "It's something to do with our genetic instincts. The feral part of our nature exists even if we never truly morph into Chanku. We've all had the same dreams. Haven't you ever awakened exhausted, feeling like you spent the night hunting on four legs? Awakened some mornings with a coppery taste in your mouth as if you'd eaten something wild and bloody the night before?"

Jazzy didn't answer him. She couldn't, not when her mind was spinning with remembered dreams and events that had never really happened.

Or had they? Might she literally have run as a beast in her dreams? Left her physical body and hunted fat rabbits in some other dimension? For some reason, the concept didn't feel all that impossible.

At least no more impossible than turning into a wolf. She scratched at her raw, itchy arms.

"That's going to go away, too," Mik said. "The itching starts about the time you're ready to make your first shift. I swear it's from your bones wanting to jump out of your skin. Once you shift, the sensation seems to just disappear."

Jazzy glanced at her raw, itchy forearms and hoped Mik knew what he was talking about.

Many gates later, they pulled into a small clearing with a perfect log cabin in the midst. Unbelievably tall trees blocked out all but the finest rays of sunlight, and huge ferns grew right up to the front porch.

There were signs of recent construction, but the grounds were immaculate and the new wood already showed signs of incipient growths of the thick moss that seemed to be everywhere.

"Anton told me he's had extra rooms added on, mainly to accommodate his packmates and the babies, so there should be plenty of space for all of us." Mik climbed out of the car and stretched. It had been a long drive from San Francisco, over six hours with a brief stop for lunch.

Tala pulled her smaller car into the clearing and parked. They all got out, craning necks and looking skyward. Jazzy shivered and rubbed at her arms. She'd had another of those big pills this morning, and already she felt different. Sound seemed to envelope her. After a moment, it suddenly dawned on her that she heard the beating of hearts, the perceptible rush of blood.

She noticed a faint buzzing in her ears, as if many voices spoke at once. When she tried to concentrate, the sound grew louder but the voices were less distinct. Shaking her head, she grabbed a small bag of borrowed clothes out of the back of the SUV and followed Beth and Nick up the front steps.

AJ had the door unlocked and they all trooped in. "We're lucky Tinker and Lisa had a set of keys to this place," he said. He pulled the window blinds open. Light streamed into the cabin.

The living area was fairly compact, with a small kitchen and great room connected beneath open beams. A standard picnic table filled the opening between the two rooms, rustic but perfectly appropriate for a cabin in the woods. One doorway led off to a large bedroom and bath; another, newer-looking door opened into a hallway with four matching doors along its length.

"AJ, Mik, and I will take the master bedroom. You guys can split the extra rooms up however you want. You're on your own. I'm beat and I'll be taking a long nap, folks. If you get hungry, Anton said the caretakers would leave the refrigerator stocked." Tala stepped back into the great room. "Looks like just four rooms and Anton said each has its own bathroom, so someone's going to have to share." Tala grinned when she said that and glanced toward Beth and Nick.

They both blushed. Jazzy decided this might be interesting. Someone else would have to double up, too. She wondered who that might be.

"Jazzy and I will take this room. Right, Jazzy?"

Logan's deep voice sent shivers along her spine. She turned and looked at him in amazement. He'd not said a word to her the entire trip.

"We'll see," she said. She walked past him and opened the first door. Nothing fancy, but definitely comfortable with a king-sized mattress on a simple frame, bedding folded on top and a door leading to a private bathroom. "I'm claiming this one all for myself. Maybe I'll want to share, later." She shrugged. "Maybe I won't."

"Beth and I will take this one."

Nick grabbed the door next to Jazzy's. She didn't wait to see what the others did. The bathroom beckoned.

5

Tala followed Mik and AJ into their room. It was by far the largest and nicest, designed as it had been for Anton's use. It felt weird, taking over his personal space, but he'd been more than generous when she'd called and asked about using the cabin.

"I think Anton's really jealous that we're here with six new Chanku and he's stuck in Montana." She glanced over her shoulder at Mik. His eyes glistened with what looked suspiciously like tears. "What's wrong?"

"I was just thinking how close we came to losing him. He almost died last month."

AJ slipped an arm around Mik's waist. "He did die last month. We brought him back. Don't forget that. We all learned something from that mess."

"I know I learned how much I love the man. How much I admire him. He was willing to give everything for us. I've often wondered if I have that kind of courage." Mik walked past Tala and sat on the edge of the bed. "Are either of you as nervous as I am about what we're doing?"

Tala sat next to Mik and bumped her shoulder against his

arm. "Nah. Nothing to it." She laughed. "Scared shitless, if you want the truth. What if something goes wrong?"

"I wish we could have taken them all straight to Anton, but Keisha said he's still too fragile. She wants him to spend some time recuperating before he takes on a project."

Tala leaned over and kissed AJ. "I have an idea of what Keisha's idea of recuperating is. She's finally interested in sex again. Lily took a lot out of her."

"She's a cute little thing."

"You sound wistful, big guy. Got the baby blues?" AJ sat on Mik's other side and threw an arm over his broad shoulders.

Mik turned and grinned at AJ. "When it was just you and me, I never thought of babies. Now we've got our very own breeder."

Tala jumped off the bed and spun around with her hands on her hips. "Don't you go looking at me that way!"

AJ frowned. "You don't want babies? I thought you loved babies."

"I do love babies. I love Alex and Lily and I will adore whatever Tia has, but I'm not ready for that. Not yet. I'm barely grown up! I've got lots of time."

AJ frowned. He leaned close, reached up and plucked a hair out of her scalp.

She slammed her palm down on her head. "Shit! That hurt! What'd you do that for?"

AJ held the long strand up for Mik. "Yep. Gray." He turned back to Tala. "You were saying?"

"Aaaarrrrgggghhh!" Laughing, Tala launched herself at AJ. He caught her, just as she knew he would. Then he kissed her, exactly as she'd hoped. Before she had time to even think of the six young people outside the door, Tala was slipping out of her clothing and rubbing against AJ like a cat in heat.

Mik flipped the lock on the door and stripped out of his shirt and pants. Then he caught Tala around the waist and held her captive while AJ undressed. She struggled, but only enough to keep the game alive. When Mik carried her to the bed, leaned back against the headboard, and stretched her out with her hands grasped firmly overhead in his, she twisted just enough to make AJ work for that first penetration.

She felt the broad head of his cock bumping against her inner thigh, and her pussy clenched. She arched her hips, waiting for AJ to fill her, but all he did was tease, rubbing his hot length between her legs, scraping his shaft over her clit with each upward and downward thrust.

"She's making it too easy, Mik. Got any ideas?"

Mik laughed. "You kidding? I've always got ideas."

Before Tala could even protest, he'd flipped her over and slipped just inside her sex with his huge cock. Her face pressed against his collarbone and she kissed the soft skin beneath his ear. Mik groaned and withdrew. Then he arched his hips again and pressed upward, deeper this time. She felt his slick glans catch at her entrance, felt the stretching that always hurt as much as it pleasured when he filled her, slowly forcing his entire length all the way inside.

Her legs stretched wide around his thick thighs, her inner muscles rippled, adjusted, welcomed his full length. Feminine juices flowed when he lifted her with each slow but steady roll of his hips, and he filled her deeper on each forward thrust. When Mik was totally engulfed in her rippling heat, he paused and grinned over her shoulder at AJ. "That the right angle, bro?"

"Oh, yeah."

She felt her ass pucker, felt the taut muscle twitch in expectation. Usually the guys did each other. It had been a long time since she'd taken both of them at once.

AJ's fingers lightly stroked her tight little hole. When Mik moaned, she knew his balls were getting the same attention. His penis jerked deep inside her.

A moment later, something cool and wet dripped down the crease between her buttocks and she picked up the subtle scent of cocoa butter and vanilla. AJ's fingertips helped the lube along, creaming her narrow cleft from her tailbone to the thick base of Mik's cock stuffed in her sex.

The cream warmed with each slow stroke of his fingers and Tala gave up all pretense of struggle. She wriggled her hips, but Mik refused to move. She felt the hot length of AJ's cock pressing into the cleft between her cheeks. He slid, hot and wet from the cream, riding up and down in the warm valley.

Tala opened her thoughts and caught the laughter in Mik's mind, the sense of AJ's big cock sliding against Mik's balls on every downward stroke. She sensed AJ's preoccupation with every sensation, the way the cream, now heated with the friction of their bodies, left a tingle on the surface of his cock. The slick, smooth skin on the inside of her buttocks, now all warm and wet, the visual of her, stretched out over the chest of the man he loved, her body impaled on Mik's perfect erection.

He could do this for hours, keeping the three of them on the edge of orgasm. They didn't have hours. They had a few stolen moments while six anxious almost-Chanku prowled around just outside their door.

Tala spread her legs a fraction wider and wiggled her butt— enough, she hoped, that AJ would feel the puckered little muscle between her cheeks and remember what he was supposed to be doing. She knew from long experience that until AJ was deep inside, Mik wouldn't move another inch, no matter how much she begged.

Her clit throbbed and the cream from her pussy was spilling out around the thick base of Mik's deeply planted shaft. The mingled scents of sex and vanilla and cocoa butter made her nose tickle. She sent a mental plea to AJ to get a move on, now!

"Bossy little thing, isn't she, Mik?"

Tala groaned. "Are you two bozos going to fuck me now, or

do I have to show you how this is supposed to work? Now get moving!"

AJ snorted, and it was Mik who moved, spinning around on the bed until he had his feet on the edge and his knees in the air with Tala planted firmly on his cock, her legs ingloriously sprawled over his thighs. Mik gave AJ a perfect target when he finally stopped laughing long enough to crawl off the bed, slip on a condom, and stand between his lover's feet. Mik lifted his hips and Tala with them, AJ pressed forward, and with all the cream and relaxed muscles, breached Tala's tight sphincter and slid deep inside her rear on the first thrust.

They all sighed when his balls hit the underside of Mik's shaft and rested on his sac, when the head of his cock rode the full length of Mik's while deep inside Tala, separated by nothing more than a moist, feminine sheath.

He held perfectly still. Tala tapped into AJ's thoughts and found a powerful blend of emotion and sensation, a maelstrom of visceral responses and feelings blended with all the emotions of a man who loved deeply, eternally.

She closed her eyes and held back the silly quip she'd intended to make. Now was not the time. Now was one of those perfect moments the three of them so often shared, their bodies linked, their hearts already beating in sync, breaths flawlessly matched as each inhaled and exhaled at the same time.

AJ was the first to move. Gently, at first, taking care not to hurt her, he withdrew and slowly thrust forward. Mik caught AJ's rhythm and Tala became the vessel through which the two men made love, the link that held them together, the one who cemented the commitment they'd made to one another so long ago.

She felt her climax building, knew she was catching both Mik and AJ's growing arousal, but something new floated in the space about them, something she'd not seriously considered until now.

She could give them a child, one borne of each man should they mate in the deep woods as wolves. Releasing an egg was a simple thing. Raising a child wasn't, but she had two fathers, men who loved equally. There was no reason to choose. She'd merely make love to both, and when her body was filled with their mingled seed, the egg would choose.

Thinking of carrying either AJ or Mik's child under her heart took her higher than she'd ever flown. A feral scream ripped from deep in Tala's throat. She arched her back and sailed over the edge of orgasm.

Her body spasmed with the hot rush of Mik's release and the deep thrust when AJ climaxed. Behind it all, she felt the gentle laughter of two men, each of them imagining their woman swollen with child.

Oops. Tala bit back a giggle. She'd let her thoughts fly free at the moment of climax. Shared a moment she probably should have kept private, at least for now, but the cat was out of the bag. Now she wasn't the only one who would be thinking about babies.

Maybe, when they shifted, when her body was in heat and it was capable of producing a viable egg, she might be willing to take a chance. In spite of the danger, despite those in the world who would do them harm . . . maybe now truly was the time.

Smiling, imagining these two perfect men as fathers, Tala collapsed against Mik's broad chest. AJ gently lowered himself over her back.

They lay there, the three of them sandwiched together, hearts pounding, minds spinning.

Filled with possibilities.

Dreaming of a future of their own creation.

Jazzy sat on the railing out front. Late afternoon sunlight bathed this one little corner of the porch, and she'd claimed it for her own. Beth and Nick hadn't come out of the bedroom for at least a couple of hours, and Matt was sleeping in one of the other rooms. She wasn't sure exactly where Deacon had gone, but he'd wandered into the woods to check out the huge trees.

Logan was the only one out here, but he wasn't exactly with her. He'd gone down to the other end of the porch where he'd commandeered a deck chair. He sat there silently, staring at the dark forest.

She might as well have been all alone, out here waiting on AJ, Mik, and Tala. From the muffled laughter and the soft scream she'd just heard from the master bedroom, there was no doubt in Jazzy's mind what was going on behind their closed door.

She felt that same ripple of sensation, the clenching of muscles, the presence of her clit rubbing against the thick seam of her jeans. Hell, she never thought of her clit. It was just there, a part of her body that usually stayed hidden until it was time to come out and play, but for some reason, lately the damn thing wanted to play all the time.

She was so not going to be ruled by her sex drive.

Like that was an issue.

Desire'd pretty much been fucked out of her after a lifetime on the streets. So many little kids, brought into the country illegally. Sold like so much property. No rights, no home, no parents. Nothing but one man after another, all with the same thing in mind.

When she was a cute little girl, they'd wanted to dress her up and then take off those same clothes. She'd had men purchase her time who wanted her to spank them. She'd actually sort of enjoyed that, especially when she was little.

When you're little, just about everything's a game.

She hadn't liked it nearly as much when *they* wanted to spank *her*. It wasn't fair. She hadn't done anything wrong. She did what they asked and they still wanted her over their laps with her pants down and her round little bottom in the air.

Damn, she was so screwed. No way in hell could she ever be a normal woman. Not now. Not after all that had been done to her over the years. Twenty-two years old, not a penny to her name, no real identification, no Social Security number, no idea what country she even came from.

She'd always figured her mom must have been Asian and her father black. Maybe a serviceman somewhere? She'd never know. Not that it would make any difference, but what kind of parent sold their child to a sex slaver?

"Penny for your thoughts?"

"Hey, Logan." She snorted, but she was secretly pleased he'd come down to her end of the porch. "You wouldn't want 'em. Not even if I paid you." Jazzy scratched her arms.

"They might be better than what I've got, which is a big, fat zero. I keep thinking I should remember something, but all I get is stuff that seems to come out of TV shows."

Jazzy frowned. "What kind of stuff?"

He actually looked embarrassed. "Some medical show. I see doctors and nurses. Sometimes an operating room."

"That's probably from when you were first hurt. You're remembering the doctors and nurses taking care of you."

He shrugged. "Yeah. That must be it."

When he looked away, though, Jazzy knew he didn't agree. She turned back and gazed out at the redwoods, but her arms and legs felt all twitchy. She stood up. "I'm going to take a walk. Want to go with me? Let's see if we can find Deacon."

"Where'd he go?"

She pointed toward a break in the forest. "He took that trail. Said he wouldn't go far, but he's been gone about an hour."

"Should we tell anyone we're leaving?"

Jazzy shrugged. "Who? Everyone else is either screwing or sleeping. Leave a note."

Logan went inside and came back a minute later with a water bottle he stuck in his pocket. "I just left a note on the table. Told them we're taking a short hike and trying to meet up with Deacon."

Jazzy laughed. "I've seen your writing. By the time they figure out your chicken scratches, we'll probably be back."

Logan flashed her a dirty look. Then he grinned. "C'mon. I need some exercise." He grabbed her hand and tugged Jazzy along behind him. She went willingly, more aware than ever of the warmth of his hand, the tingle in her palm, and the matching sensations between her legs.

"It's weird, but I can actually tell which way Deacon went."

Logan glanced at Jazzy. "You, too? I thought it was just me. What are you following?"

Jazzy grinned. "The scent of his shaving cream. My nose is so much more sensitive now. What about you?"

Logan hated to admit that all this crap about turning into wolves was actually true, but he couldn't deny facts. "I smell that, too, but I can actually see his body heat. It's a visible image, like a thin film in the air."

Frowning, Jazzy stared at the trail ahead of them. "I see it now. I think. Sort of a wavy line about waist height?" She glanced down and laughed. "We could always just follow his footprints. Look."

Logan looked where Jazzy pointed. Plain as day, there were big footprints in the mud. Deacon's heavy Doc Martens had left a noticeable trail. Logan knelt down in the mud and held up one beckoning finger. "Come, kimo sabe. White man go this way." He stood up and laughed. "He can't be too far ahead."

Talk about a man of many moods. Jazzy followed where Logan led. The trail got narrower, the going rougher, but still they followed Deacon's tracks and scent trail. Suddenly, Jazzy pulled to a stop. She held her hand up and planted it firmly in Logan's midsection. "What's that noise?"

Cocking his head, Logan caught the soft sound just ahead. "Shit, I think that's Deacon! Sounds like he's hurt."

They ran through thick ferns and an even thicker stand of pussy willows growing along the bank of a sharply cut ravine with a narrow stream at the bottom. The trail dropped precipitously.

"Logan!" Jazzy's foot slipped off the edge.

Logan grabbed her upper arm and yanked her back. Flailing for a moment, she finally caught her balance. He pulled her close. Heart pounding, Logan wrapped her against his chest and hung on tight.

"Help! Logan? Jazzy? That you?"

"Deacon?" Logan took a deep breath. He turned Jazzy loose. Her fear pounded inside his head, the words clear and panic-stricken. He'd been picking up her random thoughts for the past day or so, but not this clearly. "Wait here," he said.

He surprised himself, and Jazzy as well, when he planted a firm kiss on her full lips. She was still standing there wide-eyed, lips slightly parted, when he carefully slipped between the willow branches to the edge of the cut. Using the strong roots hanging out of the sheer wall, he lowered himself the twenty or so feet to the bottom of the narrow chasm.

Deacon's lanky six-and-a-half-foot frame lay in a crumpled heap on a sandbar at the edge of the creek. His right leg lay beneath him, twisted awkwardly. Deacon's normally fair skin was almost bluish in the shadowed light, and his hands were covered in shallow cuts and scratches. However, he'd managed to raise himself up on one elbow, which was a good sign.

"Looks like you get the klutz of the year award." Logan knelt down beside his friend and checked his pulse. A bit fast, but steady. "What happened?" He looked into Deacon's eyes and wished he had a flashlight to check his response, but at least Deacon's pupils were both the same size. Dilated, but that was to be expected, considering the pain he must be in.

Logan actually felt Deacon's pain. His leg ached so badly he could barely stand it. He consciously tried to block it so he'd be able to function. This was just too weird.

Deacon slowly shook his head. "Walking along the trail watching some neat birds," he said. His voice was thready, his pain a living, breathing entity from his toes to his head and Logan felt all of it. Deacon closed his eyes and took a deep breath. Opened them slowly. "The ground disappeared out from under me. I slid feet first until my foot got caught in some roots. Heard my leg snap. Banged my head."

"Bet that ruined your day. Did you black out?" Logan parted Deacon's dark hair looking for injuries. There was a big knot in the middle of his forehead, but the skin wasn't broken. He touched it lightly. Deacon jerked away.

"Ouch. No, I didn't black out. Son of a bitch! That hurt."

Logan laughed. "Well, at least we know you're conscious and lucid. Just hold on. Good thing you landed on a sandbar and not in a pile of rocks." Logan sensed before he saw Jazzy. He turned and saw her peeking through the branches at the edge of the ravine above them. "Can you find your way back?" he asked. "I think he's got a broken leg. We'll need Mik and AJ to get him out of here."

Jazzy's sympathy washed over him in a warm wave. Her hand covered her mouth. "Oh, Deacon. I'm so sorry." She scrambled to her feet. "I'm outta here. I'll be back asap."

Logan heard the rustle in the branches as she raced back through the willows. He turned his attention back to his friend. "Can you move your fingers? Toes . . . well, obviously not the toes on your right leg." He did a quick check, but didn't see any other obvious injury. "I'm going to have to splint your leg before we can move you. If you want, I'll do it before the others get here so you can yell all you want. It's gonna hurt like a sonofabitch."

Deacon nodded. "Might as well. Damn."

"I need some thick branches, a board, something as straight as I can find. I'll be right back." Logan headed about fifteen yards upstream to a logjam he'd spotted. Deacon's pain followed him. He dug around in the pile for a few minutes before he found a length of weathered board. It was about six inches wide and looked like it might have come from an old cabin or fence. Once he hammered a sharp rock against one end, the board split cleanly along the grain into two three foot sections.

Deacon lay back in the sand with his eyes closed. "You don't happen to have any water with you, do you?"

"Yeah. It's your lucky day." Logan handed him the small bottle he'd stuck into his pocket earlier.

"Funny. You're real funny, Logan."

Logan helped him raise his head. "Drink it slowly." Deacon took a long swallow that almost drained the bottle.

"Let's get you straightened out." Logan lifted Deacon's wide shoulders and lined his upper torso up with his good leg. Deacon cried out and bit his lip. The other leg was still twisted painfully beneath him.

"I hate to do this to you, buddy, but we can't move you without a splint, and I can't splint it twisted this way. Here . . ." He pulled his leather belt out of his pants, folded it in two and handed it to Deacon. "Bite on this."

Deacon tried to laugh, but it came out as more of a groan. "You sound like a damn cowboy doctor. Gonna cauterize something with a hot branding iron?"

Logan laughed, but he stared at Deacon's twisted leg and wondered whether or not the fracture had broken the skin. He grabbed his folding knife out of the side pocket of his jeans. "I'm going to cut the pant leg open so I can see your injury better. I'll use our belts to tie the splint."

"Just do it, man. Don't talk about it."

"Right." Logan scooted down and unlaced Deacon's heavy boot. Even though he was really careful slipping it off, Deacon moaned in pain from the slight movement of his leg.

Logan imagined he heard the sound of bone grating against bone. Then he realized it wasn't his imagination. He had heard it. Nervous sweat poured off his face and down his back. He always hated this part of emergency care. Sometimes you caused more pain, no matter how hard you tried to avoid it.

He finally got the boot off. Then he sliced the denim lengthwise, cutting through the thick hem, up through bloodied fabric to a point just above Deacon's knee. When he glanced at Deacon, he had to look away. Agony spilled out of him and it was harder to block when Logan looked directly at him.

But he had to look. Had to keep tabs on his patient, and right now it appeared that Deacon was going into shock. Where the hell were Mik and AJ?

Finally Logan finished cutting through the denim, slicing around Deacon's leg above his knee and lifting the blood-soaked fabric away from his injured leg. Jagged bone protruded from a two-inch gash below his knee. "Shit, man. You've got an open, compound fracture. You might need surgery, maybe a pin or a plate to hold it together."

"That's gonna screw with my shifting, right, Logan?"

His voice sounded much weaker. Luckily, the bleeding appeared to have stopped, but he needed medical care fast.

"Shifting is the last thing we need to worry about. Bite down on that leather." Before Deacon had a chance to worry about what was to come, Logan grabbed his ankle and slowly pulled his leg straight, twisting the bone into place as he tugged. Deacon screamed as the jagged end of bone slipped beneath the tear in his skin.

Then he passed out.

Logan groaned and shuddered with the excruciating pain Deacon broadcast. His hands froze around his buddy's ankle, but the pain lessened as soon as unconsciousness overtook Deacon's mind. Logan breathed a sigh of relief as the bone seemed to slip into position. "Thank goodness you can't feel this, buddy," he whispered. "Thank goodness I can't feel it, either."

6

Logan took off his shirt and wrapped the clean fabric around Deacon's injured leg, then placed a flat board on either side. He took his belt from Deacon's slack fingers and used it to hold one end of the boards in place. Then he carefully removed Deacon's belt from his jeans and used it to secure the other end.

He was trying to figure out what to use for a bandage over the open wound when he sensed more than heard voices. Moments later, Mik and AJ dropped down over the side of the ravine.

"How's he doing?"

"He passed out when I set his leg, but I think he'll be okay. He's shocky, but I think it's more from pain than excessive bleeding. His pulse is strong and he's . . ."

"Whoa." AJ sat back on his heels. "You sound like you know what you're talking about. You a doctor?"

Logan blinked rapidly. He turned away from AJ and stared at Deacon. Was he a doctor? Is that what he'd been? He tried vainly to remember his past. This had all seemed so natural. Setting Deacon's broken leg, fixing the splint. Why couldn't he remember? His shoulders slumped and he shook his head.

"I don't know." He turned back to AJ and Mik. Jazzy stood behind them. Nick, Beth, and Matt waited at the top of the ravine, and all their questioning thoughts bombarded him at once. Worry, confusion, concern. He took a deep breath. What was the point of keeping his past—or lack of one—a secret?

"Almost a year ago I woke up in a hospital in San Francisco. Had no idea who I was. I'd been badly beaten. ID was taken and my fingerprints aren't on record, so they couldn't match me up with anyone. I have no idea who I am or what I used to do. Never thought I might be a doctor. It's hard to say, but treating Deacon seemed to come naturally."

"After you shift, when you finally find your mate and bond with her, you might find out." Breathing hard from running, Tala slid part way down the ravine. Mik caught her and helped her to the bottom. "I had amnesia when the guys found me. When we bonded, they saw all my memories. So did I. Three years without a past and suddenly it all came clear to me."

Deacon moaned. He blinked his eyes and finally focused on Logan. "Shit, man. You weren't kidding. That hurt. Still hurts, but not as bad." He looked at everyone standing around him or waiting up on the bank. "What now?"

Mik squatted down beside him. "Now we wait for the rescue team. Tala called and gave them coordinates."

"They said they'd be here in less than half an hour." Tala stroked his arm. "There's a clearing not far from here where they can set down. I'm going to go with you. AJ will follow in the car."

"Do you want me to come along?" For some reason, Logan hated to turn Deacon loose yet. He felt as if there was more he should be doing.

"No." Tala shook her head. "Mik's staying here with you guys in case any of you are ready to shift. It could happen tonight. Since you've all been eating the grass, we don't know how close you are."

"Damn. I don't want to miss that."

Tala patted Deacon's arm again. "We'll get you healthy first. Then you can shift."

Logan stood up and brushed the sand off his pants. "Tala, no pins or plates in his leg if you can avoid it. Doctors may want to pin the bone, but I'm not sure what would happen during a shift with something that's actually affixed to bone inside a human body."

Tala flashed him a wide grin. "Will do, Doc. It sounds as if you've decided we're not all nuts after all."

Logan grinned. "I didn't say that. I still think you're all fucking crazy. Let's just say after a second day of your pills, and a whole lot of hearing other people's thoughts, I'm a little more open to the idea of shapeshifting."

Jazzy watched the taillights as AJ drove off, following the chopper that had come for Deacon. Tala'd ridden with the rescue squad; they'd all teased her about being a shrimp and not taking up any room. It finally dawned on Jazzy the paramedics knew her well.

Mik wandered out on the porch. He had a beer in his hand, but he handed Jazzy a glass of wine. He looked sort of lost with the others gone. "I wondered where you'd gone. Logan's in the shower. Beth and Nick are back in their room. I think they've just discovered sex."

Jazzy laughed and took the glass of wine. "Thank you. I think you're right about those two. Where's Matt?"

"Staring at the refrigerator. I asked if he could cook and he said 'kinda.'"

Jazzy took a sip of her wine. "That's scary. Wow, that's good." She turned around and leaned against the railing. "How come all those rescue guys know you? You're a long way from home."

"Pack Dynamics does a lot of search and rescue—sometimes,

unfortunately, search and recovery. The three of us have worked with this crew before. Mostly Tala. AJ and I are usually in wolf form on jobs, so the guys think of her as the wolf lady. They have no idea we're shifters."

"Wow. I had no idea. So what now?"

Mik grinned. "Now we figure out what to have for dinner. I'm not too sure about Matt." He grinned at her. "Can you cook?"

Jazzy shook her head. "Not really."

"I was afraid of that." He turned and leaned against the railing next to Jazzy. After a quiet moment, he asked, "What do you know about Logan?"

"Not much. No more than he knows. He said he doesn't remember much."

"Do you think he'd mind if we did a search on him? Tried to find out his identity? I don't want to overstep my boundaries, but we have a lot of contacts in law enforcement." Mik took a sip of his beer.

"You'll have to ask Logan."

"Ask Logan what?" Logan stepped out of the cabin wearing faded jeans but no shirt, but with his body totally covered in tattoos, he almost looked dressed. He'd showered and cut off his long hair. The shaved side was beginning to grow out and he'd cut the other side almost as short.

It appeared he'd removed his studs and rings, too.

"You look totally different." Jazzy turned around and leaned her back against the railing. "I've never seen all your tats. They're beautiful."

Logan laughed. "That's not all of them. I keep thinking how they're all going to fall off when I shift. All that pain turning to dust in the wind. It's sort of depressing. I figured I might as well remove the studs and rings, too."

"I don't remember you having any rings?"

"Nipple. Dick."

"Oh. Ouch." Jazzy laughed but Logan merely shrugged.

Mik hadn't said a word. Jazzy couldn't read his expression. Logan glanced at Jazzy, held his hand out to Mik. "I want to apologize. I've been a real jerk and you guys have been nothing but nice to all of us. I'm sorry."

Mik smiled and took his hand. "Apology accepted. Face it, what we had to tell you, what you saw Nick do . . . essentially, it's impossible. Shit like that doesn't happen."

Logan laughed. His entire face lit up. Jazzy decided she was liking him all over again. "So, what did you want to ask me?"

"If you'd mind our doing a search on you. Try to find out who the hell you are. If you've got family looking for you, a job somewhere." Mik paused and took a deep breath. "If you're a doctor. We really need a doctor who's familiar with our kind. We have a healer who is damn good, but he's in Montana. We're worried about Tia having a baby and no one understanding Chanku physiology, and we can't divulge our true nature. If you are a doctor, even a trained paramedic, it could make a difference. . . ."

Logan shrugged. "I know I felt really comfortable helping Deacon today. I just wish I could remember . . ."

"It'll come." Mik glanced at Jazzy. "You okay?"

"My arms itch and I feel like I'm ready to crawl out of my skin."

"Mine, too." Logan rubbed at his tattooed arms. "You got any of that cream, Jazzy?"

"Cream won't help." Mik grinned. "You're getting ready to shift. Maybe we won't have to worry about dinner after all. I'm going to get the others. Tala's going to be so pissed she missed this!" Laughing, he turned and headed into the house.

"So what does our shifting have to do with cooking dinner?" Jazzy scratched her head.

"Hell if I know." Logan leaned against the railing next to her. "As far as I'm concerned, they're all fucking nuts."

* * *

Mik dragged Beth and Nick out of the bedroom, still zipping and buttoning their clothes. He sent Matt out on the porch after them and took a spot leaning against the railing where everyone could see him. Of course, as big a guy as Mik was, standing there barefoot wearing only faded blue jeans without a shirt, with those broad shoulders and black hair flowing to his waist, he'd be hard to miss anywhere.

"Okay," he said. "Here's the deal. I wish Tala was here but she's not. You two girls are going to notice the biggest changes because you're going to have full charge of your reproductive systems. No pregnancy without the conscious act of releasing an egg. I'm telling you that so you don't do it by mistake. If you're wearing an IUD, it's going to fall out. Earrings? Studs? If you want to keep them, take 'em off now. They'll fall out, too."

He grinned at Logan. "Say good-bye to those gorgeous tats. Jazzy, that's a cute little flower on your ankle, but it's going, too. I imagine all of you are ready. You've been nibbling on those grasses for months now. I'm surprised you haven't shifted already—well, except for Nick, here, and I imagine his was the result of an adrenaline rush—but we talked about it last night and figure the nutrients might not be as strong because the soil is different in San Francisco than Tibet. No matter. You've had the pills, and that should be all you need to jump-start things."

He lifted himself up on the railing and sat there, grinning. "Are you guys all getting into each other's heads? Mindtalking okay?" He watched as everyone sort of stared at one another, and laughed. "I thought so. You've been eavesdropping and not telling each other. That brings up certain rules, sort of a 'Miss Manners of Mindtalking.' We shut people out whenever we want. We don't go crawling around in someone else's head just because we can. The upside? Sex is fantastic when you can feel your partner's experience through the mental link you'll all learn to forge."

He looked away then. Jazzy was shocked to see that his eyes sparkled with unshed tears. When he turned back to the five of them, his eyes gleamed instead with a ferocious intensity. "When you find that perfect mate or mates—when you create a mating bond which lasts for your lifetimes and starts as two wolves together in the woods, minds and bodies irrevocably linked—you will discover something totally magnificent. You will finally understand the meaning of unconditional love."

He glanced away again. It was so obvious he was thinking of AJ and Tala that he might as well have shouted it out on stage. When he turned back he was smiling. "You're also going to discover another level of unconditional love, the kind of love a mother feels for her child and then some. You will feel that love for your packmates. You might not understand it at first, but it's a powerful drive that covers both the emotional and the physical. You guys are lucky. You already know and care about each other. You might not be physically attracted to one another now, but I guarantee that will change. I can't explain it, but I can promise it.

"Another thing. You'll know when you meet the one who will be your mate. I still can't explain it, but the love I feel for AJ and Tala rocks my world. They are my world."

He shrugged his massive shoulders and gazed directly at Jazzy, then at each of the others. "You will feel love as you've never known, and a vulnerability borne of that love. It's a huge responsibility, to love and be loved by more than one person. To look at your packmates and know without any doubt you would give your life to protect them. I'm not making this up. You'll experience it, just as every one of us already has."

He slipped off the railing and rubbed his hands together. "Enough of the deep stuff. It's time for fun. I'm going to shift, but first I want each of you to link with me. Mentally crawl into my head. See if you can tell what I'm thinking."

Jazzy stared into Mik's amber eyes and broke into giggles.

He was thinking of food and hoping they'd scare up something big enough to feed all of them so he wouldn't have to cook. Within a few seconds, all of them were laughing.

"Okay. My secret's out. I hate cooking. I can do it, but I don't like it. Now that we know you can read my thoughts, I'm going to shift. I want you to see what I do in my head. Watch that, not what I turn into. Try and do the same thing."

He stripped off his jeans, folded them over the railing and turned around. Jazzy felt her insides turn to mush. The man was gorgeous. A dark Adonis with a body worthy of marble or bronze. Muscles sharply defined beneath coppery red skin, small waist, heavy thighs and, even quiescent, the biggest package she'd ever seen.

How the hell did tiny little Tala take on guys the size of AJ and Mik? Especially Mik! She glanced at her friends and realized everyone stared unabashedly at Mik's perfect body, even as she realized he was totally oblivious to their curious stares.

He stood very still and, for want of a better description, opened his mind. It was even clearer now than when he'd been thinking of hunting. Now it was such a simple thing, really, to see what he was thinking as he prepared to shift.

To see it, understand it, and apply it.

It happened so fast that Jazzy totally missed the physical change from man to wolf. She didn't miss the mental picture Mik shared with her, with all of them.

Holding the image in her mind, she quickly stripped off her clothing. There was no sense of embarrassment, no tittering about getting naked with her buds or anything she almost expected from the others. All of them were dead serious, stripping out of their clothing, each intent on the black wolf sitting patiently on the porch in front of them.

Nick was the first. "I've done this before," he said. "Now I know how I did it."

Suddenly there was a dark brown wolf with black tipped fur

sitting where he'd stood. Beth followed him almost immediately. She was smaller, finer boned with darker fur than Nick's, an all-over deep brown that was almost black. Matt shifted at the same time as Beth. He whimpered and dropped his nose almost to the ground, as if terrified by the change in his body. He was lighter colored than the others, almost a golden brown with a dark ruff around his neck.

Jazzy stared at Logan. He hadn't been kidding when he said he had tats all over. Every inch of his body was covered in art, including his penis and balls. A snake's head on the end of his dick seemed to be staring right at her.

"I had no idea," she said, biting back a laugh. She glanced over her shoulder at Mik and realized the wolf was every bit as fascinated by Logan's body art as she was.

Logan shrugged and actually grinned. "Get a good look. I hear it's all going the way of dust in the wind." He slowly turned, showing off his perfectly beautiful, lean yet muscular body with all its colorful art.

He was going to be even more gorgeous without the tattoos. No doubt about it, Logan was hot. And not nearly as young as she'd thought.

Jazzy had figured he was about her age, but seeing his musculature, the firm shape of his thighs, and the hard cut of his abs made her rethink her first opinion.

He was older. He was sexier than she'd ever imagined . . . and she'd imagined a lot.

"Okay," he said. "Show's over." He looked Jazzy in the eye and his mind linked with hers. The sensation almost knocked her flat, the intimacy of Logan's thoughts in her head.

Now, Jazzy. Shift now!

There was no thought of hesitation. Jazzy shifted. Suddenly she was shorter and balanced on four feet instead of two. Her paws were broad, the nails sharp and long and digging into the soft redwood deck. Her fur was black, like Mik's, though she thought there might be some russet highlights.

Not bad. She glanced back along her side to her full brush of a tail. She looked damn good!

Definitely not bad. You're one hell of a sexy bitch.

She swung her head around and looked right into Logan's amber eyes. He was big and dark, a pure, solid black that blended perfectly with the lengthening shadows falling across the porch.

She was immediately drawn to him. Arousal practically hummed in the air between them and she wondered if the others noticed. Logan certainly did. He took a step toward her. Then another.

Mik's voice filled her mind. Logan's spell broke. She took a deep breath through unfamiliar lungs, turned her back on Logan and watched Mik.

Very cool, he said. *So far, so good . . . you all made the shift perfectly.* Mik dipped his head, as if giving each of them a nod of respect. *Follow me. We'll start out slow so you can get your bearings and figure out how to run on four instead of two legs. Should all come naturally, but you never know.*

He turned then and leapt from the porch to the spongy, humus-rich ground beyond the steps. Nick and Beth followed, then Matt and Jazzy. Logan brought up the rear, trotting along with his tail high and his ears forward. Jazzy wanted to laugh out loud. The smells! Her perceptions of sight and sound . . . all of it so different, so vivid, so vital.

For the first time in her entire life, she felt truly alive, truly part of something wonderful.

Almost preternaturally aware of Logan following right behind her, Jazzy trotted along the trail behind the rest of her pack.

7

Logan tried in vain to find a description for this amazing new reality, but there were no words. His head filled with new, instinctual knowledge explaining the scents along the trail, the sounds he heard, the things he saw from this entirely different perspective.

The whisper of wind in the trees brought the scent of birds roosting overhead and the soft rustle in the leaves beside the trail told him where the mice and voles scurried under cover. He recognized the rich yet individual scents of his packmates. One especially called to him. He stretched out his nose and inhaled the musky scent of Jazzy Blue.

She was a witch. She must be, to have so completely bewitched him. Mik said he'd recognize his mate. Logan had no doubt in his mind. Jazzy was the one.

Of course, convincing her might not be all that easy. She truly had a mind of her own, and there were other males every bit as strong as he. Matt appeared to be as much the beta in wolf form as he was as a human, but Deacon was another matter.

Of course, if Logan moved first . . . he'd have to think about that. It would most likely be weeks before Deacon could shift.

Logan also recognized, without any need to dispute the fact, that Mik Fuentes held the role of the ultimate alpha of this small pack. Logan might take that position among his friends in human form, but there was no arguing the position of the one who led them through the damp forest teeming with unseen life.

Suddenly Beth pulled up short. She raised her nose in the air and gazed off to their left along a narrow trail.

Game.

The word floated into Logan's mind with all the knowledge Beth held from the particular scent that had caught her attention. A deer, probably a male in his prime.

Too much for you guys?

Never. Logan growled low in his throat, well aware Mik had thrown out a dare to the pack as a whole.

Beth shot a glance at Nick and raced off down the trail with the other four hot on her tail. Mik followed at a more sedate pace.

His message was clear. If the pack wanted to eat tonight, the pack better learn to hunt.

Together.

They somehow knew to come in upwind of the medium-sized buck grazing in a small clearing. Nick and Matt circled around to the left, Logan guarded the trail they'd come in on, and Jazzy and Beth quietly stalked the animal from opposite directions.

His head came up, ears twisting and turning frantically, eyes wide. The buck snorted, sniffed the air and stood perfectly still.

Logan heard his own heart pounding in his chest, sensed the other wolves hiding nearby. Almost believed he could hear the buck's heart, thundering away, but that was impossible.

Wasn't it?

After a moment, the buck lowered his head to munch once again on thick grass.

Jazzy? Now!

Beth charged the animal, leaping for his flank when he turned to run. Jazzy's body exploded out of the bushes in a flying rush of ferocious teeth and powerful jaws. She caught the startled buck under his chin. Clamping down solidly on his throat, she pulled him to the ground, overpowering the larger animal with the weight of her body and the speed of her attack.

It was over in seconds. Blood spread across the damp earth from the animal's torn throat. The buck lay still in death, dark eyes glazing over as life left its body.

Mik trotted into the clearing. Beth turned and growled at him. Jazzy stood over their kill and snarled. Mik sat back on his haunches and stared at the two females. Logan, Nick, and Matt slipped away from their hiding places in the brush and waited beside him, watching. There was something totally visceral about watching their females, successful hunters both, tear into the fresh kill and gorge themselves on the warm meat.

The sight and sounds should have disgusted him. Logan realized he'd never felt so alive, so sure of his position in the world . . . and in his pack.

His woman had killed. They would eat tonight. Soon he would take her as his mate. It was a simple thing, really.

Now all he had to do was convince Jazzy.

Sated, bellies full, they trotted slowly back along the trail to the cabin. Jazzy couldn't recall running so far last night, but it was a good two-hour trip home over rough and forested terrain, and the sky was turning shades of peach and blue in the east when they finally reached the front porch and flopped down onto the wooden deck.

Shifting seemed beyond her right now. Even though her body literally hummed with arousal and need, she decided she'd rather just lie here and pant. Logan slowly laid down next to her and rested his muzzle across her shoulders.

She felt his arousal as well, like a sweater worn a bit too tight. The need to take it off, to make the itch go away, was growing stronger by the second.

Aren't you going to say it?

Jazzy heard the laughter in Logan's voice and knew exactly what he meant, but she still managed to focus her thoughts away from her body's needs, at least for a moment. *Say what?*

I told you so. He raised his head and stared into her eyes.

Jazzy dipped her muzzle in acknowledgment. *No need. What happened tonight defies belief. It goes in the face of everything I know to be true. See? Just look at Beth, Nick, and Matt.*

Logan turned and glanced toward their friends, obviously realized immediately what was happening, and swung his head back to stare at Jazzy. *Beth and Nick I expected, but Matt, too?*

Jazzy took another look. Nick and Beth had shifted the moment they returned from the hunt and were locked together from hips to thighs, kissing passionately. Matt hugged Beth from behind, his arms wrapped around both his friends, the slow, rhythmic sway of his hips describing exactly what he had in mind.

As she watched, the three of them broke apart and moved the show inside. Jazzy figured there'd be an extra bedroom after all.

She sensed movement to her left and glanced toward Mik. He'd shifted and was reaching for his pants. His erection was hard as a bat and just as big, but he managed to stuff it into his jeans with a painful grimace.

Suddenly Jazzy understood exactly what Mik had tried to explain the night before. Slowly she turned her head and gazed into Logan's amber eyes. *I want you*, she said. *But I can't leave Mik like this. He's our packmate, just as the others are. I want you both. Logan, have you ever been with a man?*

Logan shook his head, an expression of utter bemusement on his stark, wolven face. *No, but this is definitely a time for firsts. I look at Mik and feel as if I need his touch every bit as much as I need yours.*

He shifted and stood up, reaching his hand out for Jazzy as she rose to her feet. "No tats," she said, looking at his perfectly shaped, perfectly unadorned body.

Logan sighed. "I know. Still, all things considered, I think it will prove to be worth the trade."

Jazzy laughed and squeezed his hand. Both of them turned and smiled at Mik.

"Do you want to come with us?" It seemed only right that Logan be the one to ask.

Mik nodded slowly, but his smile grew. He glanced once more at the driveway, as if expecting Tala and AJ at any moment. "They won't be home until tonight," he said, in answer to Jazzy's unspoken question. "They're waiting until Deacon can leave the hospital. Thank you for asking me. I don't want to be alone, not after such an amazing night."

He held his hands out, palms up. "Five of you shifted. Five new Chanku among us. I know it's a huge personal adjustment for all of you, but it's just as big for the rest of us. There are so few of us right now, and all of you are amazing. You had your first hunt and it was successful. You seemed to find your natural roles within the pack without any problem. I can only attribute that to the fact that you were already friends, if not lovers."

Jazzy shook her head. "None of us have been lovers . . . well, besides Beth and Nicky, but that just happened yesterday." She laughed softly, glanced down at Logan's hand holding hers, then up, deep into his amber eyes where she lost herself for a moment while desire raged inside, unchecked and rising. "Not that I haven't wanted to."

She turned then and smiled at Mik. Held out her hand.

Mik reached out, wrapped his fingers around hers. Jazzy glanced at their clasped hands. It felt right. No, better than right. It felt absolutely perfect.

Smiling, she led both men, one dressed only in jeans, the other in his now unadorned skin, through the front door and down the hall to the room she'd chosen as her own.

Connected to Mik through Jazzy's warm grasp, Logan walked with them down the hallway. He couldn't look Mik or Jazzy in the eye. He'd never felt this way. Never wanted in this way. Jazzy. Mik. It didn't matter. His body cried out for the touch of another. His heart felt the same. Open. Waiting. A sense of expectancy followed him, surrounded him.

This night had been amazing. A time of dreams. Of fantasy. His body throbbed with all he'd done. Run as a wolf. Eaten the kill brought down by the woman who would be his mate. He'd ripped into the belly of a freshly killed buck, eaten his fill of bloody, still warm meat, and felt complete.

Now he followed her lead with another man beside him. His needs almost overpowered him, the feeling that within a very short time he would be physically intimate with both the female he desired and the man who held power over him.

There was no question of the hierarchy within the pack. Mik Fuentes was the alpha male, mated to the alpha bitch, but Jazzy and Beth were both alpha bitches, powerful females in their own right. Was he deserving? Did he even belong here, following Jazzy down the long hall to her room?

As long as she believed he did, he would be there. He squeezed her hand and she responded, turning and smiling at him. Mik grinned as well. *It will be okay,* he said, his voice a soft sound of encouragement in Logan's thoughts. Logan nodded. Tonight had been one new experience after another.

What was one more?

They entered the simple room Jazzy had claimed as her own. The bed had seemed huge yesterday. Now it looked way too small for three of them, but Jazzy didn't hesitate. "I'm taking a shower," she said, dropping their hands. "Join me if you want."

She turned away and walked into the bathroom. Her perfect

little round butt had invitation written all over it. Mik grinned at Logan, shrugged, and slipped out of his jeans. He followed Logan into the small bathroom.

Jazzy already had the water hot and steaming and was stepping under the spray. She turned around and smiled at both of them and held the shower curtain wide. Logan slipped in beside her. Mik followed. The three of them laughed at the cramped quarters, but Jazzy didn't seem to mind. She made what could have been awkward into fun, grabbing the soap and lining her men up against the wall, scrubbing backs and butts, teasing their cocks until they were ready to burst, running her fingers over chests, backs, balls, and butts.

Finally Logan had enough. He turned and grabbed Jazzy, held her shoulders and kissed her mouth. He felt Mik's arms come around his shoulders and the full press of the larger man against his side and thigh.

His arousal surged as Mik's thoughts and feelings invaded his mind and his own cock filled the space between Jazzy's belly and his own. Logan's tongue traced the contours of her lips and the hard tips of her nipples pressed against his chest.

He'd not made love to her before, though he'd thought about it. A lot. Of course, in his fantasies, Logan had always been alone with her, not sharing the woman of his dreams with a bruiser the size of Mik Fuentes.

Why didn't it bother him? It really should, shouldn't it? He let the strange thoughts slip away beneath the slick skin sliding across his, the warmth of two bodies, one male, one female, each of them equally arousing. Equally attractive.

They rinsed in a tangle of arms and legs, laughing with the silliness of it all, breathless with anticipation. Logan was almost sure he'd never been with a man before, yet he felt drawn to Mik with the same level of desire he felt for Jazzy. His balls ached, his dick was so hard and thick he marveled at the sense of heaviness, its unusual weight.

Usually, when he was hard, the tip brushed his belly. Now it pointed straight ahead. At Jazzy.

She stopped at the edge of the bed, gasping from laughter, and held up both hands. "I'm gonna tell you guys straight up that I've been with a lot of men, ever since I was a little kid. That's all I've ever known, using my body to make men happy. I've done one guy with another woman, 'cause it was his fantasy. But you know what? You two are *my* fantasy. This is all for me, and I am lovin' every minute of it."

She struck a pose, hand on hip, hip shot forward, breasts high and her smile wide. She wriggled her finger in invitation and then crawled up on the bed. On all fours, she turned and looked over her shoulder. The sensuality in her pose, the invitation in her dark amber eyes, almost made Logan shoot right then and there.

He glanced at Mik and shrugged. Mik laughed. "She's looking a bit cocky if you ask me. I think this alpha bitch role has gone to her head."

"Agreed." Logan rubbed his hands together and leapt. He tackled Jazzy, wrapping his arms around her waist, rolling to his back with her back and shoulders caught against his chest. One thrust had him buried deep inside her warm pussy. Slick and wet, she offered no resistance.

Mik stood at the edge of the bed and watched them. Idly he stroked himself, running his big hand the length of his cock, cupping his balls, his gaze focused on the spot where Logan's shaft parted Jazzy's swollen sex.

Without warning, he shifted. Logan scooted back against the headboard, dragging Jazzy with him, making room for the big wolf to crawl up on the bed and lie between the tangle of Jazzy and Logan's legs.

He held them both down with heavy paws and leaned forward. First he sniffed. His hot breath brushed over Logan's testicles, damp from Jazzy's fluids. Logan moaned. Jazzy whimpered and arched away from Logan, closer to Mik's long snout.

His tongue came out, tentative at first. He touched Jazzy's clit, licked the underside of Logan's shaft. Then he scooted closer and went to work. His long tongue circled Logan's balls and squeezed inside Jazzy's sex to lick the length of his shaft. *Unbelievable.* Like nothing he'd ever experienced in his life. Logan gave up all pretense of fucking Jazzy. Both of them lay perfectly still, legs spread wide while Mik licked and stroked them long and deep with that amazing tongue.

Logan filled Jazzy with his thick erection, but Mik was the one who made it all work. His tongue and hot breath, the little nibbles with his very sharp teeth, the sense of entrapment, the way he held both of them immobile with the strength of his powerful forelegs while he worked his Chanku magic on them both.

Logan's hips moved in a rhythmic sway with each long sweep of Mik's tongue. Jazzy's jerked when he nibbled at her sensitive flesh. She moaned when he stroked long and deep. The combination of pleasure and pain, of unfamiliar sensation and unerring aim at those sensitive points, was guaranteed to take both of them to the pinnacle of pleasure.

And there he held them: slowing his sensual attack, working them with the skill of a master. Logan's breath came in short gasps; he felt Jazzy reach the same plateau, but it wasn't a smooth, comfortable spot. No, they hovered on a knife's edge of sensation, bodies straining to fly off the other side, praying for the release Mik's skillful manipulation denied them.

Suddenly, Mik was in his head. Logan sensed the tiny tendrils of alien thought, the growing familiarity of the one who pleasured him with teeth and tongue. Jazzy was there as well, and they completed a link of three, their minds so closely attuned that heartbeats and pulse and breathing—all of it worked as a single entity, a singularly aroused Chanku.

Logan was Mik, tasting the unique flavors that were Jazzy

and Logan, absorbing their arousal and taking it into himself, building on it, growing more aroused by the second with it.

Need grew and yet Logan wanted more. Needed more. The connection with Mik wasn't as deep, as complete as all of them desired.

Shifting back to his human self, Mik gazed steadily into Logan's eyes, testing his response, asking permission. Caught in the circle of need, Logan nodded. He rolled with Jazzy, placing her beneath him. She raised up on her knees and rested her cheek on her crossed arms.

Deeper was the only thing she said. Then, *more.*

Kneeling between her legs, Logan pressed forward. His cock slipped over the hard dimple he recognized as her cervix. Her vaginal canal stretched to take him completely. His hands molded her breasts, fingers pinched her responsive nipples.

He was aware of Mik behind him, aware of the orgasm hovering just beyond his reach. He heard the tear of foil and knew Mik donned a condom, felt the thick, cool cream—some sort of lubricant—gliding between his cheeks.

Expectation of the unknown took Logan higher than he'd ever flown. Fingers brushed his ass, trailed through the slick lube. Touched the sensitive portal. Mik pressed one finger deep and Logan sighed. Another finger joined the first, shocking him with the intimacy of the act, the sensations he'd not expected from a plethora of nerve endings never before stimulated.

Despite his lack of memory, Logan knew this was a first for him. Still, he spread his knees farther apart, raised his buttocks for the man kneeling behind him. Jazzy's legs spread wider to give him room and Logan realized she'd linked with him once more.

Her mind was riding his, feeling each move Mik made. When Mik inserted a third thick finger, Jazzy groaned in perfect harmony with Logan. The pressure changed, fingers slipped out slowly and the smooth head of Mik's broad latex-covered cock pressed against his sensitive sphincter. Pressure increased, and with it the first sharp bite of pain.

Then Mik was through and Logan's muscle tightened around the head of his cock. Logan almost laughed when he realized all three of them had breathed a sigh of relief.

Mik began to move, thrusting slow and deep, withdrawing at a snail's pace. Logan did the same, filling Jazzy, withdrawing and then thrusting forward once again. He'd never experienced anything like it, the sensation of being stuffed so full, the slow glide of slick flesh over nerves strung taut.

He almost wallowed in the sensory overload. Mik's taut belly pressed firmly against his buttocks, his big hands stroked Logan's back and chest, occasionally catching his nipples between thick fingers, pinching him to the point of pain, taking him higher, farther.

Logan felt the beginnings of Mik's climax. Transferred the sensations to his own and a hot coil of power built low in his groin, flowed through his balls and powered his cock for one final, balls-deep thrust into Jazzy's welcoming sex.

Her vaginal muscles spasmed around him, his own muscles clenched Mik's thick shaft, and the three of them flew from the precipice together, crying out, shuddering, bodies rigid in the power of their joined desire.

Jazzy flattened out beneath Logan's final thrust and he followed her forward. Mik came down on top of them both but he held his weight above them. His hips, though, continued thrusting slowly in and out of Logan's ass, forcing Logan's softening penis to mimic the same movements within Jazzy.

His heart thundered until it slowly returned to a level that didn't promise imminent death. Mik panted against his back, his hot breath tickling Logan's ear. Jazzy moaned and writhed slowly beneath him, obviously still enjoying more little orgasmic aftershocks.

"Okay," Mik said, drawing out the word. "That was fun."

Jazzy snorted.

Logan laughed. Compressed between Mik and Jazzy, his chest bounced off her back and he felt Mik's belly against his butt and his laughter grew . . . and spread.

Chuckling, Mik pulled away and headed into the bathroom to dispose of the condom. Logan rolled over carefully, well aware of the fact he'd just been screwed where he'd never been touched before. Jazzy merely lay in one spot, belly down, and giggled.

Mik came out of the bathroom with a warm, wet washrag. Logan headed into the bathroom to take his turn, but not before he watched Mik gently roll Jazzy to her back so he could carefully bathe away Logan's seed.

An intimate act if ever there was one. And yet, surprisingly, Logan felt no jealousy, no sense of territory.

Only appreciation that Mik was taking such good care of the woman who would be his mate.

8

Jazzy lifted Mik's big arm off her breasts and tugged her right leg out from under Logan's left thigh. Quietly she crawled off the bed and slipped out of the bedroom. She used a bathroom in one of the empty rooms so she wouldn't wake the guys. After searching a bit, she found a bathrobe hanging in the closet.

It was bright outside, but even without looking at a clock, Jazzy knew she'd slept away more than half the day.

At least, when they'd quit fucking long enough to sleep. She tried to wipe the silly grin off her face and didn't even come close. After years of sex with all the wrong men, she finally knew what it was supposed to feel like.

Damn, it was even better than she'd dreamed. Mik was an amazing lover. Logan, though he wasn't quite as big as Mik, was even better. Tender, loving, his lips and hands had been dedicated solely to her pleasure.

Her breasts still tingled from all the attention they'd gotten. Her legs felt a bit wobbly and even her jaw ached: taking a guy the size of Mik between her lips had required a lot more stretching than she was used to.

But the best part of it all had been the laughter. She'd never had sex and fun at the same time, but the past hours with both Mik and Logan in her bed had been the most fun she'd ever had with anyone.

Deacon's serious image floated into her mind. He was such a quiet, lonely kid. She bet he'd love spending a night with her and Logan. Since Matt seemed to have joined up with Beth and Nick, it only made sense.

She wondered if he was back yet. Jazzy headed for the main part of the house. The door was open into Beth and Nick's room. She glanced in just as Beth raised her head and waved. The guys slept soundly, curled up like puppies in a basket, both of them in their wolf forms.

Beth held a finger to her lips and quietly crawled out of bed. Jazzy pointed her to the empty room and the bathroom she'd used, and while Beth was using the facilities, found an extra robe for her friend. Without exchanging a word, the two of them tiptoed out to the kitchen.

"Still no sign of Tala and the guys," Jazzy said. She opened the refrigerator and looked for something to eat. There was all kinds of salad stuff, but her eye went immediately to a pack of sliced rare roast beef. She grabbed that along with some horse-radish and a loaf of bread. Beth found other condiments and they loaded their bounty onto the kitchen counter.

Finally, sandwiches made and mess cleaned up, they headed out to the front porch where they could talk without waking the men.

Beth took a big bite of her sandwich, chewed and swallowed, and washed it down with a glass of milk. "Okay," she said, grinning at Jazzy. "Was last night absolutely the most amazing time in your life, or what?"

Jazzy laughed. "You talking about the wolf gig or the sex."

"Oh lordy . . . the sex. What else? I feel like we've discovered an entirely new form of recreation."

Chewing thoughtfully, Jazzy cocked her head and stared at Beth a moment.

"What?" Beth frowned.

"For you and me, it is entirely new. I hadn't really thought about it. Sex was always work for me. My job. I never enjoyed it because it was always about the guy. He was paying for my time so I'd damn well better make it worth his while. My pimp pretty much beat that into me. For you, it's the rape thing. Hard to enjoy anything when you're forced against your will."

"I had never had sex with someone I loved." Beth stared down at the sandwich in her hand. "I love Nick. We're going to do the mating bond as soon as we can. I know Matt's going to feel left out, but he can still be with us. Just not one of us, if you get my drift."

"Sort of like Mik with me and Logan last night."

"Mik? I don't believe it!"

Jazzy grinned around her mouthful. "Believe it. He's amazing. I can see why Tala's got a big smile on her face all the time. But, like you said. He was with us, but I really felt connected to Logan more than Mik."

"Are you going to bond with Logan?"

Jazzy shook her head. "I don't know. I know he wants to. It was right there in his head whenever we linked, but I have to be sure. It's forever. I'm not sure I'm ready to commit to anyone for anything for forever. There's still too much I want to learn about me."

"What if that's the only way Logan can get his memory back?"

Jazzy shook her head hard enough to send her long hair flying. "That's Logan's issue. What if we bond and he finds out who he is during the link? What if he decides he doesn't want to be tied for the rest of his life to some little black whore? What then? I want to know the man I'm with loves me for who I am. No doubts. No questions. Then I'll think about bonding."

She took another bite and chewed angrily. No way was she going to give up her newly won independence. Free of her pimp for the first time since she was six years old! No way in hell was she turning that freedom over to another man. Not until she was absolutely sure he wanted her for herself.

The only downside was, what if he chose another woman? One who wasn't as hardheaded and opinionated as Jazzy Blue? What then?

The guys finally wandered out of their rooms, loaded up plates filled with sandwiches and snacks, and joined Jazzy and Beth on the porch. They'd all found jeans that fit, but none of them wore shirts. Jazzy rather liked being surrounded by all that muscular male flesh.

Logan parked his delectable butt right next to Jazzy's, almost as if he was staking his claim. She liked that, too, in a perverse sort of way, even when he leaned over and kissed her hard on the mouth. She kissed him back, but quickly. He quirked a brow in her direction, but didn't say anything.

It felt good to hold all the cards for once. She definitely enjoyed being so close to Logan, looking at him . . . especially now that his tats were gone. He hadn't put the studs and rings back in. It appeared as if the little holes in his eyebrows, lips, ears, and nose were already healing.

It was almost five when Jazzy heard a car coming up the drive. She glanced at Mik. He had a huge smile on his face.

AJ pulled into the parking area in front of the cabin with Tala and Deacon in the car.

Mik whispered, "Thank the goddess."

Jazzy turned and flashed him a big smile, wondering what it would feel like to have someone care so much about her and miss her so desperately when she was away.

"We're home." AJ grinned at the group on the porch and helped Deacon out of the car. He handed him his crutches and followed him up the stairs, ready to catch the younger man should he fall. Tala followed along behind. Her face was lined with exhaustion, but as usual, she was smiling.

"Hi everyone. We're home safe and sound. Logan, I have to compliment you. The doctor said you set Deacon's broken leg perfectly. He had an open compound fracture of the tibia and the bone pieces were perfectly aligned when you splinted him. No need for surgery or pins. Good job!"

Deacon leaned over and shook Logan's hand. "Thanks, bro. You really saved me." He frowned and stared at his face. "Where the hell are your tats?" He looked closer at Logan's chest. "What happened to your nipple ring?"

Logan laughed. Once he got started, he couldn't seem to stop. AJ pulled out a chair for Deacon and he sat, obviously perplexed. Finally, Logan got it under control, but every time he tried to talk, he'd laugh again. He waved a hand at Jazzy. "You explain."

It took her a minute to get her own giggles under control. "Last night, Deacon. After you left with the rescue guys? We all shifted. All five of us turned into wolves."

"No shit. Damn, I want to do that so bad."

So many emotions crossed Deacon's face, Jazzy felt sorry for him, but Logan spoke up before she could.

"It'll happen, man." Logan reached out and touched Deacon's shoulder. "Probably sooner than you think. Once you get the cast off, you'll do it, too."

Deacon closed his eyes and nodded. "So the tats . . . they just disappeared."

"Not entirely." Beth rolled her eyes and pointed to a small shimmer of colored dust caught in the porch decking. "Logan left bits and pieces of himself all over the place."

Dinner turned into nothing more than a long, drawn-out raid on the refrigerator. Exhausted from their long ordeal, Tala and AJ headed for bed. Mik followed along behind, obviously re-

lieved to have his mates back with him, but he gave one final bit
of advice.

"If you guys run tonight," he said, "don't go too far. I do
not want to have to send out a search team."

Beth and Nick shifted immediately and disappeared into the
forest.

"They're going to mate." Matt's words hung in the quiet
evening air.

Jazzy thought he sounded absolutely bereft. "That's a good
thing, don't you think?"

Shrugging, Matt stood up and leaned against the railing. He
gazed in the direction his friends had gone. "Last night I had
sex with both of them. It was the most amazing night I've ever
had. I'm afraid, once they bond, it'll never happen like that
again."

"It'll happen. Just because you're mated . . ." Jazzy's voice
trailed off. She couldn't bring herself to look in Logan's direction.

"Jazzy's right," Logan said. "Mik was with us last night,
and . . ."

"Mik?" Deacon's head whipped around. "You guys had sex
with Mik? He's like the uber alpha male."

Jazzy giggled. "He's just like any other guy when you're
sucking his dick. Logan, did you notice him going all alpha?"

"I'll answer that once it doesn't hurt to sit."

They sat outside in the growing darkness and talked and
laughed, telling Deacon about their amazing night while he'd
been stuck in ER getting a cast on his leg.

Jazzy wanted to take the feelings of the four of them together and hold them close to her heart. She'd never felt anything like this. *Pure, unconditional love.*

Mik had definitely known what he was talking about. She
loved them all. Mik, AJ, and Tala, three people she hardly knew,

yet knew so well. Deacon and Matt, two young men she fully expected to know a whole lot better before too long.

Nicky and Beth . . . especially Beth. Since making their shift last night, since their talk this afternoon, she realized Beth was the sister she'd never had, the best friend she'd always wanted.

And then there was Logan. She took a quick glance at him out of the corner of her eye and caught him watching her. He didn't look away. Instead his smile grew, a smile she'd rarely seen before now.

He still didn't know who he was. Still wanted to discover his missing past, but he'd not pressed her at all for something she wasn't certain she could give.

Herself. Forever.

For that alone she felt herself falling deeper in love with him. Falling deeper under the power of another man.

This time, though, maybe it was right.

Maybe she was falling for the right reasons.

And maybe, just maybe, Logan was the right man.

Nicky trotted closely behind Beth through the dark woods. Sounds of the night were exactly as they should be: the whoosh of an owl overhead, the soft squeak of bats, the rustling in grass along the trail that told him mice and rabbits scattered at their approach.

Nothing out of place and the world felt right. So why did he feel so tense? He hadn't wanted to pressure her, but he wanted this with a visceral need. Wanted Beth as his mate. He knew she was young, but even at twenty-one, life on the streets aged a person, whether they were male or female. At twenty-four he sometimes felt positively ancient. Beth was wise beyond her years.

Too wise. Maybe too smart to want a loser like him?

That's not true, Nick. I love you. I've loved you since the first time I saw you over at the memorial garden.

You never said a word. He sat back on his haunches and stared at her. Beth dipped her head, almost in apology.

I was afraid.

You don't ever have to be afraid. Not with me, Beth.

I know. That's just one of the reasons I'm here with you right now.

What are the others? He knew he was pushing her, but he couldn't help himself. He had to be sure. Had to know Beth was sure. Mik said this was forever. What did you know about forever when you were only twenty-four?

I know that if my life ended tomorrow and you weren't my mate, it would be my greatest regret. My reasons are simple, Nick. I love you. I'm happiest when I'm with you. You complete me and I know my life would not be right without you in it.

I feel the same. Beth? Why is it easier to say these things when we're animals, but almost impossible when we're human?

When we speak with our minds, we can say what's in our hearts. When we use our voices, it's too hard to say the words. Make love to me, Nicky. Make me your mate.

Instinct was such an amazing force. He'd only had sex with a woman a couple times in his life and last night had been his first time with two people. Never had he mated as a wolf, but it was so easy to rake her shoulders with his paw, to turn Beth's body and mount her from behind. He'd wondered what he'd do about her tail, but it moved out of the way and he entered her on the first thrust.

He hadn't known about the knot in his penis. Had no idea they'd be locked together, but Beth didn't seem at all surprised. He felt her joy, her arousal, her curiosity about this fascinating act . . . and then he felt Beth.

As the knot swelled inside her and tied the two of them together, a link formed in their minds, a joining unlike anything Nick had ever imagined. He didn't just feel her arousal, as he'd done last night. He suddenly realized he *was* Beth, just as she became him.

Her entire life spread out before him. Her close relationship with her mother, her childish fear of her stepfather that had proven itself when he raped her. Nick felt her pain, her terror during the attack. Silently he vowed the man would die if he ever had the chance to kill him.

The years since Beth left home had been hard, but she'd maintained her integrity, worked at honest jobs, avoided drugs and casual sex. She'd been taken against her will on a couple of occasions, but in both cases she'd learned from the experience and moved on.

She was a survivor. Quiet and intelligent, yet powerful in her sense of self, a loyal friend, a true love. And he saw how very much she loved him. How much she respected him for the hard choices he'd had to make in his own life. All of this knowledge, these memories, washed through him in a heartbeat, yet Nick knew they would stay with him forever.

Just as his mate would stay.

Age had nothing to do with unconditional love.

He shifted. Beth was so perfectly attuned to him that she shifted at exactly the same moment. Nick's arms were wrapped around her middle, his chest pressing into the warm length of her back. He rolled with her to one side until they lay together in the cool grass. Panting, hearts pounding, minds and bodies still linked, their path forever joined.

"That was amazing."

Beth's soft whisper expressed exactly what he was thinking. "Will we always be this closely linked?" He had to clear his voice first to get any sound to come out.

"I hope so," she said, turning to smile at him. "Oh, Nick. I sure hope so."

They lay there in the sweet grass, their convoluted pasts forgotten, hearts and minds set firmly on a perfectly joined path into the future.

Deacon yawned. "I need some sleep," he said, struggling to his feet. Obviously the use of crutches didn't come naturally to someone well over six-and-a-half feet tall. Laughing, Matt helped him untangle his cast from his crutches.

"C'mon, big guy. I'll help you to bed. I'm not going to run tonight. I'm tired, too."

The night fell into a preternatural silence when they left, as if they took all sound with them. It left Jazzy even more aware of Logan's silent presence beside her. She swallowed and the sound seemed to echo in her ears. When she glanced up at Logan, he smiled and rubbed his cheek against her hair.

Jazzy turned, wanting so badly for him to kiss her, needing the taste of his lips against hers. Suddenly a rustling in the bushes at the edge of the forest caught her attention. Both she and Logan turned to look.

Beth and Nick trotted out of the trees, tails high, ears forward. Each of them shifted as they reached the stairs to the porch, going from wolf to human as if they'd done this same thing all their lives. Their steps were in sync, they grasped one another's hands at the moment of their shift, glanced briefly at Jazzy and Logan, smiled in greeting, and headed directly inside. It was obvious what they were going to be doing in a very short time.

Jazzy saw the love on their faces and the light in their eyes. She knew she'd never been so jealous in her entire life.

Not of Beth and Nick, not of their love. She was jealous of their certainty. The irrefutable conviction that they'd done something exactly right and held no regrets.

She wanted that same feeling.

The only one she wanted it with was sitting next to her.

Jazzy turned and glanced at Logan. Her lips parted when she saw the longing in his eyes. She opened her thoughts, startled when she realized Logan's needs mirrored hers. He wanted Jazzy to love him. Wanted her to believe strongly enough in their love to give herself to a man without a past.

Are you willing to give yourself to a woman who has a past? One as miserable as mine?

For all you know, I'm an ax murderer.

She slapped her hand over her mouth to stop the nervous giggles. "I very much doubt that."

"It's not our past we should be thinking about. It's the future." Logan took a deep breath and stood up. Then he surprised her completely by going down on one knee and taking Jazzy's hands in his. "It's not hearts and flowers, but I do love you, Jazzy Blue. It's not a promise of marriage, though if you want the traditional ceremony, so do I. I believe this is something even more powerful. This is forever."

Once again he said, "I love you." His voice had gone gravelly with emotion and tears sparkled in his eyes. "Will you be my mate, Jaz? Will you go into the woods with me tonight and make love under the stars? Commit to me for the rest of our days?"

Jazzy slipped down on her knees beside him. Her fingers trembled in his big hands. His fingers were fair, hers dark. His hands were large, hers small and slim, but he deferred to her and her status as the alpha bitch. He loved her in spite of her past, and he was right.

They needed to think about the future, and she couldn't even imagine one without Logan. "Yes," she said, nodding her head slowly in agreement. "Yes, I will be your mate, for now and for always."

When she stood up and pulled Logan to his feet, it was with a sense of conviction that all was finally right with her world.

* * *

They talked about their decision long into the night. Questioned the validity of their feelings, the goals they had, the kind of love they expected. Jazzy finally led Logan into the trees just before dawn, trotting confidently on four legs through the glorious old growth redwoods. Her sense of unreality faded as she became more attuned to the primeval forest around her.

The night was still though the ancient trees had a voice of their own, a voice that called out to both of them. Words of promise and hope, a sense that what happened tonight would have a more powerful effect on Jazzy and her mate than any single act she'd ever done in her life.

With a sense of awe she stopped in a small clearing, turned her head and gazed over her shoulder at the beautiful dark wolf behind her. Her mate, Logan. The one she chose.

The one who chose her.

When he mounted her, when his sharp nails raked her shoulders and his powerful jaws clamped down on the thick ruff of fur at her collar, Jazzy gracefully submitted.

It was only right.

Her arousal grew, expanded and consumed until the link forged between them solidified. She was Logan, a man lost in a mind damaged by injury. She forged ahead, found his memories locked behind scars, found his amazing skills, his compassion, his past.

And in a moment of pure sharing, Logan did the same for Jazzy. Showed her the single mother she'd forgotten, the one who had loved her and died much too young. Showed her the neighbor in that foreign land, where forest grew thick and polluted waters fouled the streets—the neighbor who had promised to care for her, yet gave into greed and took gold in payment for a frightened little girl alone in a heartless world.

So many details, memories exposed and recalled, theirs to sort and try to comprehend when the time was right. Now though, it was time for a joining like nothing either had experienced. A bonding of hearts and minds and bodies.

Locked intimately, bodies in sync, hearts beating together, tongues lolling and mouths wide and panting, Jazzy finally understood what Mik had tried to explain.

What she'd seen on Beth and Nick's face. In Tala, AJ, and Mik's eyes. *Unconditional love.* The forever kind. Sighing, she shifted and realized Logan was right there with her, leaning over her and grinning like a fool.

"I have to say I love you, only the word doesn't seem powerful enough."

"And I love you, Doctor Pierce. You really are a doctor. No wonder you knew what to do for Deacon."

"Yeah, but my first name is Rupert. Can you actually love a guy named Rupert?"

Jazzy laughed and kissed his nose. She loved his nose, even without the ring in his left nostril. "Your middle name's Logan. I'm good with that."

Logan sat up, leaned against a fallen log, and pulled Jazzy into his lap. "I must have recognized it on the nurse's badge. I was there to volunteer my services at Glide Memorial. Didn't tell anyone at Good Samaritan that I was leaving. I'll need to contact them, tender my resignation, let them know where I've been all this time."

Jazzy frowned. "You're not going to go back? You had a really busy practice."

Logan shook his head. "No. You heard Mik. The Chanku need a doctor. My place is here. With my pack. With you."

Jazzy stood up and grabbed his hand. "Just so long as we're clear on that." She pulled him to his feet.

"Perfectly clear, Jazzy, my love. Perfectly clear." He kissed her lips, held her close, and then both of them shifted.

Running shoulder to shoulder, they headed back toward the cabin, racing the sun into a new day.

Animal Instinct

Lydia Parks

1

"What . . . who the hell are you?" Gary scrambled to his feet.

The young woman approaching one slow step at a time didn't answer. She wore absolutely nothing as she tiptoed through knee-deep snow.

Emerging from a crystalline forest, she looked like a fairy. Ice glistened in her white hair and on her creamy skin. Even in the sub-zero temperature, she didn't appear to be cold.

"Are you okay?"

When she didn't answer, Gary glanced around, convinced this must be some kind of practical joke.

Nothing but silence accompanied her approach. As he watched, he realized all he could hear was his own breath puffing, and blood rushing past his ears.

"Look, if you're lost or something . . ."

She smiled and shook her head.

The woman was beautiful, with perfect little breasts and a slender waist. She couldn't be more than twenty. She wore her shoulder-length hair in a stylishly wild and uneven cut. The weird thing was that all the hair on her body was white.

She continued to approach and Gary took a step backward, stumbling over the log he'd been sitting on. As he struggled to regain his balance, he kicked over his Coleman and coffeepot, and warm liquid hissed in the snow.

"Shit." He righted the stove and coffeepot and closed the propane valve, then rose to face the strange woman. "I, um, will have radio contact in an hour." He ripped the snaps open on his down coat, shrugged it off, and walked toward her holding the coat out like a bullfighter's cape. "Here."

She smiled at him through his clouds of frosty breath and shook her head again.

"Aren't you freezing?" he asked.

"No." Her voice was quiet, as if she were sharing a secret.

He gulped. This had to be the most beautiful woman he'd ever seen, but she also had to be nuts. Why else would she be walking around naked in the middle of Denali National Park? And in March?

She took his coat and spread it on the ground, then stepped close to him.

"I, um—" Gazing into her silver-blue eyes, he couldn't think of a thing to say. It occurred to him then that he must be dreaming, especially since he didn't feel particularly cold anymore. Instead, his body seemed to be heating like a freshly stoked wood stove.

She reached up and touched the side of his face with slender fingers.

Her touch felt real enough.

Still, she must be a fantasy. It had been too cold even in his sleeping bag to jerk off this week; his dick now rose in protest.

Her hand slid down to the collar of his flannel shirt and she began to unbutton the garment.

"What are you doing?" He followed the progress of her fingers until the shirt lay open to his grimy long-John top.

The woman stepped closer and eased his shirt off with her

warm palms sliding across his chest and shoulders, and down his arms.

Gary closed his eyes at the intense pleasure of her touch, even through the cotton.

When her fingers grazed bare skin at his waist, he inhaled sharply, taking in the scent of spruce, spiced with some kind of musk. Most women he knew smelled of shampoo or perfume, not wild animals and trees. Still, her scent only added to the fantasy; he loved the outdoors.

She slid her warm palms up his sides and arms, pushing his thermal shirt off over his head. She added the garment to the growing pile next to his jacket.

He should have been shivering with cold, but his internal heat kicked up a notch as she spread her hands across his chest.

She urged him around and backward toward his pile of clothes.

"I'm not complaining, but what—"

"I'm here for you," she whispered.

His knees buckled, and he went down, landing on his jacket. She followed him, kneeling gracefully between his legs.

He watched her remove the rest of his clothing, unable and unwilling to stop her. He'd never had a fantasy like this. The whole thing left him confused.

His prick pointed skyward as he lay naked on his back, and she rose to her feet. Gazing down at him, she ran her hands over her own body, caressing her nipples into tight nubs, and then sliding one hand between her legs.

The world around him faded to a dull gray with this woman standing in the center of it, soft, warm flesh sprinkled with ice crystals. His body tightened with need, and he fought to catch his breath.

She crouched, reached out, and touched his dick. He jumped.

She quickly withdrew her hand and frowned as she studied his face.

"Sorry, I just wasn't expecting . . ."

Apparently reassured, she leaned forward and wrapped her hand completely around him.

He nearly lost it then. Her unfamiliar touch, her incredibly sexy silver eyes, were almost too much.

Before he could come, she released him and crawled forward on all fours to straddle his hips. His swollen prick rose in front of her, and her white pubic hair teased the sensitive skin.

All he could think about was grabbing her and fucking her, but he couldn't move.

Holding his dick, she rose up and pointed it into her, and he closed his eyes as the head pressed against wetness so perfect it almost hurt. She pushed down onto him.

As hard as he was, though, he didn't slide right in.

Gary opened his eyes to find her studying him with a steely gaze. She wriggled, working the tightest cunt he'd ever felt over the head of his dick. Was she a virgin? Why the hell would he fantasize about a virgin? He'd never done so before. He'd always fantasized about big-breasted whores giving him blow jobs. This was totally out there.

Frowning, she grunted softly with effort until suddenly her cunt swallowed his cock all at once. She cried out as if in pain.

He would have gotten soft if all this were real; he'd never wanted to hurt anyone, especially during sex. Instead, he responded to the tightness squeezing his prick by getting even harder. He grasped the liner of his coat in his fists.

Her thighs gripped his sides as she moved forward and backward, very slowly, cruelly rubbing his buried dick. Thick cream slid down between his balls.

Cum pooled deep and heavy as his dick prepared to erupt.

Suddenly her cunt squeezed tighter, and she threw her head back. Her fingernails dug into his chest.

He couldn't hold back the flood. In spite of the pain of her nails, he exploded inside her, lifting his hips off the ground to get deeper.

Her gaze snapped to his and she narrowed her eyes as he pumped what felt like gallons of cum.

She drew her fingernails down the front of his chest, scraping flesh.

He continued to come, and his vision blurred.

Her face seemed to distort, elongating, her eyes moving apart, until she looked like some kind of animal.

He tried to scream, but he couldn't. His dick still throbbed with the last of his release, and his head swam. Tendrils of confusion snaked through his brain.

She leaned forward and sank her teeth into his shoulder with a feral growl.

Rachel stopped inside the doorway of the smoke-filled building to stomp snow from her boots, stuff her wool cap into her pocket, shrug off her heavy coat, and let her eyes adjust. Half of Siberia seemed to be crammed into the bar, all raising glasses of vodka, screaming at each other to be heard, and chain smoking. She scanned the room, expecting Inspector Volsky to stand out in the crowd, undoubtedly sporting silver hair and a pressed uniform with lots of metals and braids. Maybe he hadn't yet arrived.

Ten feet in front of her, two large men jumped to their feet, red-faced and yelling, and grabbed the fronts of each other's shirts. People around them raised glasses and bottles out of the way as the two men bumped into tables, each trying to topple the other. One finally succeeded and followed his opponent to the floor.

In the space left by the brawlers, Rachel had a clear view to a back table where a man sat alone, long legs stretched out in front of him, boots crossed. He had wavy black hair that faded at his broad shoulders into dark clothing, and he held a glass in one hand.

He stared at her.

For a moment, she couldn't look away. All she could do was return his stare.

His eyes looked almost yellow, like a cat's eyes, and seemed to reflect nonexistent light. He didn't blink. The rest of the room blurred into nothingness around him.

As she watched, his gaze ran down her body and back up, and a shiver followed it.

"I've found him."

Rachel jumped at the voice beside her and tore her eyes from the strange man at the back of the room. She turned to face her guide. "He's here?"

"*Da.* This way."

Trying to ignore the man she was sure still stared at her, she followed Sergei along the length of the bar and around crowded tables, dodging stumbling drunks and waving arms. Sergei stopped, then stepped aside.

"Inspector Rachel McNeil, this is Inspector Volsky."

She sucked in a breath of surprise as the man who had been staring at her rose and nodded. "Inspector McNeil," he said, extending his hand.

This was Inspector Volsky? No pressed suit or silver hair. Instead, golden eyes studied her from a ruggedly handsome face. A hint of a smile tugged at the corners of his mouth.

Rachel mentally shook herself and accepted the handshake, pretending not to notice how commandingly strong his hand felt as it wrapped around hers.

"Inspector Volsky."

He motioned toward a chair. "Please, call me Nikolai. And I will call you Rachel, if you don't mind."

"Uh, no, I don't mind." Rachel draped her coat over the back of the wooden chair and sat.

Sergei, with no place to sit, cleared his throat.

Volsky glanced up at him. "Thank you, Sergeant. I'll make sure the Inspector gets back to her hotel."

Sergei shifted from one foot to the other, obviously annoyed at being dismissed but unsure what to do. After a moment, he turned and left.

Rachel tried to size up the man across from her as he sat back and studied her again. She usually managed to read strangers within about twenty seconds, but this one was different. Not just because he was Russian. In fact, his accent was a little odd for a Russian.

"Where did you learn to speak English, Inspec—uh, Nikolai?"

"From my mother."

"Your mother's from England? Australia?"

He shook his head. "No. She's from Siberia."

"And your father?"

"Also Siberian."

"I see."

"And you? What is your lineage?" The hint of a smile from earlier bloomed into a full-fledged grin.

Heat rose in Rachel's neck and cheeks, and she felt as though she were a toy mouse being batted around by a mischievous house cat. She absolutely hated that feeling. Simon had made sure he left her feeling small and inconsequential after every argument. Damn him and his stinking psychology degree.

She took a deep breath, surprised to realize Simon could still piss her off after nearly a year. She hadn't even cared about him all that much.

Tucking a strand of hair behind one ear, she decided to get down to business. "What can you tell me about the case?"

"The one where eight young men were found at various locations in the wilderness, dead?"

She nodded. "Yes."

He shrugged. "That's about it."

"You solved the case."

Nikolai shook his head. "No, I stopped the killings."

"But you must have solved the case in order to stop the killings."

His grin widened, and she realized just how luscious his mouth looked.

Rachel dropped her gaze, swallowed hard, and then looked him evenly in the eye. "I came a long way to talk to you, Inspector Volsky. This is not a game. If you can't help me—"

Nikolai's smile faded. He glanced away and sighed. "Perhaps I can, I don't know."

He nodded to someone behind her who unceremoniously delivered a bottle of vodka and a glass to the table. Nikolai filled the new glass and his own, then slid the new one to Rachel.

"I don't drink vodka," she said, cringing at the memory of a particularly bad screwdriver hangover in college.

He raised his glass and his smile returned. "In Russia, inspectors drink vodka together before sharing secrets."

She got the message. If she wanted information, she'd have to drink.

Just one. She could do that. It wasn't as if she were a teetotaler.

"*Na zdorovye*," he said.

She clinked her glass to his. "*Na zdorovye*."

The first sip of vodka was surprisingly mild compared to the stuff she'd had in college. She just might be able to make it through the whole glass without embarrassing herself, if she drank it slowly enough.

"Tell me about your case," she said.

He leaned forward, resting his arms on the table, and looked her in the eyes as he spoke. "We found eight men over the course of three months. All were out in the woods for one reason or another. One was a geologist, scouting gold. Two were hunters. One had simply stopped his car to relieve himself. Three were university students doing fieldwork."

"That's only seven."

He nodded. "Yes. One was a police officer investigating the deaths."

"Someone you knew?"

"No."

"Common denominators?" She sipped from the glass as she fought the urge to squirm under his scrutiny.

"All young, all naked, all dead." He refilled their glasses.

"Had they been mauled?"

"To some extent." He emptied half his vodka, then studied the glass as he rotated it slowly on the table. "Now tell me why you're here."

"We have a similar problem."

His gaze snapped to hers. "How similar?"

"All young, all naked, all dead. Six so far."

His eyes narrowed and visibly darkened to brown. Even without the golden eyes, he was handsome. His chiseled features reminded her of ancient royalty.

"You said you stopped the killings. Are you going to tell me who's doing this?"

He looked out at the crowd as if searching for an answer. "It isn't so much who as what."

"Excuse me?"

"Let's dance." Nikolai rose suddenly. His chair screeched across the concrete floor.

"What?"

He offered his hand.

Rachel felt something odd, something primitive and indefinable. Her gut knotted with longing as she gazed up into eyes revealing both strength and vulnerability.

What was it about this man?

Even as she asked the question, she took his hand and let him lead her to the far end of the room, a dark corner where a small area of floor had been cleared for dancers. He gripped her in a possessive manner, as if they'd already been intimate.

Already? Why had she thought that? She had no intention of becoming intimate with this man, or any other for that matter. Simon had cured her desire to open her heart when he'd snuck out of their apartment in the middle of the night to run off to Vegas with a stripper.

Nikolai turned and drew her into his arms without asking permission.

Rachel stiffened against him, her hands on his chest, trying to push away without being obvious. "What are you doing?"

"I'm dancing with you," he said with his mouth near her ear.

He stood a good four or five inches taller than she did, which put him well over six feet. He didn't wear aftershave. He didn't need it. His scent whispered of masculinity forgotten in modern times. When she closed her eyes, she saw castles and horses. She felt the shadows of thick woods and heard clashing swords.

Weird.

"Much better," he whispered.

She suddenly realized she'd slid her hands down to his waist and relaxed against him. Her head rested on his shoulder as he swayed gently to music she could barely make out above the din.

Rachel stiffened again. "Why are we dancing?"

"You don't enjoy dancing?"

"Not with colleagues."

"We are not colleagues, yet. We're simply strangers meeting on a dance floor in a crowded bar."

A shiver ran down her spine.

She shouldn't have had the vodka; it was doing strange things to her system.

"I came here for help in a murder investigation," she said.

"Yes, I know. I'll help you." He eased one hand down the middle of her back nearly to the base of her spine and drew her closer.

Rachel gulped back a groan as desire writhed in her stomach.

His body felt hard and lean beneath the thick shirt, and he moved so gracefully she couldn't even feel his steps. His breath caressed the side of her neck.

"How?" she asked.

"Hmm?"

"How will you help?"

"Take me with you, and I'll stop the killings."

"How will you stop them?"

When he didn't answer, she leaned back enough to look at him.

His eyes smoldered as their gazes locked, and she felt as if all the air had left the room. Some traitorous instinct urged her to taste him, to lean into a kiss.

Fortunately, she fought the urge and looked away.

"I can't tell you," he said. "I can stop the killings, or you can return home alone. That's all I can offer."

She stepped back, out of his arms. "Is this some kind of military crap?"

He shook his head. "No."

"Then tell me who's doing it."

He frowned. "You have my offer. It's all I can do."

A wave of dizziness hit. Rachel took another step backward and grabbed a chair. The combination of heavy smoke, vodka, confusion, and being near Nikolai overwhelmed her. "I, uh, need to find the restroom." Without waiting for directions, she turned and started toward the only alcove she could see.

Noise and smoke lessened as she pushed open the door to the women's restroom. The large room held two wooden stalls, two sinks, ancient mirrors, and, fortunately, no other visitors. Coolness from concrete floors and walls seemed to ease the heat in her skin left by Nikolai's touch, and she felt some semblance of sanity returning.

Rachel stepped toward one sink as the door squeaked open. She glanced in the mirror.

Nikolai walked in, letting the door close behind him, and strode directly to her.

She spun around. "What are you doing in here?"

He didn't say anything. Instead, he grabbed her arm, slid one hand behind her neck, and drew her mouth up to his.

She gasped as his lips found hers. She pressed her hands to his chest intending to shove him away, but somehow she couldn't.

He pinned her against the sink with the weight of his body.

His mouth opened, and hers responded, opening, too, welcoming him.

He tasted her, swirling his tongue around hers, caressing her from the inside out.

Her body began to tremble, starting at her knees and moving up to her chest. What was she doing? How could she stand in this foreign bathroom and let this man she didn't know kiss her as if they'd kissed a million times?

He wrapped his arms around her, drawing her tightly up against him.

She felt his hardness pressed against her abdomen, and a groan rose in her throat.

He tilted his head and dove deeper into her mouth, and she drew hard on his tongue. She needed more of him, so much more. His hands moved over her body with slow, maddening sureness, touching, adoring her.

Somewhere deep inside her, embers that had appeared when she first spotted him in the bar burst into flames. Heat rose, chasing away the tremors, turning all her thoughts and concerns to boiling liquid.

He must have felt it, too, for he tightened his grip, pushed one leg between her knees, and raised it to her crotch.

The liquid spread through more of her, oozing out between

her legs where she straddled his muscular thigh, rubbing with a primal rhythm.

He squeezed her ass through her pants and drew her in closer, returning her groan with a low, steady growl that vibrated from his chest to hers.

Her clit swelled and scraped against her wet panties as if they were sandpaper, and her entire body stiffened. She clung to the back of his shirt.

The flame blasted forth, creating an inferno that threatened to consume her as she rubbed harder, faster, every muscle tightening.

He pushed against her and matched her rhythm, drawing her to the edge of the blaze.

Rachel tore her mouth from Nikolai's and pressed her face to his shoulder as her body erupted. Spasms ripped through her vagina as she clamped his leg between hers and ground her pulsing muscles into his thigh. Gasping, she rode out the waves of scorching release, holding him close, filling her heightened senses with his scent and his presence.

She slowed as the need waned.

One by one, the flames flickered out, leaving her spent and shaking again.

He held her, still now, except for a slight tremor in his arms. Then he turned his face to hers and kissed her lips and cheeks.

He lowered his leg and leaned into her, harder than before.

He straightened, and released her completely.

Gripping the edge of the cold sink behind her, Rachel stared up into his golden eyes, trying to read the emotions flashing in them.

He took a step back. "I'll get you a car," he said, his voice rough and deep.

He turned and hurried away.

She stared at the door as it slammed shut behind him. The noise echoed through the empty room.

What the hell had just happened?

More important, why?

She'd never been a particularly sexual person, certainly not prone to episodes with strangers. Yet, if he'd asked her to, she would have ripped off her clothes and let him fuck her raw in the women's restroom, not caring what would have happened if someone had walked in on them.

Even Simon hadn't come close to making her feel like that, and he'd been the best she'd ever had.

Until now.

"Oh, shit," she muttered, turning to face the mirror again.

The face that stared back had puffy red lips and mussed hair.

After taking a few minutes to compose herself, Rachel left the bathroom, her legs still wobbly. She walked slowly and deliberately across the room, avoiding stares of men from every table she passed. She felt as if every one of them knew what she'd just done.

She found the table she'd shared with Nikolai empty except for her coat, thankfully still draped over the back of a chair, and a note scribbled on a napkin. "Tomorrow at 10, at the airport. N."

Crap. She'd agreed to take a man back to Alaska with her that she'd practically had sex with the first time she met him. What would happen the next time they were alone?

Tucking the note into her pants pocket, Rachel pulled on her coat as she scolded herself. *Nothing* would happen the next time they were alone. They were colleagues now, not strangers meeting on a dance floor. They had a case to solve.

2

"This is it." Rachel opened the door and pressed it to the wall. "It's not a suite at the Captain Cook, but my budget only stretches so far."

Nikolai stepped into the hotel room with his duffle bag slung over his shoulder and looked around.

Having him so close sent her senses into overdrive. She'd managed to sit halfway across the plane from him on the flight back, and share the front seat with the taxi driver as they crossed town. This hotel room didn't give her all the space she needed to keep between them.

"Quite nice." Nikolai flung the bag into an upholstered chair, walked to the window, and shoved back the curtains. He stood looking out, studying the view.

"We'll head to the park tomorrow." Letting the door close, Rachel slowly crossed half the room, fighting the desire to run to him and spread her hands across his back. Just the thought of touching him made her belly flip with excitement. Why did this man evoke such strong reactions in her?

Fortunately, when they'd met at the airport, he'd acted as if nothing out of the ordinary had happened between them the day before. Maybe he was used to women throwing themselves into his arms. God, he was gorgeous enough. A black sweater clung to his lean torso, and black jeans hugged his tight butt and muscular thighs. Her mouth actually watered as she watched him.

When he turned his head, she studied his profile and modified her earlier opinion that he'd descended from royalty. He must have descended from gypsy royalty; he had the mystique thing down.

He glanced over his shoulder.

She mentally shook herself. "I just want to make sure you have everything you need."

"Like?" He turned to face her.

"Like water glasses, and a coffee maker." She hurried to the sink outside the bathroom door and moved things around. "You know, the basics. Sometimes they forget things when they clean the room."

What the hell was she babbling about? Why couldn't she just hand him the card key and leave?

Her entire body wanted to stay.

"I don't have *everything* I need."

Rachel screeched as she spun around. How had he crossed the room without her hearing him?

Nikolai stood a breath away, watching her with his amber eyes as if waiting for her to make a run for the door so he could pounce.

Her heart thundered in her chest and her hands shook as she reached back to steady herself against the counter.

"Like . . . what?" Her voice came out as a croak.

"Like, *you*."

She gulped as the shaking in her hands spread to her insides. "I, uh, don't think we should—"

He slid one hand behind her neck and drew her mouth up to his, just as he had in the Siberian restroom.

His mouth was warm and greedy as it took hers with more confidence this time.

She melted against him, welcoming his already familiar taste and scent, realizing just how much she'd wanted this to happen. Closing her eyes, she released every ounce of resistance she'd nurtured since their first encounter.

He wrapped her in an embrace of barely leashed power, and she felt his heart pounding to match her own. His hands spread across her back and sides. He drew her closer than she thought possible.

His tongue slid across hers, stroking it, suggesting more, starting a rhythm that her brain latched onto.

Her body responded by relinquishing all control. Her knees gave out as her limbs turned to Jell-O, her crotch swelled with need, and her nipples tightened against her nylon bra.

The bulge in his pants grew between them, an undeniable sign of his desire. Could he possibly feel the same need that blossomed in her belly? She wanted him, all of him. The idea of feeling him enter her sent a shiver up her spine.

No matter how much she wanted him, this was insane.

Rachel turned her face away from his and pushed herself from his embrace.

They weren't lovers. They were strangers, coworkers at best. Nothing more.

Gripping her arms, he kissed her jaw and her neck.

She held the front of his sweater in her fists. "We shouldn't be doing this."

He slipped his hands under her sweater and to each side of her waist—smooth palms on bare skin. She groaned at the pleasure of his touch.

When he straightened, she looked up into golden eyes, smoky with longing, and her resolve fizzled.

His hands moved slowly, deliberately up her sides. She raised her arms and let him draw her sweater off over her head. Then he leaned forward and kissed her again.

Feeling more than just seminaked, but not caring, Rachel lifted her hands to his shoulders and returned his kiss, drawing hard on him, demanding more. When her bra popped loose, she shrugged it off, relieved to feel his palms crossing her bare back.

His fingers traced her jeans to the front and slipped the button from its buttonhole.

There was no turning back. She was about to have sex with Nikolai Volsky, and she couldn't think of anything she wanted more.

He lowered the zipper on her pants, and she peeled his sweater off and dropped it to the floor. Then she took in the sight of him, a little at a time, starting with his muscular shoulders, moving down the line of dark hair marking the middle of his wide chest. Her fingers followed her gaze, raising goose bumps in his smooth flesh.

His nipples were small and hard, and she feathered her fingers over both. A strange noise, like a strangled groan, rose in his throat.

She continued down, following the indentations of his ribs to his lean, hard stomach, tracing the middle of his torso with her thumbs. At his waistband, she slid her hands around to his hips.

He eased her pants to her legs, then wrapped his arms around her and lifted her from the floor, pressing his mouth to her throat.

Rachel pushed off her boots and kicked off her pants, suddenly anxious to be rid of everything between them.

Nikolai's tongue drew slow, sensuous circles in her skin. She arched her back to give him access to more.

Cold linoleum rose under her butt and she sat as he placed her on the counter. He pressed his forehead to hers. His breath caressed her face in rapid bursts to match her own.

"You are beautiful," he whispered. His hands skimmed her body with quick, gentle touches across her shoulders, and waist, and the tender sides of her breasts.

Her breath came faster as excitement bubbled inside her.

Her body felt as though it swelled and stretched her sensitized skin from head to toe.

He teased her nipples with his thumbs, pushing the hard nubs in circles. Then he took her mouth again as he held her around the waist with one arm.

She tasted his need now, knew how it built in his gut like a gnawing hunger. She felt the same need.

Burying one hand in his silky hair, she clung to him, her arms around his shoulders.

His body moved with action she couldn't see, and then he pulled her to him, lifting her to the front of the cool counter. She wrapped her legs around his thighs.

Warm skin met her heels at the backs of his legs and she realized he'd gotten rid of his pants. He tilted his head to reach deeper into her mouth, offering her more, taking more.

Muscles between her legs twitched with anticipation. Damn, she wanted him badly.

He drew her closer and leaned forward, pressing one hand to the mirror behind her head.

Hard warmth nudged between her legs. Her thighs quivered in response.

His hand slid down to her ass, and he pulled her forward.

She opened her legs, ready, anxious, needing to know the next moment.

He pushed against her waiting heat, sliding easily in the gush of wetness he caused. The head of his erection eased into her folds, finding the hard nub of her clit and stopping.

She tilted her hips, but couldn't move forward on the counter. What was he waiting for? God, she wanted to feel him filling her, ached for the invasion of his body into hers.

Instead, he moved slowly side to side, pivoting the head of his penis against her clit, stroking it with a velvety touch.

Every nerve in her body jumped to attention as the stroking continued.

Muscles in his back and shoulders bunched under her hands, and she felt the heat building in his skin as it built in her. How could anything feel so damn good?

He released her mouth and she gasped for air. Her back arched against the intense pleasure.

"Your body is exquisite," he said, his breath licking her ear. "Your cunt weeps for me."

Muscles hardened, ready to explode. She dug her heels into his thighs, trying to draw him in deeper.

Still he held back, easing the hard head in, then withdrawing, shoving her swollen clit back and forth. She rocked to the rhythm and he moved to match her speed.

A line of heat sizzled up the backs of her thighs, across her ass, and into her crotch.

Her head went back and she cried out as her world exploded.

Orgasmic release rolled through her body in the most amazing waves, long and hard.

Up and down her torso they went, crashing over her senses. She lifted her body into his. Her thighs trembled, and muscles pulsed.

He groaned softly, his mouth on a sensitive spot below her ear.

Her release continued. He pressed against her clamping muscles, torturing her clit, stroking. Too much, too intense.

As she clenched her teeth against the need to scream, everything slowed to low, rumbling rolls of bliss.

The orgasm eased away, leaving her weak.

He withdrew. Kissing her jaw and neck, he straightened.

She clung to his shoulders, her senses still clouded.

His erection poking against her abdomen testified to his remaining need. Rachel touched the velvety skin, surprised at how large he was. Perhaps he'd worried about hurting her.

She shuddered at the thought of feeling him sheathed inside her, and felt absurdly angry that he had deprived her of that experience.

What now? Was she supposed to just get dressed and leave after this strange encounter? For the second time in two days, she'd reached a climax in this man's arms. Would he leave her sitting naked on his bathroom counter, again wanting more?

"Incredible," he whispered.

She looked up into his face and found him watching her with feverish intensity, his brow furrowed, his eyes nearly black.

Her brain shut down. She had no idea what to do.

He released her and stepped back, raking his hair back with both hands.

Rachel hopped from the counter onto shaky legs and stared at him. The only thought that seeped from her muddled brain was, *Dear God, he's good looking.*

He moved to the sink beside her, turned on the water, and filled his cupped hands.

Nikolai drank his fill of cold water, then splashed a handful on his face. In the years since Sasha, he'd forgotten just how difficult control could be. And it had never seemed as difficult as it was with Rachel.

Something about her touched him. It wasn't just her wonderful scent or amazing body. It had to do with the honesty in her eyes when they were close. As an inspector, she had mastered the art of illusion. He'd seen her don the mask. Yet, when he held her in his arms, her mask crumbled. He saw her needs and wants reflected in eyes as green as spring tundra.

Intoxicating.

Nikolai buried his face in a towel and took a deep breath. Could he take the next step and remain in control?

As he dropped the towel and glanced in the mirror, he was surprised to find Rachel plucking clothes from the ground. She'd already slipped into her underwear.

He spun to face her. "What are you doing?"

Her eyes opened wide. "I'm, uh, getting ready to leave."

He closed the distance between them and gripped her wrist. "I'm not finished with you yet, Rachel. Would you leave me in this state?"

She glanced down to his cock and her eyes widened more. Her gaze snapped back to his. "I'm not . . . I mean, I, uh—"

There it was again, the honesty. He saw her confusion and uncertainty, her fear of ridicule. He had to remind himself that she didn't know the ways of his people.

He touched her smooth cheek and smiled. "Please don't go. Not yet."

The clothes tumbled from her arms.

Nikolai walked, guiding her in front of him to the oversized bed, and urged her to sit. He knelt in front of her and kissed her willing mouth. Her taste left him hungry.

He loved the smoothness of her skin. She was young, so much younger than anyone he'd known this way. Her reactions were honest, unrehearsed, and unrestrained.

After easing her satin undergarment down and tossing it away, he touched her body as he kissed her, exploring each sensitive spot, enjoying the way she squirmed.

She shivered as he nipped at her neck, and her breath quickened when he moved across her breastbone. Her breasts were small, but responsive, and the saltiness on his tongue made his cock stiffen more.

He drew her close as he suckled, listening for her soft moans of pleasure, rewarded as he drew hard on her nipples and flicked them with his tongue.

The scent of her aroused cunt whispered to him of bliss, and he abandoned her sweet breasts.

She hesitated when he kissed her thighs, but he continued, easing her legs apart until he had full access. He lapped at her thick juices, enjoying the taste, both new and familiar.

Rachel finally lay back on the bed and propped her cold feet on his shoulders, and he cupped her firm ass to lift her to his mouth.

He savored her cum, nearly losing focus as he did, but settled into nipping and licking her cunt lips as he strove for command of his reactions. *Center, focus.*

She trembled, deliciously excited by his attention.

He moved to her swelling clit, licking softly at first.

She pushed against his shoulders, lifted her hips, and her breath came in stuttered gasps.

Slowly, he drew her to the edge, feeling the connection with her desire.

Her clit hardened, and her entire body shook.

Sucking softly, closing his teeth gently on the nub, he took her over the cliff.

She cried out, raised her cunt against him, and clamped down hard on his tongue as he plunged it into her. He imagined how wonderful her cunt would feel on his cock and groaned.

But it wasn't yet his time. Probing deeper, he lapped up her juices, relishing the perfection of her taste.

Much too soon, her muscles relaxed and she collapsed. Her feet slipped over his shoulders and rested against his back.

Nikolai kissed the tender insides of her thighs, giving her time to enjoy the aftereffects. She cooed softly.

"I can't believe you did that," she said. "I've never . . . you know, reached a climax twice in one day."

He smiled. *Twice?* That was child's play.

"What?" She rose up to her elbows and frowned at him. Apparently she'd felt his smile against her tender skin.

"You think we've reached your limit?"

She nodded.

He grinned. "We'll see."

She gulped and sat up. "Look, Nikolai, this is crazy."

He gazed up at her, wondering what kind of experiences she'd had with men in the past. She certainly wasn't comfortable, in spite of her wonderful body. Although she obviously enjoyed their activities, she continued to protest.

He sat on the floor and crossed his legs.

Watching her eyes, he drew her forward by the ankles until her ass slipped off of the bed. She held herself up with her hands on the mattress.

"Hey!"

He grabbed her waist and lowered her onto his lap. Her heat resting against his cock drew an unintentional growl from his throat.

Giving in, she released the bed and wrapped her arms around his shoulders, relinquishing control. He saw the precious moment of surrender in her eyes.

Holding her lovely, firm ass, he kissed her tender lips, and she drew his tongue into her mouth again. Her right hand fisted in his hair, and her legs circled his waist. Joined thus, he slid her wet cunt up and down the length of his cock, thrilling to the anticipation of entering her at last.

The friction he enjoyed began to work on her again, and her juices slicked his cock. She pressed her breasts to his chest; the hard nipples dragged across his skin each time he raised her.

Her kiss became more adamant. He felt her level of desire rise until it nearly matched his own. He tasted the beginning of her desperation.

Tearing his mouth from hers, he lifted her higher and she tilted her hips forward, ready for him. Every bit of him wanted her now, craved the feel of her wrapped around his pulsing cock as he filled her with his seed.

Reverting to the teachings, he began to chant inside his head, making the old sounds, centering himself. *Kah, shawut, gugan, dis.* If he withdrew from the desire, he could hold out for her again. His body fought his mind, but he knew his mind would win. It always had. *Kah, shawut, gugan, dis.*

Easing her down, he nudged against the opening to her cunt. Her heat surrounded the tip of his cock, drenching it with her fluids. *Kah, shawut . . .* he eased her lower, letting her swollen cunt swallow the head . . . *gugan, dis.* Her muscles tightened, clamping around him, and he clenched his jaw against the need. He held her close and rocked. *Kah, shawut* . . .

Her fingers dug into the muscles in his back and her legs tightened around him. She grunted softly in his ear.

. . . gugan, dis . . .

Her cunt bit down hard with the first wave and she came, screaming through clenched teeth as pleasure wracked her body.

Burying his face between her damp breasts, he chanted one word for each pulse until her climax finally eased.

Rachel clung to him, panting against his skin and shaking.

Nikolai waited, holding her, listening to her heartbeat and feeling it in her flesh. Her cum rolled across his balls like a torturous tongue, making him ache for release.

Not yet, not yet. Kah, shawut, gugan, dis.

He lowered her slowly. Her tight cunt strangled his cock, and he worked harder at centering. He felt the eruption building, in spite of his best efforts, and worried he would come too soon.

Not . . . yet.

Halfway now, her wondrous cunt swelled around him. Deeper and deeper he went, until he felt the first hint of resistance. Holding her, he rocked, working against her tightness, waiting for her to adjust. Sweat beaded across his back and chest as he shook with desire.

He felt her finally close around the base, taking the last. She groaned softly in his ear and held him tighter, and he knew she approached the edge once again. Turning his head, he took her mouth, circling her precious tongue with his own in time to the rocking of their bodies.

The moment neared, and he reminded himself not to expect too much. It wasn't as if they'd been mates for years, practicing the joining of bodies and souls. This was simply sex with a beautiful woman, nothing more.

Even as he said it, his vision filled with white light, and his soul burst forth to entwine with hers. His body tingled, poised on the edge of the abyss.

With the first pulse of her cunt around the base of his cock, he fell. Spreading his arms, free falling, diving into the depths of bliss, he fused with her.

His semen erupted, exploding into her womb.

Her cunt milked his cock for more, and he gave it, pumping hard.

On and on it went until he felt his soul straining for freedom.

Holding her, holding on, he reached the last.

And then he drew his soul back.

The world stilled to silence, broken only by their panting.

"What the hell was that?" she whispered.

He held her, amazed by what had just passed between them, wishing he could explain it to her. But she wasn't his mate. They came from different worlds, and he would eventually return to his.

He smiled and kissed her shoulder. "Nice."

Rachel leaned back and stared at him. Sweat matted her auburn hair to her face, and her green eyes glistened. "Nice? How about, unbelievable?"

He nodded. "Yes."

Rachel shook her head as if trying to clear a fog. With his help, she crawled off of him, and collapsed at his side.

Nikolai lay back on the carpeted floor, spread his arms, and closed his eyes to enjoy the last tingling sensations of pleasure. The backs of his fingers found her sweet ass, and he stroked her soft skin.

He was glad he'd stayed on the outside a little longer. After all, no one waited for him in the village. He had nothing but a lonely house to return to. He would pass many nights reliving this encounter.

Besides, he had to find out if a Cushakna had truly escaped from Siberia, before it was too late.

3

"Set it down over there," Rachel said, pointing to a clearing.

The pilot nodded and shoved the stick to the side. The helicopter tilted forward and sideways and dropped from the sky.

Once they landed, Rachel peeled off the headphones as she pushed open the door.

Nikolai climbed from the backseat of the aircraft and smiled. "Beautiful day," he said, yelling over the mechanical whine.

"Yes." Rachel slipped her can of pepper spray into the holster on her hip, opposite her Glock. "There's a can for you, unless you'd rather something else." She pointed to the emergency rifle mounted under the backseat.

He waved off her offer as if it were silly.

Fine. As soon as one of Denali's mountainous grizzlies lumbered up on them, they'd see what was silly and what wasn't.

Ducking, Rachel trotted under the slowing blades and quickly caught up with Nikolai. He shot a sexy smile in her direction, and she forgot her annoyance.

Her ears rang in the quiet that replaced the helicopter's steady engine roar. As they walked toward the edge of the woods, the ringing finally gave way to sounds of Alaskan wilderness.

They both looked up at the call of an eagle, and then Rachel glanced over at Nikolai. He watched the magnificent bird circle for a long time before looking down again. When he did, his smile had faded, replaced by a strange expression of sadness.

Trying not to wonder about it, Rachel started toward the edge of the woods in long strides, following an old game trail through dead wet grass, newly uncovered from winter's blanket of snow by the recent warm spell. Nikolai followed so quietly, she had to look back to make sure he was there. She found him walking with his chin raised as if he were sniffing the air.

Strange man.

His eyes met hers briefly, but she couldn't read him.

Stumbling, Rachel returned her attention to the trail. She wished she were following instead of leading. Nikolai moved with such graceful ease, he probably fought to keep from laughing at her clumsiness.

"We found him right here," she said, stopping at the campsite. In the short time since the discovery of the body, the scene had already started to disappear. Short spring grass had grown to cover the bloodstained trail, and a large animal had rolled the log Gary Campbell had apparently used as a chair. "He was laying on his back, naked, his head in that direction." She nodded toward the north.

"He'd been camping here?"

She nodded. "Six days. He was a biologist for the park service."

"Doing fieldwork, like our students."

She nodded again.

Nikolai circled the site slowly, searched the ground. After one round, he crouched and fingered a broken, dried stalk of fireweed, then rose and continued. He examined each aspen carefully, leaning close to the trunk as if searching for microscopic evidence hidden in the peeling bark.

"We had a crime scene unit out here. They went over everything with a fine-tooth comb." She decided not to mention that she'd also spent a full day investigating the site. The only thing she'd found had been signs of a few animals—probably a pair of wolves—circling the camp. Fortunately, neither had been hungry or brave enough to drag the body off.

He didn't appear to hear her as he continued. At one point, on the edge of the sparse forest, he stopped and searched the horizon to his left and right.

After nearly an hour, he sighed heavily, glanced at Rachel, and started back toward the helicopter.

"You've seen enough?"

"Yes, for now."

For now? What more could he hope to find in the wilderness? If he was expecting a murder weapon or a suspect, he'd be disappointed. Surely he knew that.

"Learn anything?" She pulled open the door and motioned for the pilot to start the engine.

"Perhaps," Nikolai said, as he popped open the back door and leaned close to her.

She caught a whiff of him and had to gulp at the lump in her throat. He still wasn't wearing cologne; he smelled of rugged, natural, sexy man.

A shiver danced through her as she remembered their unbelievable encounter in the hotel.

It couldn't happen again. If the department found out, she'd be laughed out into the street. No one would ever take her seriously as an investigator.

She'd worked hard to get where she was. She would not let this man, no matter how gorgeous, ruin her career.

Besides, he was pissing her off again with his aloofness. It was bad enough that he wouldn't tell her who the killer was. This was her case, not his. *She* would decide what was important at the site and what wasn't. What the hell did he mean by *perhaps?*

After climbing in, buckling up, and positioning the headphones over her ears, she glanced at the pilot. "Ready."

"Clear on your side?" the pilot asked.

Rachel looked out her window. "Clear."

Tops of trees shrank below them, and Rachel studied the majesty of Mount McKinley, unusually free of clouds and monopolizing the landscape.

At the tap on her shoulder, she slid her headset forward and leaned back.

"Do you know what the biologist was looking for?" Nikolai asked, yelling near her ear.

Rachel shook her head.

"Could it have been foxes?"

She shrugged and craned around to see him frowning at her. "You think that's important?"

"Yes."

"I don't see how," she muttered.

"What?" He leaned closer.

Too close.

"I'll find out." Turning her back to him, she covered her ears again and watched the ground slide by, willing her heartbeat back to a normal pace.

Picking up the Cushakna's scent had disturbed Nikolai's senses. He felt disoriented and on the verge of melancholy.

The panther's heart began to beat—softly, faintly, but there nonetheless. It produced a steady cadence in his soul, and he felt his own heart speed up to match it.

If he were smart, he'd have returned to the village as soon as he'd completed his mission, but he couldn't resist learning more about the outside. Things had changed so much since he was young. He'd told himself he was doing it for the good of his people, but he knew better. He was doing it because he wanted to.

At one point, when he'd first seen Rachel step into the bar, he'd wondered what it would be like to stay on the outside. That stray thought had terrified him enough that he almost returned home that night, in spite of his promise to help her.

Now, here he was, flying through the air in a helicopter— much noisier than he'd guessed it would be—studying the back of Rachel's head, recalling how softly her hair brushed against his cheek when he kissed her neck. His heightened instincts allowed him to distinguish her scent among the strange mechanical smells of the aircraft, to feel her apprehension, to picture every hand movement in the subtle motions of her shoulders. He wanted to draw her under him and mount her with the urgency swelling in his groin. He wanted to give her his heart.

He must control these urges before they pushed him into forbidden confidences. He could hardly risk the existence of his people to satisfy his own insane desires.

Nikolai gazed out the small window to his right and watched the tops of dwarf trees wave below them. He thought of Sasha. Is this how she'd felt soaring far above him, her feathers glistening in the sunshine?

Old hurt rose in his chest, but it didn't stay long. He'd learned to deal with the loss many years ago, long after she'd quit returning to their house to watch him from the rooftop.

Emotions simmered in his heart, bubbling heat to his skin. He unzipped his jacket and drew the sweater away from his neck with two fingers.

How would it be with Rachel if he managed to get her back to his hotel room? He'd been close to the panther today, close to animal form, and that proximity threatened his control—not nearly so much as it would if he had changed, but enough to worry him.

Still, he wanted her. He wanted to feel her flesh against his, to taste her skin, and her mouth, and her thick, salty cum. He wished they could spend every moment in each other's arms until he had to return.

Even as a young man, he'd never felt such desire. Was it only his long stretch of abstinence playing games with his thoughts? Or was his heart truly healed and in want of a mate again?

A mate. As if this human could be that. Even her strength and honesty were nothing compared to what was required of his kind. She couldn't truly release her soul to him, could she?

No, it would be impossible.

Still, he *wanted* her to the point of agony.

Purposely remembering the peace of home, the joy of resting under the trees in his yard and watching summer clouds race by, he looked out the window and tried not to think about Sasha, Rachel, or the Cushakna.

As they approached the hotel, Rachel felt as if she were walking through invisible gates of intensifying arousal. She ached for Nikolai's touch. She couldn't take her eyes off him when he wasn't looking in her direction. The swish of his clothing against his skin with every step made her want to groan.

What the hell was wrong with her? His first kiss had infected her with some kind of mental illness that seemed to be getting nothing but worse every time they touched. It was all she could do to keep from ripping her clothes off halfway down the hall between the stairwell and his room.

The closer they got to the door, the more he watched her. She couldn't read his expression, but his eyes seemed to get darker and darker with each step. Could he be feeling the same kind of desire?

He slipped the plastic card into the reader, opened the door, and moved back to let her enter ahead of him.

She hesitated for a long moment before stepping inside.

This whole thing was crazy. She wasn't supposed to be sleeping with the visiting Russian inspector. She should be grilling him for answers, not dropping her jeans. The very idea—

Nikolai caught her arm as she passed and drew her around to face him. His mouth found hers before the door had even closed behind him.

Devouring her with a feverish kiss, he sandwiched her between his body and the wall.

She hooked one leg around his and clung to him, shaking almost violently, savoring every sensation his mouth produced.

He tore off his coat without breaking contact, then unzipped her coat and peeled it from her body.

All restraint he'd exhibited before seemed to have vanished. She didn't care. She wanted him to ravish her, rip her clothes off and take her without asking. She wanted to feel him enter her with the urgency sizzling through her own body at that moment.

What the hell was going on? She'd never experienced this kind of raw need.

Nikolai tore his mouth from hers and backed away, but he didn't release her. Instead, he held her in a smoldering gaze and made quick work of her clothes and his own, until every stitch had been discarded. Without a word, he wrapped her in his arms and lifted her from the ground.

Her thoughts merged into warm, flowing desire as she locked her legs around his bare hips. His body was powerful, hard against hers. Muscles bunched and relaxed under smooth skin, and she floated through the air kissing him.

He pressed her to the cold wall again, rubbing his engorged erection against her sensitive pussy.

She tilted her hips toward him, desperate to have him inside her, needing him.

Soft skin skimmed across her swelling clit, then back to her anus, and forward again. She imagined his swollen penis traveling the same path inside and shuddered.

He kissed her face with warm, soft lips, nipping at her jaw playfully as if he suddenly felt no urgency at all.

Once again, anger at the one-sidedness of her need rose inside her, and she tightened her grip on his hips. "Take me, now."

He drew a stuttered breath against her cheek and groaned as he pressed her harder to the wall, muttering something she couldn't understand. Then he whispered, "Don't tempt me, Rachel."

Her name in his deep, strained voice jolted right through her. She suddenly realized he wanted this every bit as much as she did. Why did he work so hard at holding back? Granted, anticipation made the experience even more exciting, but she wanted to be able to make him lose his cool. She wanted to have the same effect on him that he had on her.

Grabbing a handful of his thick hair, she pulled his face away from hers.

He gazed at her with black eyes.

She raised one eyebrow. "Fuck me, Nikolai."

He dropped his forehead to hers, grabbed her right thigh, and pushed, easing the head of his prick into her swelling pussy.

She held his out-of-focus gaze, watching a frown of determination tug at the corners of his mouth.

He pushed deeper, apparently determined to go slowly in spite of her slickness.

She wanted to feel him buried as far as he could be, reaching for her very core. She dug her heels into his tight buttocks.

He groaned as he pushed his hard prick deeper still.

Her pussy stretched to take all of him, sending waves of pleasure up through her torso. Her spine dissolved into jelly.

His grip tightened on her thigh.

A strange vibration entered her body through her breasts, pressed against his chest, as if he trembled.

No, it wasn't a tremble, it was more like a sustained growl.

He turned his face from hers and drew her earlobe between sharp teeth as he buried himself in her, filling her completely.

And he filled more than just her slick, swollen vagina; he filled her need, brought her home to their union with a joy so intense, it terrified her.

Even in her fear, she wanted nothing more than to stay locked in his embrace.

As if sharing her joy, he kissed her, opening her mouth with his own, tasting her all over again, and she welcomed him, clinging to his vibrating body.

He started the movement so slowly, she almost didn't notice until it grew in strength. His thrusts were long, slow, exhilarating. He withdrew and buried himself anew with each.

Her body reacted by tightening, starting between her legs, muscles knotting. Her fingers dug into his tight shoulders.

His long thrusts stroked her clit as completely as his tongue had the day before, lifting her into an erotic haze.

She closed her eyes and dropped her head back to the wall.

He nipped at her neck and pushed deeper, faster.

More. She needed more.

As it had the last time, the entire world seemed to suddenly vanish into whiteness. She floated on a cloud, aroused beyond belief, aching for release, a fuse under the flame's first kiss.

He wrapped around her as if they were two columns of smoke merging into one shaft of white light, spreading together to fill space and time. She felt his tenderness, and desire, and hunger, emotions without flesh.

And then her own flesh ignited, the fuse crackled, and her body exploded with blissful release.

White light muted to sunshine and she rose into his glorious thrusts, her body pounding and squeezing.

He crushed her with his release, molding his body to hers, grunting softly in her ear with each thrust.

A strange happiness flowed over her as they stood together, sharing ecstasy and damp flesh, hands caressing bare backs, buttocks, and shoulders. Slowly the need ebbed until she felt nothing but her pounding heart.

They panted against each other, groaning softly. She feared he might disappear if she opened her eyes, so she held on and enjoyed the last of the bliss rolling in her belly.

With sudden movement, he drew her from the wall and carried her across the room.

Rachel opened her eyes, met his wild gaze, and felt a strange and terrifying sense of possession. Why the hell would she think she had some claim on this man?

Why did she suddenly want such a claim?

He held her to him with one arm as he lowered them to the bed, and then he kissed her tenderly.

She knew better than to open her heart, but she felt the hinges straining.

He covered her face with sweet kisses, then rose up onto his elbows and brushed her hair from the side of her forehead.

She stared up into golden eyes studying her face as if trying to memorize it.

For some reason she couldn't begin to identify, tears welled in her eyes. She turned her head so he wouldn't see.

He kissed the side of her jaw, and then nibbled the tender flesh of her neck as his hand slid down her bare side. When his mouth found a nerve bundle, she raised her hips into him, and he pushed against her.

Still inside her, he hardened and groaned softly against her ear. "Shall I fuck you again?" he whispered, his voice playfully deep and sexy.

Smiling in spite of her tears, she nodded.

"I hoped you'd say yes." He turned her face toward him and took her mouth.

* * *

Nikolai lay on the bed on his side, his head propped on one fist, watching Rachel dress. After coming three times in less than two hours, he felt drained and pleasantly tired.

She stumbled twice as she tried to step into her pants. "Don't laugh," she said, glaring at him.

He smiled and her glare softened.

"I wouldn't dream of it."

But he felt much more than tired. He felt connected to this woman, as if she were his to love. She was not, of course, and never would be, but he couldn't stop the soaring sentiment.

Once she'd replaced her clothing, she sat on the edge of the bed.

He drew her hand to his mouth and kissed the palm. It smelled faintly of their union, in spite of her effort to "rinse off." He liked the scent very much, and felt his body reacting.

"Nikolai."

He laced his fingers into hers and raised his gaze to her lovely face. "Yes?"

She frowned this time, her green eyes glistening in the fading light from the window. "I don't know what's going on here, and I'm not sure I'm ready to talk about it."

He waited, unwilling to press her into a conversation they shouldn't have anyway.

"But we need to talk about the case. What did you mean when you said *perhaps* you had learned something at the site?"

Sighing, he studied their joined hands. How much should he reveal to her? How much would satisfy her need for knowledge?

"I saw signs of something out there. It's a rare animal related to the arctic fox, a Cushakna."

"A *fox*? You think Campbell was killed by a fox?"

He shook his head and looked up at her. "Not a fox. A Cushakna, a distant cousin."

"How big is this . . . this Cushakna?"

He shrugged. "It's hard to say."

"The size of a fox? Or a wolf? Bigger?"

He shrugged again.

Her expression hardened, and she withdrew her hand from his. "Look, I don't like getting jerked around. What the hell's going on? Talk to me."

He studied her face, wishing he could simply reveal the truth to her. If he did, not only would he be threatening the entire village, he'd most likely risk having Rachel question his sanity. Society had long forgotten the old ways.

"I'm sorry I can't tell you more," he said. "I promised to rid you of the killer, and I will. I must return to the site tomorrow. Alone."

She frowned. "No way. If you go back out there, I'm going with you."

"Rachel, I must—"

"Don't even think about it. You're here on a visa I signed. If you fly into Denali tomorrow, you're flying with me."

He saw determination in her eyes and knew she wouldn't back down. She had too much courage and stubbornness for her own good.

He nodded. "All right."

She rose and walked to the door, all signs of unsteadiness gone from her step. "I need to run by my office."

He wanted to jump up and take her into his arms for one more kiss, but he didn't. Instead, he watched her leave.

She stopped in the doorway. "I'll pick you up tomorrow at nine."

As the door clicked into place, Nikolai rolled onto his back and closed his eyes. He drew a heavy breath into his lungs, held it, and slowly blew it out. Centering himself, he repeated the process twice more.

Rachel had touched his soul once again, this time with more certainty. How would he be able to leave her behind?

The thought of staying crept back into his brain, and he savored it for a moment before sending it away.

He needed to focus on the task at hand. If he faced the Cushakna as a man, he'd probably die, but he couldn't change in front of Rachel.

In one movement, he rolled off the bed and to his feet.

He needed to start his preparations. Tomorrow, he'd find a way to lose Rachel long enough to track down the Cushakna.

Questions nibbled at the base of his skull. How had the Cushakna escaped Siberia? It couldn't maintain human form long enough to cross the Pacific. Perhaps there was more than one. How many would he have to face? One could be difficult enough; two would be a challenge.

More important, how would he keep his secret from Rachel while keeping her safe?

Nikolai drew the sacred bundle from his bag and carried it with reverence to the middle of the room where he sat cross-legged and placed it on the floor in front of him. He closed his eyes, raised his palms, and began to quietly chant the sacred words.

4

Rachel sat in the back of the helicopter this time, wishing she could be alone. Even a good cry—something she never did—hadn't released her from the overwhelming feelings of impending loss and pain. How could this stranger have stolen her heart in such a short time?

Christ, she was a ninny. She didn't even know who the man was.

She knew things about him she'd never known about anyone else, but she couldn't begin to explain how she'd gained the knowledge. She knew he was caring, tender, and intent on doing the right thing. And she knew he had suffered great loss bravely.

Or did she just want him to have these qualities?

Enough. She had a case to focus on.

Her sergeant had given her extraordinary leeway on this one. It wasn't that he necessarily believed in her; he had the governor breathing down his neck and was desperate to catch a break. She hadn't been exactly open about Nikolai's promise to "rid them of the killer," either. She hoped to figure out what was going on by sticking to him, not letting him out of her sight. Had he really thought she'd let him come out here alone? Maybe they did things differently in Siberia.

Staring out the window, her thoughts drifted to one of the least spectacular men she knew: Jerry White. A fellow investigator, Jerry got into the troopers not because he particularly enjoyed fighting crime and helping people, or investigating cases, or even solving mysteries. Jerry liked to "play" on the computer, and couldn't find anything else that gave him the chance to do so and get paid. He was truly a wizard at getting information.

After leaving Nikolai the evening before, Rachel had gone home, taken a shower, changed clothes, and then hurried into the office to check e-mail and call Fish and Game about foxes. She'd had to leave a message; it was well after seven when she arrived.

Most of the desks at the Bureau had been empty. After running through her e-mail, she'd picked up several pages with a yellow sticky note on the front from the top of a pile of files. The note said, in Jerry's handwriting, *Curiouser and curiouser.*

She'd pulled the note off and read the information below, a summary of several database searches ranging from Interpol, to the Russian police files, to the Web. In each case, Jerry had searched the name Nikolai Volsky. Each search had returned the same results: *no record found.*

A chill had crawled up her back.

She'd glanced at Jerry's empty desk.

What difference did it make whether Nikolai's name popped up on an Internet search? Her name probably didn't show up often either, and she was a good investigator. And not in some remote part of the world.

Why had Jerry been searching for information on Nikolai? Had he figured out that something was going on between them?

The chill had dropped into a knot of fear in her belly. If Jerry knew, everyone knew.

She pressed her forehead to the small Plexiglas window and watched the ground blur below.

"Crap," she whispered. If Nikolai did something illegal while getting rid of her problem, she'd not only lose her job, she'd probably be charged as an accessory.

She should have had a heart-to-heart with Sergeant Williamson long before this.

The pilot glanced back and pointed.

Rachel looked down at the same landing zone they'd used on their last visit, and made an OK sign. The pilot maneuvered the aircraft to the ground.

Nikolai offered her a hand, which she ignored as she crawled out of the helicopter. Turning back, she handed him one of the bags she'd brought and her backpack from the backseat, then drew out the rifle. She pulled a radio from the front, turned it on, and tested the reception by clicking the transmitter a few times with the speaker pressed to her ear. A reassuring beep echoed in her head.

The pilot leaned forward so she could hear him over the engine noises. "You've got everything?"

She nodded.

"See you in twenty-four hours."

She nodded again, backed out, and firmly closed the door. Slinging the rifle over one shoulder, she hurried behind Nikolai to the edge of the clearing, and they watched the helicopter rise into the clouds.

Taking her backpack, she led the way to the campsite Gary Campbell had once occupied, and propped her stuff against a log. Nikolai did the same, very carefully placing the strange bundle he'd been carrying on top of the log.

He'd brought a small duffle bag and this bundle with him. When he'd climbed into her car and she'd asked about it, he'd shrugged. "Things I need," he'd said. And then he'd changed the subject, asking about her inquiries into fox studies.

The bundle appeared to be wrapped in old leather, ornately decorated with beads and dyes. It was about the size of a sleeping bag, but she guessed from the way he held it that it wasn't a sleeping bag.

Once again, he didn't appear to have any interest in carrying a weapon. Rachel, on the other hand, placed the rifle where she could easily grab it, and slid a canister of pepper spray into its holster on her hip. Although her Glock was relatively useless against a grizzly, she felt better wearing it. She stood the radio beside the rifle.

"What do you want to do first," she asked, "have another look around?"

He shook his head. "First we should have tea, then start."

"Start what?"

He smiled, opened his duffle bag, and drew out a red and blue metal can. "I brought good Russian tea."

Rachel sighed. "Fine. Tea it is." She unzipped a side pocket on her pack and pulled out the Coleman and a camp pot. After lighting the stove, she filled the pot with water from a plastic canteen.

Nikolai squatted beside her, watching her work. The silence between them grated on her nerves, and she purposely didn't look at him. How could she be so asinine as to risk letting this man ruin her life? Even amazing sex wasn't worth that.

Placing the pot on the stove, she moved the lever to adjust the flame.

Nikolai rose and she glanced up. "I need to, um, visit the woods," he said, blushing slightly.

Rachel nodded and returned her attention to the small bag where she'd stashed a couple of mugs, spoons, forks, and cans of food. She hadn't trusted that Nikolai would bring food with him; he didn't seem all that concerned about basic necessities.

His footsteps rustled through the grass behind her as he walked toward the trees, obviously to relieve himself. Funny that needing to pee embarrassed him, after all the intimacies they'd shared. He had walked around his hotel room naked as if it were the state he preferred, and even peed without closing the bathroom door.

She glanced to her left and frowned at the empty spot on the log where he'd carefully placed his leather bag. Then she jumped up and stared at the line of woods. None of the trees were large enough to hide his wide shoulders.

"Son of a bitch."

He'd ditched her and she hadn't even noticed.

After dousing the stove, she slung the rifle over her shoulder and dashed off along the trail of crushed grass, running as quietly as she could. Her father had spent many summers teaching her to track game, and she had no problem picking up Nikolai's trail.

He ran north along the tree line, leaving behind broken twigs and branches, and heavy indentations in damp earth. Rachel followed, ducking under whiplike branches and stumbling once or twice over heavy brush. The trail led deeper into the woods as it went.

And then it stopped.

Rachel skidded to a halt. She turned a circle, checking the woods, then studied the ground for the slightest sign.

He couldn't have disappeared into thin air.

Starting in the direction he'd been heading, she made slow, careful, widening circles. After a good five minutes or more, she found a very slight indentation.

He'd turned left about forty-five degrees and suddenly become careful about his trail, after starting out with all the care of a charging elephant.

What the hell was he doing? And where was he going?

She continued to follow him, but at a walk.

* * *

As Cushakna's scent strengthened, Nikolai's animal instincts surged. He caught whiffs of numerous other beasts, sorted out sex and size, as the sounds of the wild whispered to him in an ancient voice. Above the caw of a raven and huffing of a distant grizzly, he heard Rachel crashing along through the brush behind him. As he'd hoped, her progress had slowed significantly when he'd stopped purposely leaving a trail. Unfortunately, she was apparently capable of following the slightest signs. He hadn't expected such ability in one who lived on the outside, and in a city, no less.

Still, he had the lead he needed.

The Cushaknas' scent doubled in strength, and he stopped. Their den must be close. He'd discovered there were three, not one, and knew he must be careful. Three Cushaknas could be dangerous.

Searching quickly, he found a dark spot where the skimpy woods thickened and hurried to it, untying the sack as he went. He tore off his clothes and shoved them into a tree, then drew the skin from its cover, deposited the cover safely in an aspen fork, and draped the skin over his head and shoulders.

The Change tingled through his body already as a result of his preparations. It wouldn't take long. For a moment, he'd be vulnerable, but then he'd be ready to face the vicious beasts.

Somewhere deep inside, he felt pity for the Cushaknas. They did only what was in their nature and necessary for survival. The original sisters were more to blame, but according to legend, none of them survived.

Crossing his legs as he sat, he pushed away the pity and focused on the hunt. No Cushakna could be left to feed on a human society unable to protect itself, or to reveal the secrets of his people, if any of the old knowledge remained in the creatures.

He raised his hands, palms up, and repeated the sacred words, this time releasing his hold and letting them carry his soul from his body.

He rose above the ground, above the trees, and into the safety of the air. And he watched as the Change occurred. Body stretched, lengthened, legs shortened, and hide molded into skin. Teeth elongated to glistening white fangs, and claws grew to lethal daggers.

The senses awoke then, taking in everything at once, and he released a sound of joy to echo across the wild landscape.

Dried grass and rotting leaves felt cool under wide pads. He lowered his face to the ground and sniffed, then raised his nose and opened his mouth as he sampled the air.

Cushaknas were close, perhaps curled in midday rest. He started slowly one way, then turned into the scent.

His body surged with strength, primitive needs, and primal urges. He would find them and do what must be done.

Regret and pity had vanished completely from his focused thoughts.

Rachel froze in her tracks.

What the hell was that? Denali didn't have big cats, but she could have sworn she'd just heard a mountain lion.

It must have been something else. Birds of prey could make a lot of noise, and marmots had an incredibly loud whistle. Or maybe she'd heard a wolf crying out in pain.

There were no mountain lions in Denali.

Taking a deep breath and tiptoeing, she continued.

Nikolai's nearly invisible trail continued through the woods, stopping at a patch where the evergreens gave way to aspen. She crouched and held her hand out over a place where the grass had been crushed in a large circle, as if he'd stopped to rest and sat on the ground. Could she really feel warmth, or was it her imagination? She searched for any sign of which way he'd gone.

Her heart leapt into her throat when she spotted the large feline prints.

She *had* heard a mountain lion!

"Shit."

Jumping up, she pulled the rifle around and threw the bolt, shoving a round into the chamber. How the hell had a mountain lion ended up in Denali?

She turned a slow circle, trying to calm her nerves by sorting out the trails, and realized the cat's trail simply started, as if the animal had dropped from the sky.

Stranger still, she saw nothing of Nikolai leaving the spot.

Maybe he was following the mountain lion for some reason. Or maybe the mountain lion was following him. Holding the rifle in front of her, she started on the big cat's trail.

Footprints led out of the trees and into rocks forming one of McKinley's minor cousin peaks. Rachel stopped at the edge and glanced up the face where the snow line had risen to about fifty feet above the trees. She saw nothing of Nikolai or the cat, but spotted wet prints leading over the first rock ridge.

Stepping carefully, she moved forward as quietly as possible. She heard a low rumble from the cat up ahead, but couldn't tell how far. At the ridge, she stopped.

Below her, sand had filled in a hollow from which another rock face rose about twenty yards away. The hollow formed a small canyon, not more than ten feet deep, but extending into boulder fields on each end, gifts left by retreating glaciers.

At the cat's warning yowl, she dropped to her knees.

At first she couldn't see it because it was as black as soot and stood perfectly still in a shadow. Then the movement of three other animals caught her eye. The three stood in a circle around the black cat, trapping it against the rock wall. Were they wolves?

They didn't really look like wolves, although they were about the right size. Solid white, they had long, pointed snouts and bushy tails, like foxes, but they weren't.

"Cushaknas," she whispered.

The black cat suddenly raised its gaze to her and her heart pounded wildly. Then it returned its attention to the Cushaknas.

The three foxlike creatures moved back and forth, approaching the cat carefully, yipping softly as if talking to each other. One would dash in and pull the cat's attention away from the others, and the other two would jump forward, snapping at the cat's flank.

The black cat—a panther?—slapped at one and then the other as the Cushaknas continued trying to bait it forward. None of the lethal swipes or bites seemed to quite connect.

Rachel had a strange desire to shoot the Cushaknas, in spite of the fact that she couldn't believe these creatures had killed six men in the Alaskan wilderness. It was just that she hated seeing the cat cornered. It was a beautiful creature, and completely out of place. It must feel lost and so alone.

She picked up a rock and threw it at one of the Cushaknas. The creature yelped and spun when the rock hit its leg, and stared up at her with ice-blue eyes. The other two followed suit, also staring at her, and the hair on the back of Rachel's neck stood on end.

The panther growled, and struck out at the fox creature she'd struck with the rock, knocking it down with one blow, then leapt forward and bit into its neck. Rachel heard the cracking bones from her perch. The fox let out half a yelp, then fell silent, obviously dead.

The other two Cushaknas charged forward, leaping onto the cat's back and sinking teeth into its flesh, and the big cat spun, trying to dislodge its riders. Dust rose as the three creatures became one swirling ball of fur, claws, and snarling teeth.

Panic drove Rachel to her feet and she yelled. "Hey! Stop!" Desperate, she drew her Glock and fired a shot into the air.

The fight went on as if she weren't there. Although it seemed like an hour, it probably lasted two or three minutes, and then everything stopped.

Dust settled onto three white foxlike bodies covered in blood, and the black panther leaning against the rock wall, studying them as if waiting for one to move. Blood ran down the big cat's side where vicious bites had torn its hide, and a nasty cut on the side of its face bled profusely.

After a moment, the cat raised its yellow gaze to Rachel, and she suddenly realized she was standing alone in front of an injured wild animal—not a smart place to be. She slid back down the rock face she'd climbed and turned toward the woods, listening for movement behind her. She heard nothing.

In the trees, she stopped, her arm wrapped around an aspen trunk, and tried to slow her breathing. What the hell should she do? She'd just witnessed a fight to the death between four animals that shouldn't exist, at least not in the Alaskan wilderness, and she had no idea where Nikolai was.

A horrible thought occurred to her. What if the panther was stalking Nikolai, ready to kill again? How could she stop it? She might get off one shot, but if she missed, she could be the cat's next meal.

Maybe this panther was the killer she was looking for.

The radio. She needed to get back to camp and use the radio to call for help. She needed a search party, no matter what the result to her reputation.

Releasing the tree, she ran as quietly as she could, hopping over piles of brush and swatting at thin tree limbs.

At camp, she dropped to her knees in front of the log, gasping for breath. She laid down the rifle and picked up the radio, but when she depressed the transmitter button, nothing came out of her mouth. Lowering the radio, she continued to gasp for air, and looked around. She drank a quick sip of water from the pot she'd started to warm, and then another. Her breathing finally slowed enough to allow her to talk.

A feline yowl spun her around.

The panther stood less than ten feet away, facing her, its mouth open.

Rachel reached over very slowly and raised the rifle. Her hands shook violently.

The cat watched her, its ribs rising and falling quickly, its tongue moving in and out as it panted. A drop of blood fell to the ground from its chin, followed by another.

Rachel pulled the rifle around until she felt the cold trigger under her forefinger, and slowly swung the barrel toward the beast.

The panther raised its gaze to hers and stared without blinking. Its eyes were yellow-gold, just like . . . *Nikolai's?*

All the air vanished as Rachel stared into the cat's eyes.

Without lowering its gaze, the cat took one step toward her, and then another.

She knew she should shoot. With one bite, the creature could take off her head.

The cat continued to approach.

A strange vibration filled the space between them, a loud, deep, persistent growl. Muscles bunched and stretched under sleek black fur as it stepped. Even injured, it moved with an indescribable grace, as if floating on air.

When it stopped, the creature stood less than a foot away. Its warm breath brushed the front of her bare neck.

Rachel looked down to where she'd dropped the rifle. Her hands lay uselessly in her lap, and she found no will to fight. She had only seconds to live, and all she wanted to do was touch the panther.

She reached out.

The gigantic cat stretched forward, sniffed her fingers, and then licked them, caressing her hand with its warm tongue. And then it suddenly dropped to the ground, stretched out, and placed its massive head in her lap.

Rachel stared at the animal lying in front of her, at least six feet long, with paws as big as her head, and three-inch fangs. The coat she'd mistaken for solid black was actually spotted, like a leopard's, and soft as silk. She ran her hand down the solid neck to the shoulder.

The low rumble from the cat softened to a strange purr, and she stroked its shoulder and the top of its head. When it opened its eyes and gazed up at her, she saw its pain, and her heart broke.

She saw something else, something that should have terrified her. She saw a familiar look of desire as the cat's eyes darkened.

"Nikolai," she whispered.

The cat grunted softly.

Tears burned behind her eyelids as she continued to stare. There must be something she could do to help him.

As she watched, the cat's body changed, lightened. Lines blurred and twisted.

Dizziness and confusion swirled around her.

Rachel cried out, wanting to scream but unable to. Her universe tilted away from her as she stared down into Nikolai's face, marred by several long scratches down his cheek.

"Oh, my God," she whispered.

He smiled at her and then closed his eyes.

His body, stretched out on the ground in front of her, was completely naked and covered with dirt. Several nasty gashes in his side oozed dark blood that ran down his back and stomach.

Without trying to figure out any of it, Rachel scrambled out from under him, gently lowering Nikolai's head to the ground, then crawled over to her backpack. Partially blinded by tears, it took her a few difficult moments to locate the first-aid kit.

She grabbed a clean T-shirt and the pot of water, and hurried back to his side.

He didn't move as she wiped the wounds with her wet shirt, and only flinched a little when she poured peroxide into the deepest ones. Once she was sure the cuts were as clean as she could get them, she closed the widest gash with butterflies, then used all the Band-Aids she had on the others.

As she moved him around to reach the worst cuts, she realized he hadn't passed out. He simply lay still and quiet, and trusted her to help him.

He didn't say a word.

Finally, she finished what she could do and knelt beside him. "I need to get you to a hospital."

He opened his eyes, looked up at her, and shook his head. Fear flickered in his eyes.

"Christ," she muttered, combing her hair back with her fingers. "How the hell am I going to explain this?"

He closed his eyes again, rolled over on his side, and curled into a ball, shivering.

"You must be freezing," she said. "Where are your clothes?"

He didn't respond.

Then she realized what lay in the grass beside him was a hide: the hide of the black cat. She touched it and found it still eerily warm. As she drew it over him, he smiled weakly.

Rachel rose to her feet, staggered a step, and then regained her balance. She looked around. If he didn't want her to call for help, at least she could set up camp. Maybe he'd feel better in a warm sleeping bag with a cup of something hot to drink.

If nothing else, she'd feel better going through the motions of normal activity.

She erected the one-man tent she'd brought along, and spread out her arctic down bag. Then she warmed water and brewed tea.

With a little help, Nikolai sat up and drank the tea. He hadn't uttered a word, and he looked terrifyingly pale, but at least he'd quit shivering and his wounds didn't seem to be bleeding anymore. In fact, the cut on his face almost looked like it was healing as she watched.

Two hours earlier, she would have said that was impossible. Now she didn't know what was possible and what wasn't.

The sun started its dip into the horizon, and the air temperature dropped noticeably. As soon as Nikolai had finished his cup of tea, Rachel knelt beside him and held his arm.

"Can you make it into the tent?"

He nodded, and groaned as he struggled to his feet. With an arm over her shoulders, he walked slowly to the tent and released her as he crawled in. He drew the panther skin in with him.

Rachel followed him inside to help him get settled, and held the sleeping bag open.

With trembling hands, Nikolai reverently folded the hide and placed it beside him, then he stretched out in the sleeping bag.

As she started to zip it, he stopped her with a hand on hers. "What?"

He rolled onto his side and patted the sleeping bag.

"We can't both fit in here," she said.

He moved back against the bag to make room for her.

Rachel huffed, then sighed. "What the hell."

She removed her holster, rolled the belt, and shoved it into the corner, then stripped off her clothes and hurried in, thankful for his warmth.

He drew her into the curve of his body and wrapped his arms around her, groaning softly into her hair.

She hadn't realized she was tired. After all, it wasn't even nine o'clock. But as she listened to his steady breathing, she found herself drifting off into dreams of chasing a large black cat through the woods.

When he woke her, the inside of the tent was too dark to even make out his silhouette.

5

The need, the desire was undeniable. No amount of self-discipline could have stopped him from taking her.

Nikolai felt the strength of the leopard surging through his muscles. Rachel's scent sang to him in a clear, sweet voice, drawing him up to all fours. He straddled her, letting the cover fall from his shoulders. Cold air felt good and roused him completely. Leaning down, he nuzzled her silky hair, inhaling the warmth rising from her neck.

Rachel rolled over to her back and looked up at him. "Nikolai? Are you okay?"

His human soul, barely holding on, had little voice. "No."

"What's wrong?" Her hands rose to his chest. Cool fingers spread across his heated skin.

He pushed her legs open with his own and knelt between her tender thighs, then lowered his mouth to her ear. "I want you. Now."

She made a soft noise, either of surprise or need.

Licking a slow line up the front of her neck, he worked one arm under her, around her waist, and drew her hips up to him.

His cock, already hard, found its target immediately, and he shook with restraint. She was his—his to take.

But enough of the human survived that he couldn't allow himself to mount her immediately. He couldn't hurt her. A low growl rolled through his chest.

He found her mouth as the head of his cock rested against her warm labia, easing into the blessed opening to her body, her heart, and her soul.

When she reached up and grabbed his shoulders, he felt the feline greed rising. Her legs spread wide for him, welcoming him. He could take her now, release his seed into her, claim what was his.

"Nikolai," she whispered against his lips.

He felt cream coating the head of his cock and could wait no longer.

"Mine," he said, the growl escaping from his throat. Rachel drew in a quick breath against his cheek.

He dove into her wet cunt and her body rose up against him in surprise.

He withdrew and thrust into her again. Then he stopped, buried inside her, sheathed in her taut heat. Her muscles tightened around him as if to draw him deeper.

His body tingled, and the leopard's soul expanded, threatening to take over and force him to change.

"No." *Not now.*

Nikolai shook with fear. After all this time, he couldn't lose his connection to humanity, now that he'd found his mate.

"What?" She reached up and pressed her warm hand to his cheek. Her beautiful eyes moved side to side with sightless concern. She couldn't see him in the darkness.

But he could see her. The cat's vision allowed him to study her face, make out the lines of worry in her forehead.

"Nikolai?"

His name, whispered in her sweet voice, soothed him as surely as her touch, drew his human soul back into his body and banished his fear.

He turned his head and pressed his lips to her smooth palm. Then he licked a line to her wrist and covered her soft pulse with his mouth.

Slowly, he drew out and pressed back in, sliding in her wetness, savoring every sensation. She pushed against him, taking his entire cock without hesitation. He continued a slow, steady rhythm and tightened his arm around her waist.

Her pulse quickened.

A rumbling growl echoed in his chest.

Her body stiffened against his, and then she cried out as her muscles contracted around him, biting his cock from the base to the tip. The scent of her release surrounded him, igniting his senses.

She was *his*.

Refusing his own release, he rode out her marvelous, gripping pulses until they slowed and stopped, and she collapsed.

He could have filled her then, but he needed more.

He needed her total surrender.

Rachel lay still, enjoying the last of her orgasm. She'd never felt such a completely draining release. Not that she'd experienced the strange out-of-body sensations she had in Nikolai's hotel room. That mostly seemed to happen when they shared a climax.

Nikolai hadn't come yet. She felt his hard prick buried in her, larger than it had been when they'd started, unmoving.

And then he suddenly withdrew. She whimpered at the sense of abandonment.

"Turn over," he said, his voice deep and gravelly near her ear.

A shiver ran up and down her spine. If only she could see what was going on, see his expression. He certainly wasn't exhibiting the total restraint he had before. She knew he'd nearly lost control, and that knowledge had thrilled her, pushed her to a climax.

The weirdest thing was that she wasn't sure if she was having sex with a man or an animal, or maybe something in between.

No, the *weirdest* thing was that she didn't care.

Obeying, she turned to her belly.

He slid his arm under her again and drew her up to her hands and knees, into the curve of his body. She marveled at the way they fit together, as if they'd been poured on opposite sides of the same mold.

He held her in one arm and nuzzled the back of her neck. His body vibrated like that of a giant house cat purring. His breath warmed her shoulder.

Drawing her up tighter, he curved around her and pressed his prick against her pussy. In spite of the intensity of her orgasm moments earlier, she trembled with desire, waiting for his entry. He didn't ask permission; she knew he would take her when he wanted to.

She lifted her backside into him, giving him better access.

The head of his penis pressed against her pussy and then slid away, teasing her. She bit her bottom lip to keep from whimpering.

He eased his hold on her waist and slid his hand up to her breasts, caressing, touching.

Her nipples tightened, aching for attention.

He gripped one between thumb and forefinger and pinched as the head of his prick pushed into her cunt.

She gasped at the pleasure.

He withdrew.

God, he would drive her nuts at this rate.

He reached to the other breast and repeated the process, rolling the nipple as he pinched it, and entering her at the same time.

Her entire body tightened. Something about the hint of pain heightened her senses, and intensified the pleasure.

Juices dripped down her thighs, cooling in the night air.

He held her waist again, drew her up tight, and buried his massive prick in her in one steady thrust.

She sucked in a breath of surprise.

His stomach and chest pressed against her back and buttocks, hot, as if he ran a fever, nearly scorching her skin. Sweat prickled between their bodies.

He withdrew and thrust again and again.

She felt the promise of orgasm tightening the muscles in her legs and arms as she countered his movements.

He growled and clamped his mouth onto her shoulder, pressing into a nerve bundle. She squirmed against intense pleasure that derailed her attention, and the approaching orgasm faded.

He slid his hand down to her abdomen, and she felt the friction of his erection against his palm through her flesh as he fucked her. The glory of him filling her so completely took her to the edge again, and she drew in a stuttered breath.

He bit harder into her shoulder.

She bucked at the erotic pressure of his teeth threatening to puncture her skin.

He released the pressure and her body tightened.

Each time she neared release, he bit down.

Minutes lengthened until she felt like a cartoon character, dangling in midair after the ground had opened, knowing she's about to fall but unable to do anything about it. He had total control over her. He could decide when and if she'd come, and she had no say in it. All she could do was wait, open and ready.

Never in her life had she surrendered so completely to another person. If he'd wanted to, he could have ripped her throat out. Nikolai wouldn't hurt her, of course. But she didn't know what the panther would do.

Sweat ran along her ribs and tickled the sides of her swollen breasts.

She closed her eyes and focused on him. His stomach muscles knotted and eased against her back with each movement.

And then, almost imperceptibly, his movements quickened.

Her arousal shot up to a new level, knowing that he approached release. She craved not only the orgasm rocketing through her body, but also the mental joining she knew would happen. She needed to feel him fusing with her, body and mind, taking all she had to give and giving all of himself.

The vibrating purr grew into a deep growl, and his prick seemed to swell to an impossible size, stretching her with each plunge toward her center.

Her body liquefied as if made of molten metal, and she leapt past the point of return.

A wild, feline yowl echoed in her ears and her head.

Her back arched as the orgasm broke over her, taking control, driving her to scream at the first pounding spasm. Wave after wave rolled through her, dark and hard, wet and hot.

Blessed release.

On and on it went, the ecstasy approaching pain.

And then she left the physical plane completely.

Swirling around him, part of the same light, created from the same breath, she rose to a place without bounds. She felt his joy as her own, tasted his tears on her tongue, heard his sighs rising from her own chest. And she smiled, but not with her mouth. Her entire being smiled.

Pure, perfect happiness flowed from and to her.

She would stay with him here, where nothing could come between them. Remain in the heavens as one being made of two. Pain would never find them . . . no loss, no death.

Together.

Forever.

Then she felt the gentle tug at her center, pulling her down, drawing her back.

Slowly, she floated into her skin, into the liquid pleasure.

Joy flooded her body as he filled her with his seed. His voice, both human and not, cried out in delight, matching hers.

Her arms and legs gave out.

He fell with her, pumping the last of his release, his mouth near her ear.

They lay stretched out together, panting, groaning softly.

Just as she started to complain about his weight making it hard to breathe, he rolled them both over and gathered her into his arms.

Fitted in the curve of his body, sweat cooling on her skin, she listened to his breathing, and to the sound of blood pounding in her ears.

The spot where he'd bitten her shoulder tingled.

He tenderly kissed the same spot and drew her closer. Then she felt him draw in a deep breath and sigh.

Rachel closed her eyes. How strange was this relationship?

And just what the hell was Nikolai?

The only thing she knew for sure was that his wounds seemed to have healed in record time.

When he opened his eyes to find daylight filling the tent, Nikolai considered taking her again. He certainly wanted her badly enough. At just the thought, his cock hardened and rose against the warmth of her smooth ass.

Rachel moaned softly, just starting to wake.

Perhaps it was the fact that he'd had trouble releasing the leopard this time that kept him in this state of heightened arousal. Certainly holding onto the sacred feline soul had allowed him to heal from what could have been lethal wounds.

No, he knew better. Rachel produced this desire in him. He let himself daydream of waking with her in his arms for decades to come, of making love to her in morning sunlight, of raising a family with her, of kissing away her fears and sorrows, and of letting her heal his heart.

But it was only a daydream, and a dangerous one at that. Watching her walk away would rip open old wounds and load them with salt. Perhaps this time, those wounds wouldn't close.

Nikolai closed his eyes and listened to sounds outside the tent. He heard several birds, and the scratch of a curious ground squirrel on the camp utensils.

He remembered his encounter with the Cushaknas. They'd heard him, or smelled him, or something, because they'd slipped from their den before he arrived and waited for him in the rocks. With fangs slashing the air, they'd cornered him against the rock wall.

He hadn't worried about them doing any major damage when they first surrounded him. They were fast, but smaller than the leopard. He'd known he could wait for them to make a mistake, or to tire. Then he'd take them out, one at a time. Rachel's arrival had ruined his plan.

The Cushaknas had spotted her just after he had, and he'd known they would use her presence against him. He couldn't risk getting her injured, even if it meant facing all three of the beasts at once. As he'd taken the first one down, he'd known he was risking death to save Rachel.

Somehow, it had felt right to do so, as if she were his mate. Could it have been the strength of his feelings for her that surged through him as he fought the Cushaknas?

He heard another noise, something foreign to the moment, and opened his eyes. Morning light, softened by the blue tent fabric, gave Rachel's hair an eerie, icy glow.

Rising up on one elbow, he kissed the side of her head, drew her hair away from her face, and whispered into her ear, "Rachel, wake up. We're about to have company."

* * *

By the time the helicopter arrived, they were both up and dressed, but barely. Their ride back wasn't due for hours yet. Why had it arrived early?

Nikolai's pale complexion had Rachel worried, in spite of his apparently miraculous healing. They could probably excuse his appearance as food poisoning or something, but that didn't make her feel much better. What would she say if anyone asked her why she thought the killings would now stop?

And was Nikolai right about that? She really had no way of telling. In spite of the bite marks on the victims, it looked like they'd had human company at the time of death.

She glanced at Nikolai and considered the fact that she'd watched him change from a panther into a human. Had these foxes had that ability, too? If so, where had they come from?

For that matter, where did Nikolai come from? Did the Russian government know about him?

She suddenly remembered Jerry White's note and the database search results he'd left on her desk. Maybe no one knew about Nikolai.

Except her. She knew. It couldn't be knowledge he wanted her to have.

Shit. What had she gotten herself into?

The helicopter landed on the far side of the clearing, about thirty yards from their camp. As the engine wound down and the rotor slowed, the passenger's side door opened and long legs appeared, clad in slacks totally inappropriate for the bush. The rest of the body followed, resulting in a tall, strikingly attractive blonde crouching under the aircraft's blades.

"Who the hell is this?" Rachel asked the question to no one in particular.

Nikolai's only response was a low growl.

The woman seemed friendly enough as she approached with outstretched hand. "You must be Inspector McNeil. I'm Dr. Letsa. Elena."

"Rachel." She accepted the firm handshake, and turned toward Nikolai. "And this is my associate—"

"Nick," he said, interrupting. "Nick Phelps. Nice to meet you, Doc."

Rachel frowned. Not only had Nikolai's Russian accent disappeared, he sounded like he'd left Dallas just moments ago.

Shaking herself mentally, she returned her attention to the woman standing before her. Elena Letsa had a faint Russian accent, stood nearly six feet tall, and couldn't be more than forty. Something about her appearance, as strange as it was in the wilds of Alaska, screamed authority. She studied both of them but pretended not to. *Odd.*

"Uh, Dr. Letsa—"

"Elena," the woman insisted.

"Elena. I don't mean to be rude, but what are you doing here?"

The woman released a friendly laugh. "Of course, you were not expecting me. I was contacted by Earl Stanton of the State Fish and Game. He said you were looking for information on fox sightings in this area."

Rachel felt a cold hand wrap around her heart.

Elena continued. "I'm heading up a project to reintroduce the rare Russian Arctic fox into the park. They were wiped out fifty years ago by hunters, and are only found in northern Siberia in the wild. I hope to change that." She smiled as she looked from Rachel to Nikolai and back. "I understand you contacted Mr. Stanton."

Rachel nodded. "Yes, but I didn't say it was an emergency. You didn't need to fly all the way out here."

The woman waved off the statement dismissively. "It is no problem. I'm very concerned that the . . . *specimens* survive."

"So, you've already released some of these foxes?"

"Yes, several months ago."

"How many were released?"

"I'm afraid that's confidential."

"I understand," Rachel said, "but I'm working on a murder investigation. Any information you can give me may help, no matter how insignificant it seems."

"Murder?" Elena raised a hand to her chest. "Really? Well, then I guess I should get my records. I have information and release locations on each fox in my briefcase."

She turned and started back for the helicopter at a fairly brisk walk in spite of wearing heels.

"Nikolai—"

He raised one finger to his lips and then motioned toward Elena.

Rachel frowned. No one could hear her from that distance.

Nikolai stepped forward and stood between Rachel and the helicopter, his face very close to hers. "Where's your weapon?"

She reached for her hip, found it bare, and frowned. "In the tent." Then she glanced to her left and spotted the rifle. "But we have—"

A shot rang out.

Nikolai lurched forward, knocking into her and spinning as he fell. He yelled a string of what must have been Russian curses through gritted teeth.

Rachel dropped to all fours and stared at the blood oozing out from between his fingers where he held his thigh. "You're hit."

"Grab the rifle and run. Get to the woods."

She reached for him. "Nikolai, you're hit."

"Now!" The order came out as a roar, deep and lethal.

Rachel snatched her hand back and stared at the danger flashing in his golden eyes, then spun away toward the rifle.

The second shot went over their heads, thudding in soft ground. She could barely see the blond head of the shooter over the log. Why hadn't the pilot stopped her from trying to kill them?

Rachel decided not to consider the obvious answer as she

grabbed the rifle. She rolled with her back to the log and watched Nikolai scrambling toward the tent.

"I can get her from here," she said to him, checking for a chambered shell.

"Run," he said. "You won't kill her."

As he crawled into the tent, a shot ripped through the nylon well above his head.

Certainly her Glock wasn't going to do any more good against Elena than the rifle. If she were some kind of—

A low growl, totally feline and wild, startled her, and Rachel realized he hadn't gone in after her weapon. A black head emerged from the tent, flashing long white teeth.

Gripping the rifle, she crawled toward the woods as fast as she could. Whatever the hell was going on was way out of her league. Besides, she could take a better shot if she could stand.

6

———————

He caught her scent now, and was certain. She was Cushakna. But she was more. He tasted more human in the air than fox.

A shot followed him across the field. Ignoring the burn in his left leg, Nikolai ran as fast as he could, eating up the ground in long strides. He stayed too low to see her, but he knew where she was.

As he neared her location, he prepared to lunge, anxious for the kill.

He skidded to a stop beside the helicopter where the rifle lay on the ground beside a pile of clothes.

Testing the air, he looked around but caught no hint of her.

He stood on his back legs to see into the helicopter and found the pilot slumped forward with a pool of fresh blood spreading around his feet. A large gash glistened across the side of the man's throat.

He turned and scanned the horizon.

This Cushakna acted as no other.

Lowering himself to the ground near her clothes, he sniffed and caught the musky scent of the fox. He picked it up all around him and followed the wide circle, scanning side to side, until he found the path leading out.

At first, she headed south through the trees. He trotted along, keeping her scent in front of him. Before long, he was headed north, having made a sweeping circle. She crossed a boulder field, leapt over snow, and cut back and forth several times, but he followed. She ran like Cushakna.

The pain in his leg lessened as the wound closed, and he picked up the pace. He kept his eyes on the trail ahead for any hint of white fur.

He caught a whiff of Rachel in the air. The Cushakna was headed toward the site of the earlier battle. He must reach Rachel before the Cushakna did.

He raised his head as a yelping scream pierced the woods, followed by silence. All other creatures fell quiet at the sound.

Abandoning the trail, he raced toward the small canyon, making the first rock ledge in one leap.

There below him, the three Cushakna corpses lay where he'd left them the day before. In the middle of the bloody circle stood Rachel, her hands empty at her sides, dirt and scrapes marking the side of her face. Her wide green eyes reflected the early sunshine.

Behind her stood Elena Letsa in human form, naked, holding Rachel's rifle pointed at the back of Rachel's head.

"Change, shaman," Elena said.

He studied them both, noting every movement. Rachel's nostrils flared, and she stared directly at him. A soft breeze lifted a strand of her silky hair. Elena held her shoulder, gripping tightly. He saw the murderous rage in the Cushakna's blue eyes.

The leopard's fury filled his chest, urging him to attack, ignoring what remained of human reason.

"Change, damn you! Or I'll kill her now!"

With a growl of frustration, Nikolai closed his eyes, took a deep breath, and released his hold on the cat's pure soul.

It didn't leave him easily, but peeled away one layer at a time, ripping with it his strength and instincts. His hide grew heavy and hot, and then lifted from his skin as his body knotted and his legs stretched. The familiar discomfort became more painful as the process continued, taking much too long. Perhaps it was because he knew Rachel watched.

Perhaps it was because he was close to his final state.

Not now.

Change!

One last push and the soul finally disappeared.

He lay still, feeling the cold ground beneath him, hearing with human limits.

Holding the sacred hide, he rose to his knees, and then to his feet, drawing the leopard skin around his shoulders.

"There, now. Much better." Elena gave Rachel a shove. "Sit."

Rachel eased down to the ground and drew one leg up in front of her. Her gaze went from Elena to Nikolai and back. Even without enhanced vision, he could still see anger flashing in her eyes.

"You'll pay for this." Elena glanced down at the swollen corpses. "My beautiful children," she whispered.

Nikolai stumbled down the rock face, needing to be near Rachel. When everything went to hell, he hoped to save her. She didn't deserve to be caught in this, not with so much of her young life ahead.

"That's far enough," Elena said, pointing the rifle at his chest.

"Let her go," he said, nodding toward Rachel. "She isn't part of this."

Elena smiled, her insanity easy to see now. "Interesting thought." She crouched and stared at Rachel through narrowed eyes. "She isn't one of us, but she knows. How is it she doesn't fear you?"

Nikolai clenched his jaw, biting back an angry growl. He knew how easily Elena—or whatever her name was—could pull the trigger.

Why hadn't she?

He frowned.

"What is it you want, Cushakna?"

The woman shot to her feet and glared at him. "You use a name from long ago. Do you even know how it came to be? Do you know the tragedy of our story?"

He straightened and studied her. Perhaps he could disarm her, if he was ready when the opportunity presented itself. He couldn't run the risk of slapping the rifle aside and getting Rachel shot.

The woman snorted. "Of course not. How could you? The old ones lied to you, told you vicious stories of us. They only wanted to make sure no one would help us. Did you know that?" She pointed the rifle at Rachel again and drew a fingernail across Nikolai's bare chest.

It suddenly occurred to him who he was standing before. Could it be? Had one of the sisters survived all this time?

"You're one of Alexandra's," he said.

She laughed dryly. "Oh, so you know about us." She nodded as if pleased. "Yes, my dear sisters and I were ostracized from the village long ago. Do you know why?"

He decided not to answer. Perhaps he'd already said too much.

"For simply giving in to our nature. That's all. Can you imagine such a thing?"

"Your mother broke the first rule," he said.

She snarled. "A rule made by a self-righteous bigot, already dried up and useless. He couldn't begin to understand her or us, yet he condemned us all. My mother died of a broken heart. She left us to fend for ourselves, and so we did."

"You're supposed to be dead."

That made her smile. "Am I?" The smile faded. "Well, I'm

not. My sisters were taken one at a time years ago. Were you the one who hunted them down?"

Nikolai shook his head slowly. "No."

She leaned close to his face. "Too bad. I would enjoy this even more."

She walked away from him, keeping the weapon trained on Rachel. "You seem attached to this one. Is that why she doesn't fear you?"

When he didn't answer, she grinned at him. "Cat got your tongue, shaman?" She laughed.

The hair on the back of his neck stood on end.

"Fine. Let's get on with it." She motioned to Rachel. "You want me to let her go?"

"Yes."

"And you'd do anything for that, wouldn't you?" She waved her free hand. "Don't bother. I'm ready to make you an offer. I'll release the woman in return for your help."

"What kind of help?"

Her gaze ran down his body. "The kind I believe you're *equipped* to give, shaman."

Nikolai swallowed hard. "And that is?"

"You will give me your seed in return for her life. If I'm right, the child will be unlike any who have come before. She will be able to maintain human form, and will have the same abilities I have. She will be the one to save our line."

He knew what this meant. He'd heard the stories of men who had given in to Cushakna. Even someone with his training would be unlikely to survive, and the death would not be fast or merciful.

For Rachel's life, the sacrifice was nothing.

"All right. I accept."

"Nikolai, what the hell's going on?"

He looked at Rachel, taking in the beauty of sunshine on her face, regretting only the time they would not have together. Then he glanced at the Cushakna.

"Go ahead, tell her," she said.

He walked slowly to Rachel and drew her to her feet, then he cupped her face in his hands.

"Listen to me, Rachel. Get to the radio and get out of here. Don't come back."

"But, this doesn't—"

He stopped her by kissing her precious mouth, tasting her one last time.

She drew in a breath of surprise, but returned his kiss.

Then he stepped away, turning his back to her. "I'm ready."

The Cushakna strutted toward him, smiling. "Not yet, but you will be. And when you are, she can leave."

Nikolai let the sacred skin fall from his shoulders. It no longer mattered what happened to it; he'd never get the chance to release its powers again.

With one hand gripping the rifle, the Cushakna used the other to grip his flaccid cock. She squeezed and lifted, as if taking his measure. Then she nodded. "Yes, I think you'll do. On your knees."

Trying not to think of Rachel standing behind him, watching him, he eased down to his knees.

The Cushakna stepped closer, her white bush inches from his face. She raised one leg and rested it on his shoulder, releasing the full force of her scent.

It was the scent of both female shaman and animal, blended into a force no man could resist. More than just woman, her scent drove all rational thoughts into the shadows. He wanted more of that scent, to bury himself in it, to roll in the pleasure of it. He leaned closer and inhaled.

Hunger rose inside him, hunger for something timeless, primeval. His cock swelled in a rush, and he reached for her. Gripping her thigh and her ass, he drew her cunt to his mouth.

The taste exploded in his brain, leaving him weak and drunk. He lapped at the rich cream, reaching deeper.

She held him by the hair. "Yes," she said, "you cooperate well."

He heard movement behind him. *Rachel.* The thought of her drew him back just inches from the shadows.

He must hold out long enough for her escape. If he could re- member the sacred words, he could give her more time. *Kah . . . shawut . . . gugan—*

Ancient heat, primal forces whispered to him in a language he couldn't understand, seducing him and pulling him. He gripped tighter, digging his fingers into pliant flesh, sucking hard. He needed all of her.

Darkness rose around him, drowning all thoughts, taking him under.

His universe focused down to one need: to mate.

Rachel stood at the edge of the woods, panting, trying to catch her breath. The noises coming from the other side of the rock ledge made her wonder if she was doing the right thing. Had she lost her mind? After all, they were simply screwing, weren't they? Hardly a capital offense.

Unsure, she climbed the rock face as quietly as possible. It had taken her a good fifteen minutes to get back to camp and return, running as fast as she could. She hadn't known what to expect to find.

What she found was Nikolai, lying on his back, holding Elena's waist. She gripped his shoulders and rode him with total abandon. His penis, enlarged to amazing proportions, glistened in the sunshine with Elena's fluids each time it emerged and dis- appeared inside her.

Rage made Rachel shake, and it took a moment for her to re- alize the rage was mostly jealousy. She'd run from the camp, hoping to save Nikolai's life, only to find him screwing his brains out with one of the most attractive women on the planet.

Even through jealous eyes, the two formed an amazing pair: her sleek lines and smooth, pale skin against his dark, muscular body. They moved together in perfect rhythm, grunting with each thrust.

As she watched, Elena drew her fingers down Nikolai's chest, ripping flesh with her fingernails. He didn't even seem to notice as he thrust up into her, lifting them both off the ground each time. Blood pooled and ran down his sides.

Shit. This wasn't good old-fashioned sex, it was something else, something dangerous.

Something lethal.

Elena threw her head back and her grunts changed to yelps, like the sounds of an animal on the trail of prey.

Hoping she'd found the right moment, Rachel rose to her feet and charged, letting momentum carry her down the slope with the force of a boulder. She held the Glock in both hands, waiting for just the right moment, and squeezed the trigger.

The shell ripped through Elena's head as Rachel vaulted past, landing on her side on the ground just beyond them.

Elena flew sideways off of Nikolai, landing on her back in the dirt. Rachel sat up, the weapon still pointed, and shot twice more, nearly severing the woman's head.

Elena lay in a spreading pool of blood, her face unrecognizably mangled, undoubtedly dead.

Rachel *had* been able to kill her.

She lowered the Glock as Nikolai rolled over and scrambled to his hands and knees. He glared at her with wild yellow eyes, noises rising from his throat that sounded like a mixture of growls and wounded screams. Blood dripped from his chest.

He suddenly jumped to his feet and charged forward, knocking Rachel onto her back and the air from her lungs. The Glock skidded across a rock beyond reach.

His hands circled her throat as he straddled her chest and glared down at her, teeth bared. She gripped his bulging arms and gasped for breath.

His eyes flashed with murderous rage.

He planned to kill her. She saw it in his wild expression. He was in worse shape than someone on PCP, and she would die for saving him from Elena, from the Cushakna.

"Nikolai," she mouthed, unable to get air past his grip on her throat. "Nikolai."

Suddenly he froze and his eyes widened. Recognition seemed to be struggling to get in, and he loosened his grip just a little.

"Nikolai. It's me, Rachel." The words barely made it out.

He slid off of her and backed away, wiping his mouth with the back of one hand. His black hair brushed across his wide, muscular shoulders as he looked from her to Elena and back. His chest heaved with rapid breaths.

"Rach—?" His voice broke. He tried again. "Rachel?"

She sat up, massaging her bruised larynx. "Yes."

He said something in Russian, and then crawled over to her. With a gentle touch and trembling hand, he caressed her face, and sanity finally filled his eyes.

She touched his bleeding chest. He sat, drew her into his arms, and held her as he rocked. He whispered her name over and over.

Rachel wrapped her arms around his neck and chest, closed her eyes, and pressed her face to his warm skin. His scent filled her with a feeling of security she found strange at that moment, but savored nonetheless.

The Cushakna's body shimmered silvery white as she walked toward him, her ice-blue eyes staring from a seductively lowered head. Her lips parted, and the tip of her tongue slid across her upper lip.

Every inch of him reacted as desire smoldered deep in his belly and groin. One thought, one need, it was all he felt. Nothing else in the world existed.

He lay back as she stood over him, her swelling cunt drawing his focus. Slowly—painfully slowly—she lowered herself down, down, down, until her heat covered the tip of his aching cock.

He whimpered when she stopped.

Her hands pressed to his chest as she leaned forward, snaring him with her gaze.

Dark heaviness floated over him like a blanket, weighing down his arms and legs, and he couldn't move, couldn't fight, couldn't drag her to him.

Her fingers sharpened to silver claws, piercing his skin. She smiled, flashing white fangs, and leaned closer.

Her scent fanned the flames blazing in his gut, flames of need.

She drove her claws into his chest, ripped out his beating heart, and held it up where he could see it.

Nikolai gasped as he sat up.

He stared at a white tile wall.

Warm water splashed against his sides and back, and he frowned down at his chest where his hand covered the spot over his heart.

No, the Cushaknas were dead. It was over. Elena's hold on him had been broken.

Taking a deep breath and releasing it, he lay back in the tub and stared at the textured ceiling as small waves of water died against his flesh. Steam rose to caress his neck and face.

The echo of water dripping from the faucet took him back to a day of great joy, so many years ago, and he smiled, taking comfort from the memory. . . .

Spring's sun shone on the valley as he waited in the warm pool of blue water. Friends laughed quietly, remarking on his anxious state. He'd sported an erection since waking hours earlier. He didn't mind. He'd waited for this day, trained for this. He could endure the pain for the lifetime of pleasure to follow.

A soft breeze whispered through red and white flowers lining the path down from the main house. Bare feet moved almost silently on the grass as the mating party approached.

Two young girls in front wore white robes and tossed flower petals into the path. They giggled and exchanged glances as they walked. It would be their turns to walk behind the party someday, but not for many years yet.

The girls parted to circle the pool, revealing the rest of the approaching party. The group of four women came first, followed by their respective or perspective mates. All wore blue robes, laced in gold.

Then came Sasha, beautiful Sasha, clad in red velvet, and holding the arm of his best man, Andrei, who also wore ceremonial red. She smiled at Nikolai, her dark brown eyes sending messages of happiness, excitement, and love, and he smiled back.

Once they'd passed him, he rose from the pool and stepped into the waiting robe, then was led by the crowd to the den. Most of the village waited outside as Nikolai ducked into the small opening, following the mating party.

Inside, steam warmed the air and dripped from sweating rocks. Torches lined the walls, and shadows from the firelight danced around him.

Two dozen people—the mating party and the village elders—formed a loose circle that opened to allow him in. They smiled and wished him well, and patted his shoulders encouragingly.

In the middle of the circle on the round altar, Sasha lay on her red robe, gloriously naked, one leg drawn up seductively, smiling.

Nikolai winked at her, and laughed. She'd been through this before, but he'd never had a mating ceremony. In spite of his calm exterior, he was nervous about his performance.

"Let the ceremony begin," one of the elders, Vera, said, her voice reverberating ominously in the damp air.

The women of the mating party stepped forward then and drew his robe from him, leaving him standing several arms' lengths from the altar, naked.

Sasha glanced down at his cock and nodded approval.

Heat rose in his face in spite of all he'd been through in preparation. He couldn't help it. Sasha's approval meant more to him than anything.

Then Andrei stepped forward, shed his robe and knelt on the altar. Sasha turned her attention to him.

Andrei, a few years older than Nikolai, had been a dear friend for as long as Nikolai could remember. He was marvelously well-formed and handsome. In his changed state, he became a lion, proud and ferocious, powerful and fast. He'd taught Nikolai much about understanding the cat's soul, and they'd wandered the Arctic plains together many times. He was a good choice for the ceremony.

Andrei moved with the lion's grace while in human form. He crawled forward, admiring Sasha's body first with his eyes, and then with his hands. He touched her legs and sides, and then caressed her full breasts. Sasha made small movements of pleasure. Then, on all fours, he leaned forward and licked her, circled her breasts with his tongue, and he sucked. Sasha's breathing grew louder.

As Nikolai watched, the women touched him, stroked him, kissed his shoulders and chest. Their touches heightened his arousal to the point of pain. He took deep breaths to maintain his focus.

Andrei covered Sasha's body with attention, moving from her neck slowly down to her thighs. He spread her slender legs to expose her dewy labia to Nikolai's gaze. Then, with a quick grin over his shoulder, he buried his face between her legs.

Sasha's eyes closed and her back arched as Andrei audibly sucked and licked.

Warm moisture coated Nikolai's cock, and he glanced down to find two women licking it, laughing as they matched movements up and down each side with their tongues. One of them took him into her mouth, sliding wet lips down his length. In his state, he nearly forgot everything he'd learned. He was ready to come, ready to explode, as fingers flicked across his nipples and drew sensuous lines down his back.

Mentally shaking himself, he found the words then, and started his silent chant. *Kah, shawut, gugan, dis.* He chanted in time with the wonderful mouth sliding up and down his cock.

Sasha groaned as the first release started, and lifted her hips against Andrei's mouth. Andrei's growl vibrated through the den, a counterpoint to her cries of joy.

Nikolai smiled, relieved that he'd made it through the first round. He'd heard stories of some who hadn't.

Andrei drew back, glanced over at his friend, and nodded with approval. Then he crawled forward and stretched out on top of Sasha, kissing her neck and throat as he eased his massive cock into her. He did so while leaning to one side so that Nikolai could watch it slide in, disappearing a little at a time into Sasha's rosy cunt.

Damn, he wanted to be in Andrei's place, taking his mate with long, slow strokes, feeling her welcoming heat. They'd spent the last month apart, as required.

Kah, shawut, gugan, dis. One of the women licked circles around his balls and his knees shook. *Kah, shawut, gugan, dis.*

Andrei's back roped as he rose up to his hands, burying his cock and withdrawing all but the head. The dark skin of his hard shaft glistened in the torchlight. With slow, steady strokes, he continued until Sasha's back arched again, pushing her tightening stomach up against his. Her hands fisted against Andrei's arms and she cried out.

Nikolai staggered back half a step, steadied by feminine hands. His heavy cock rose to point at his mate as the women turned their attentions to other places, finding nerve bundles to nip and kiss. His entire body began to tremble. *Kah, shawut, gugan, dis.*

Andrei withdrew, well lubricated now with Sasha's cum, and kissed her belly.

Flashing a grin of impending victory at Nikolai, he urged Sasha to her hands and knees. He leaned down and licked all the way from her clit up to her lower back several times before straightening. His sounds of pleasure lowered to something like a deep, rumbling purr.

He parted Sasha's luscious ass, revealing her tightest opening. He used one finger to draw cream from her cunt up to her anus and carefully, tenderly, lubricated the sphincter. As he worked deeper, his cock seemed to enlarge even more, rubbing against her thigh. Then he drew Sasha to him and held her waist.

Andrei's body rocked with Sasha's, matching a back and forth rhythm, drawing closer with each movement. Nikolai felt fingers pressing against his own anus as he watched Andrei's phallus slowly disappear. Once he was sheathed, Andrei leaned forward, molded himself to Sasha's body, and groaned.

Nikolai felt his knees buckle, but caught himself before he went down. Semen welled in his balls, ready to erupt. *Kah, shawut, gugan, dis. Kah, shawut, gugan, dis.*

Their bodies glistened with sweat as their rhythm increased in speed. Sasha raised her head, her eyes closed, breathing in soft moans. Andrei's body swelled and muscles rippled; he pressed his forehead to Sasha's back. His golden hair fell forward, brushing her damp skin. His breathing grew ragged, and he drew Sasha up tighter.

She cried out, louder this time as her body tightened and jerked.

Nikolai curled his fingers and held his fists at his side, working as hard as he could to stay centered. Thick air swirled around him, laden with sex, and others in the den groaned as they kissed and petted each other. The women squeezed his cock with strong fingers, caressed every bit of him, nipped at his flesh and kissed him, and he shook. *Kah, shawut, gugan, dis.* He silently mouthed the words in time with Andrei's quickening thrusts.

Andrei rose up, gripped Sasha's waist, and roared his release, and the whole den seemed to quake. Nikolai whispered the sacred words, closing his eyes to focus, throwing everything he had into it. He *would* hold out. He *would*.

And then the air stilled and his attendants moved away.

Nikolai held his ground, sweat running down his chest and neck, and he opened his eyes.

Andrei kissed Sasha's pale shoulders as he eased from her, and stood, wiping his hair back from his face with both hands. Grinning, he swaggered to Nikolai, gripped his upper arms, and kissed his cheeks. He met Nikolai's gaze evenly. "Go to your mate, my friend. You have earned the respect of all here." Then he winked and gave Nikolai's shoulder a shove as he released him, sending him in the direction of Sasha.

She lay on her back, propped up on her elbows, smiling and waiting for him.

He crawled across the altar and settled between her legs, burying his cock in her tight, wet cunt in one motion, savoring the feeling of belonging, and he kissed her willing mouth.

Sasha wrapped her arms around him and drew his tongue in as she lifted herself against him. Kissing her, enjoying her taste, he let her lead the rhythm and said a prayer of thanks as he felt her cunt tighten around him. She tore her mouth from his, and groaned softly in time with the rippling spasms.

He held her, pressed his face to her neck, and let go. With all the cum erupting from him, he vaguely wondered if this first time would produce a child.

And then he rose into the light.

"Nikolai?"

He opened his eyes to find Rachel standing in the doorway.

"Looks like you're feeling better."

He followed her gaze to where his swollen cock broke the water's surface. Then he smiled up at her. "I will be, if you cooperate."

7

Rachel watched Nikolai emerge from the bathroom, buck naked and fully aroused. The sight of him took her breath away. Water dripped from the ends of his dark hair, streaking his massive chest and shoulders. Washboard abs rippled as he walked slowly in her direction. Each silent step reminded her of the black cat stepping toward her, unblinking and sure.

Her heart pounded like a fist against her ribs.

In spite of the wetness pooling in her crotch, they needed to talk. He seemed to be returning to his old self, and she had to know exactly what had happened in the park. Official questions had been asked, and more would follow.

He crawled onto the bed and sat on his heels. "You have too many clothes on."

Standing across the room, she folded her arms, trying for nonchalance. "We need to talk first."

"*First?*"

"We need to talk," she said, correcting herself. It annoyed her that he seemed to think he had some kind of right to her. "I killed a woman. Her body might be found at any moment. If I can't explain what happened out there, I could face charges."

"No." He turned and sat, his playful smile fading. "She was not woman. She was Cushakna. Her mother was one of my people, and her father was a fox. And I hid her body where no one will find it."

Feeling the weight of the truth at last, Rachel sat in the desk chair. "Who are your people, Nikolai? Who . . . *what* exactly are you?"

He dropped his gaze to his hands and frowned, then raised it back to hers. "I am a shaman."

"Like, a medicine man or something? I don't understand."

He shook his head and looked away.

After a moment, she realized he wasn't going to continue without prodding. "No bullshit this time. I need the truth."

Nikolai sighed. "I'm breaking all the laws of my village by telling you any of this, but I understand your need. You've seen things you thought impossible. And you wound up in the middle of a fight that wasn't yours. You saved my life. I owe you the truth, at least, even if it puts me at risk."

He drew one knee up to rest his arm on, and Rachel tried to ignore the fact that he put every Greek statue ever carved to shame.

He studied her with his intensely golden eyes. "Many thousands of years ago, when civilization as we know it began to take hold, there were shamans, men and women of great power, scattered across the globe. They helped their people as healers and guardians, and spiritual leaders. When modern religions came into existence, the shamans were ousted from many parts of the world, and could easily have disappeared forever.

"Instead, a group from what's now western Europe got together and struck out for an isolated place to make their own. They took human mates, packed up what they needed, and walked for years. When they finally found the right place, they built their village and have lived apart from the rest of the world ever since."

She frowned. "You're trying to tell me that you and your people live in a town no one else knows about, even with satellite imagery?"

He nodded.

"How?"

He shrugged. "I can't give you details, Rachel. Only those who plan to stay forever, who have agreed to be life mates, know the location, or how it's hidden."

She shook her head to clear it. This would have been impossible to believe if she hadn't seen what she had in the past two days.

"Okay," she said. "You come from a secret village of shamans. Is everyone like, you know, a shapeshifter, or whatever you call it?" She felt silly just asking the question.

"Not everyone. Those who are born in the village and carry the shaman bloodline are able to take on the soul and shape of an animal. Each of us is sent out to find our animal guide when we first reach adulthood."

His eyes darkened as he spoke, and Rachel felt as though she were pushing her way into territory he didn't want to share. Still, he hadn't refused to answer her.

"Tell me about the Cushaknas."

He glanced toward the window, breaking eye contact. "When we change—"

"Into an animal?"

"Yes, when we take on our animal's form, we carry the animal's soul and instincts. The drive to mate is a powerful instinct. In the early times, shamans mated with animals, and the results were sometimes tragic. Offspring would be either monstrous or pathetic, neither shaman nor animal, but something in between. The first thing all shamans are taught is that we must not mate while in animal form."

"That's what you meant when you said that Elena's mother had broken the first rule."

"Yes. According to the stories, Alexandra was a headstrong young woman whose guide animal was the Arctic fox. She thumbed her nose at the rules, changed whenever she felt the urge, and ran wild outside the village. On one such outing, she mated with a fox and was impregnated. She gave birth to four offspring, one of which was born dead, the only male. The other three survived."

"Elena and her sisters."

He nodded.

"You were surprised when you realized who she was." It wasn't a question; she'd heard amazement in his voice when he'd said, "You're one of Alexandra's."

"Yes. We believed the original sisters had died centuries ago."

"*Centuries?*" Her throat tightened.

He nodded slowly, frowning.

"She couldn't have been forty."

He didn't answer.

"How old was she, Nikolai?"

He swallowed hard. "About three hundred and fifty."

"*Years?*"

He nodded again.

"How old are you?"

"Is it important?"

This time, she nodded, a little afraid of what he might say.

"I'm nearly two hundred years old."

"Holy crap!" She jumped up. "Tell me you're joking."

"I'm not joking."

"You're like . . . immortal?"

"No. We simply have a longer life span than humans. Usually."

"What do you mean 'usually'?"

Nikolai stretched out on his side, propped his head on one

hand, and smiled at her. "The animal's soul is seductive in its beauty, its simplicity. Some are seduced."

"They stay as animals?"

"Yes. If we change too frequently, coming back becomes more difficult. If we're not careful, it becomes impossible."

"Then what?"

He sighed. "We live out the life of our spirit animal and we die."

She enjoyed the long, powerful lines of his body, and realized how much like the panther he looked. "How did you choose the panther?"

His gaze snapped up to hers. "Leopard," he corrected. "I didn't choose him. He chose me." Warning flashed in his eyes again, though probably not consciously.

Rachel rose and walked to the window. She stared down at traffic, building for the lunch rush. "What were you smiling about in the bathtub?" She turned around and found him watching her intently.

"I was recalling the day I took Sasha as my mate."

"Your mate? Is that like a spouse?"

"More. We mate for life. Once we've given our hearts to another, there is no going back."

She swallowed hard. "So, this Sasha, is she waiting for you?"

He smiled and shook his head. "No, Rachel."

"She . . . what, died?"

"Most likely. The last time I saw her, she was circling high above me, and then she flew away." Tears glistened in his eyes. "We had thirty wonderful years together, and I'm thankful for that. Sasha's guide animal was a golden eagle. Her first mate had been human. They'd never borne children, and some speculated that she needed a shaman mate. I was fortunate enough to be chosen.

"Unfortunately, we had no children. I don't know why. She wanted children so much, I think it broke her heart. And maybe

188 / *Lydia Parks*

part of her heart had never completely healed after Michael's death."

"The human?"

He nodded. "She told me how wonderful it was to fly high above the trees. She talked about how sweet the air was, and how the wind whistled across her wings. I knew she would change forever at some point."

"How long ago was that?"

Nikolai stretched, sat up, and swung his legs over the side of the bed.

"Long enough," he said. He watched her from a lowered head, and she suddenly remembered the feeling when she first met him of being a toy mouse. How appropriate.

"I should get to work," she said, starting toward the chair where she'd left her coat. "I still have to figure out what I'm going to write in my report."

"Don't leave, Rachel."

She stopped, the collar of her coat in one fist, and turned to look at him. Every cell in her body screamed for him, craved the feeling of his bare skin against hers.

But the whole thing was absurd.

If she could believe what he said, the man sitting in front of her was two centuries old, and not even a man but some kind of different species.

"Please, Rachel," he said, his voice a notch lower, "don't leave."

She swallowed hard and dropped the coat.

He held out his hand, palm up.

She stared at it, this graceful, powerful hand, knew the thrill of feeling it caressing her breasts, remembered the fingers stroking her clit.

"You're the one leaving," she said, slipping her hand into his. As she said the words, tears spilled from her eyes and ran down her cheeks. Through all of the insanity, she couldn't bear the thought of him going away.

"Not yet," he said, drawing her steadily closer.

When she stood right in front of him, he wrapped his arms around her thighs, pulled her close, and pressed his face to her belly. Even through the sweater, his lips felt hot on her skin.

He looked up at her with eyes sparkling with emotion she couldn't begin to read. "Come to bed, Rachel."

She couldn't have resisted if she'd wanted to.

Holding his muscular shoulders, she kicked off her boots and let him help her from the rest of her clothes. His fingers, brushing her skin as he pushed her pants down and peeled off her sweater, started a strange fire just under the surface.

Once free, she straddled his hips, wrapped her arms around his neck, and kissed him.

He opened her mouth, offering his familiar taste, and she took it, holding him tighter. Her breasts swelled against his chest, and her nipples puckered.

No matter what her brain thought, her body knew the pleasure he produced and craved it.

He buried his fingers in her hair and turned her head to reach deeper.

She drew hard on his tongue, enjoying his desire. His prick swelled between them, pressing against her pubic bone. She pushed against it.

He groaned. With one arm around her waist, he rolled around and stretched out on the bed, drawing her under him.

She ran her hands over his shoulders and down his arms, tracing lines of hard muscle bunching under warm flesh. Her fingertips recalled the silky feel of the leopard's fur.

Without breaking the kiss, he gripped her thigh in one hand and started into her. She felt her own juices coating the head of his penis as he rubbed her clit, inflicting sweet torture that made her heart race.

He tore his mouth away and rose up to gaze down at her. Holding her gaze with a magical intensity, he entered her in one long, slow thrust.

His eyes closed for a second, then he opened them again and studied her face as he stroked, slowly, gently, reaching her depths and withdrawing.

The fire under her skin spread to the core of her body, bursting into flames. She clung to him and lifted her hips into each lunge.

His breath slid across her lips and face, cooling the tear tracks, quickening as he continued.

Her body tightened, the flames intensifying, searing cruel lines up the backs of her thighs and across her buttocks. She pressed one palm to his chest and his heartbeat pounded against it, matching her own.

She heard the whoosh of an exploding inferno and threw her head back as her body erupted. Heated contractions started in her pussy and shot up through the rest of her, rolling away as the next one started. She pulled him closer.

He pinned her down with his weight, matching her speed, filling her need.

Deeper, harder, faster.

Until the flames spread away, leaving her charred.

She held him, afraid to let go.

He lay still, breathing against her neck, hard still inside her.

She took a deep breath and sighed it out, smiling at the sense of completion. "Damn, you're good at that."

He kissed the tender spot below her ear. "I'm glad you approve."

She wondered how he always seemed to be in control. The only time she'd seen him close to losing it was the night in the tent, just after he'd fought the Cushaknas. Perhaps he'd still been part leopard then.

The mark he'd left on her shoulder tingled at the memory.

She pushed him to his side.

He rolled over and smiled at her. Dear God, he truly was gorgeous.

She rose up to her knees and moved between his legs. He watched her, questioning her intention without words.

She stroked the velvety skin of his prick, slick with her cream, and his eyes rolled shut. She circled the thick base with her fingers and squeezed.

"Nice," he whispered.

Wanting all of him, she leaned over and drew the head of his penis into her mouth, tasting herself on his skin.

He jumped and hardened even more.

She took more of him, sliding down the shaft until the head nudged against her throat. She slid up and back down, then bit carefully.

He groaned.

Egged on by the feeling of control, Rachel sucked hard and swirled her tongue around the head.

Nikolai's hips rose off the bed and fell back as she released him.

She persisted, thrilling to the way she could make him jump or groan, and the way he continued to swell until it felt as if his prick were carved of warm stone. She licked the salty pre-cum in a long lap that elicited a low growl.

Raising her head, she crawled up his body on all fours until she gripped his shoulders and centered herself on him, ready to slide down the shaft with her pussy.

He opened his eyes and stared up at her, something between fear and joy lighting his golden eyes.

She moved side to side, hinting at letting him in, but not.

His eyes darkened.

She grinned, pressing down on him just a bit, and rising back up.

He reached up and grabbed her waist, and tried to urge her down, but she held herself poised over him, her arms stiff.

The growl vibrated through him again, and his eyes went black. In one sudden move, he tossed her over, spread her legs, and entered her.

Rachel gasped at the pleasure of him filling her all at once.

He didn't stop, but continued to thrust, one hand wrapped around the back of her neck, the other gripping her ass and drawing her up. He pushed hard and fast as if he'd lost control.

She dug her fingers into the muscles in his back, holding him close as her body hardened. With each thrust, he moved deeper into her, claiming her, marking her as his. His mouth locked onto her shoulder.

Sweat moistened the space between them as his thrusts grew stronger still. His skin heated under her hands.

She felt the first explosion of his cum into her as he cried out against her skin. Her back arched as her own release started, rolling over her as steady, pounding waves, opening her legs wider, sweeping her up against him.

He held her closer, pumping against her pulses.

She yelled at the intense pleasure, waiting for the rest of it, aching for the closeness.

And it came in a rush of light as bright as the sun.

They rose together, wispy shadows of themselves, wrapped in each other's arms, closer than possible in life. Higher and higher they went until the earth was little more than a thought.

She heard his thoughts of love and desire as if they were words, spoken in a language she'd known since birth but never heard.

Her heart overflowed with perfect joy.

As he drew her back down, she felt a pang of disappointment, but she went because he held her. She'd go wherever he led.

She slid back into her body in time to feel the last of his seed pumped into her pulsing pussy.

They both collapsed.

After a few moments, Nikolai rolled to his back, drawing her with him so that she stretched out at his side, her head on his shoulder, her hand splayed across his heaving chest. His scent and the soft vibration in his chest made her smile.

"Come to my village," he said softly.

She raised her head and stared at his face. He stared back, his eyes a light gold again.

"You said no one gets to see your village unless . . ."

The thought of spending her life with Nikolai made her dizzy. Was she prepared for such a commitment?

Even as she asked the question, she knew the answer.

"You've been my mate since the first time our souls touched," he said. "I couldn't have chosen better."

She understood what he meant, but was she ready to walk off the face of the earth with this man? Could she give up life as she knew it and step forward blindfolded?

If Nikolai led the way, she could.

She smiled and lowered her head back to his shoulder. "Yes."

Wrapping both arms around her, he held her close, kissed the top of her head, and purred.

Wings of the Swan

Anya Howard

This story is written with much appreciation to the following people:

My editor, Hilary Sares, for her faith. Author and friend Devyn Quinn, for her continued encouragement. Friend Pam Lake, who took over a headache I look back fondly upon. Writer Marianne LaCroix, whose enthusiasm has helped me more often than she knows. And my gratitude is especially extended to my family, who have lovingly tolerated the peculiarities of a writer's habits, and made sure I never ran out of coffee.

I dedicate this story to my husband, Robert Perry, warrior, lover, and best friend.

The dreams of the Saxon chieftain Rulf had rarely been anything except reflections of the overwhelming concerns he faced everyday as the leader of his people. But earlier this evening, mentally fatigued after a lengthy meeting with his councilors, Rulf had sought out the sanctuary of his own bed to sleep. He'd not meant to sleep long, but this slumber lasted longer than he'd intended, and was deep indeed. His sleeping visions this time were every bit as poignant as the usual reflections. But this time they were of a nature very different and pleasantly arousing.

In the dream the chieftain had stood atop a lolling hill overlooking a heavily shaded dale. He had listened to the gentle lapping of the stream that cut through the bottom of the dale, and the smell of wildflowers and apple blossoms had filled his senses. All these things filled Rulf with a languorous sense of happiness. But it was the woman that sat in the grass in the dale that captivated him.

Reclining in the grass with her back to him, she was slender and fair skinned, and the breeze whipped her long black hair about her small shoulders. Rulf was overcome with raw carnal desires as he stared at her. He had begun walking down the hill toward her, and just as his shadow fell across her he caught the flash of something overhead. Looking up, Rulf saw it was two white swans sailing side by side across the horizon.

"They say swans mate for life," he heard a melodic voice say. He looked at the young woman and saw she was smiling up at him. Her fair features were petite, almost feline in their gracefulness. Her innocent smile somehow sharpened his lust.

Rulf knelt to one knee and could not resist caressing one of her rose-dusted cheeks. Her skin was fine to his touch. "Who say this, my dear?"

"My mother and her folk," she answered, her eyes lowering. "They who have allowed you to visit."

"I do not know your folk," he said, suddenly afraid the admission would make her run off like a rabbit. The chieftain wanted her so very much; he could almost feel himself inside her, driving in and out of her nether mouth that he was doubtless was as tight as she was delicate.

A bold smile lit her face. "Ah, but it is for the piety and constancy you've shown them that you are here."

Rulf was still confused. The girl rose to her feet, and his desire hardened for her tempting body. But she took his hand most timidly and asked him to walk with her. He followed as she led him to a tall, chalice-shaped stone fountain he had not noticed before. It stood beneath a pear tree heavily laden with blossoms. He gave it a casual glance and noticed the clear water in its goblet was so calm that their reflections were like looking into a polished looking glass. The girl dipped a forefinger into the water and immediately the surface quivered.

"In my innocence I had forgotten that truth," he heard her say. "But this truth, coupled by the immortal and eternal soul, have made us always one flesh."

The water moved gently beneath the almost-whispery breeze; forming wide circles that moved outward from the center, revolving out and over, one crest skimming over the other like the caressing limbs of lovers. Rulf was spellbound by this movement, and as he stared at the swirling circles Rulf began to see something new in the pristine water.

It was an image of himself, an image from his life when he'd been only a boy. He was standing inside the grove of the old land, that which had been sacred to his people until the Franks had come and razed it by ax and fire. Rulf could still remember the feel of being in the grove, the air permeated with the wisdom of his ancestors, the energy of the great oaks and rowans imparting silent testimony to the sacred rites that had been performed under their branches.

Rulf had come alone to the grove that day in order to kneel before the altar of Freyja. This had been located beneath the single mulberry tree that grew on the bank of a narrow stream that ran through the middle of the forest. A large white stone it was that graced the bank, perforated in the center by a natural hole. Rulf had brought an offering to lay before the altar. It had only been a small loaf of rye bread he'd baked in his mother's oven that afternoon. His reasoning for this unfamiliar activity had been simple: his mother, who had recently been very ill, had broken of her fever early that morning. His father had already thanked Thor and Freyr for sparing her life. But whilst she'd been sick Rulf had heard her pray to the goddess. And now that she was to live, Rulf knew Freyja should not be forgotten in the family's gratitude. So the young Rulf had come to convey his deeply felt appreciation by offering the goddess the humble loaf. Except for a few clay toy warriors and his miniature ax, it was all Rulf really had worth giving. Quite frankly the loaf of bread had turned out misshapen despite his efforts and his grandmother's advice on the making, and was in fact the best of the three attempts he'd made that day. That by his own hands it had been made and baked he had hoped would at least show his sincerity to the gracious Lady.

Rulf felt nostalgic fondness for the boy he had been. And yet he wondered why this vision was being shown to him. But as he turned his eyes away from the scrying water and he looked at his beautiful companion, Rulf thought he understood. It was not an understanding he wanted to be duped by; he had never been so full of his own worth that he thought the blessings of the gods his to wield.

"No," he said at last. "I am only a man, and not a perfect one. Hardly that."

A beaming smile came to his lovely companion's lips. Her entire body shimmered and she grew white with this power; her fair flesh brandished silver; her dark hair was aglow with ebony radiance. Rulf was filled with awe and fell to his knees. And yet the piquant desire for her was there even more fully than before, and his eyes fell in shame for this carnal craving.

"Do not be ashamed," he heard her say, "for if not by mutual passion you would never recognize me . . . and I should never know happiness."

In a blaze of senses and visions Rulf was no longer kneeling but making love to this beauty. Exquisite beyond measure was the feel of this virginal woman, and for a moment Rulf feared he had died and was awakening in the pleasure gardens of Vanaheim. He could not stop this divine pleasure, and dove in and out of the woman until his seed exploded into her white-hot depths.

Her deep moan echoed in Rulf's ear as he awoke.

The chieftain was in his own bed and he knew company was expected soon. Rulf sat up and wiped the sweat from his face and brow, and felt the singing last tremble of the visionary orgasm. For a time he sat on the side of the bed, until at length his erection had eased and he was ready to see the expected visitor. Soon enough a knock at the doorway announced his visitor, and Rulf put the dream out of his mind while he greeted her. She had come prompted by her own dreams, he knew, and this in itself struck him as mocking irony.

Rulf did not want to be rude to the Vitki; it was disrespectful for even the highest chieftain to dismiss these Freyjan priestesses. To discount the visions of a Vitki was surely a very stupid decision to say the best. But Rulf was drained by decisions. For the last month he'd had to deal with increasing numbers of spies, sent to bring back tidings of the tribe's whereabouts to the powerful Frankish mayor. These were all men who wielded the fate of their conquered, and because of their threat, the fate of his own tribe was one Rulf held in his hands. And Rulf, called "Rulf the Just" by his own devoted people, simply had no stomach this evening to hear any tidings about more spies; he had no taste to sentence any more men to be tried and executed. As deeply as Rulf despised the Franks' amoral grasp for power, he took no pleasure in taking any man's life.

In his heart Rulf already knew what must be done; he would have to uproot his people for a second time and lead them into the wilder forests north, where Pepin and his Christian forces had not yet penetrated. It was not a task he could ignore, but it was one that, for this night at least, he wanted to forget.

And no Vitki comes after dark to seek conference with the chieftain unless it is ill tidings, Rulf thought.

Nonetheless, Aeyani was here in his own room. Lovely she was, this wife of Thorm, who had been a lifelong companion of Rulf's father. She wore a shawl over her shift, and her usually plaited golden hair cascaded down her back all the way to her hips. Rulf had invited her to sit on the bench with him before the low flame of the hearth, and he was self-consciously aware of the scent she wore: meadowsweet and apple blossoms, with just a hint of some luxurious woody resin. Thorm was understandably jealous of his pretty wife; Rulf imagined whatever news Aeyani wanted to deliver must be urgent for the old warrior to let her come so late. And patient she seemed now as she contemplated the fire; the air about her not so grim as one might expect from a seer with a warning.

"Aeyani, we have no need for ceremony between us," he said at last. "I am going to suppose your reason for coming is to tell me your visions bring grave news of new spies or marauders?"

The Vitki looked at Rulf and smiled. "No, although you and I both know you have reached a decision that unfortunately must be made. The vision that gripped me tonight is of a much different nature, but one I hope will prompt you as quickly to action as a threat to our people."

Rulf felt relieved. "You certainly intrigue me," he said, bemused. "So tell me, what visions have the hearth flames given you tonight?"

Aeyani offered her sage, guileless smile, the one that had enchanted Rulf when he was only a boy. She was only a couple of years older than he, and they had been companions. But she'd never liked the rough play of boys, and Rulf, beset with stirrings he'd been too young to understand, had played her champion. After they'd grown Aeyani had little interest in the boy champion and it had broken his heart when she'd married Thorm. But he'd wished her well just the same and it wasn't until he'd met his wife, Dauhredei, that the old stirrings finally quieted. And when Dauhredei had died Rulf often found himself feeling envious of Thorm and his happiness. But happiness, Rulf had come to feel, was not what the gods had called him to experience in this life.

At length Aeyani said, "You are to take a respite, Rulf. Away from the village and pressing worries. For too long have you engaged in earthly politics, and while you are a wise and decent ruler, your identity has nearly been lost beneath the constant regard for the welfare of others. You are to go hunting in the wood where flows Freyja's sacred waterfall."

Rulf was pleasantly confused. "You wish me to go hunting," he said dubiously. "This is the message the gods delivered?"

Aeyani reached over and laid her hand on his. Her touch stirred only fondness in Rulf now; there remained no secret passion or even nostalgic sense of what could have been had only he'd been old enough to challenge Thorm for Aeyani's love. This knowledge almost saddened him. He could not remember the last time he'd lusted for a woman or even brought one of the pretty housemaids or slaves into his bed. *Have I been so obsessed with politics and the safety of the tribe that I've forgotten the pleasures of life the gods expect us to pursue?*

"You must be wary, Rulf," she said somberly. "In your struggle to keep us free of the Christian yoke you must not unwittingly become the ascetic half-man our enemies would have you be."

Rulf sighed. He knew she was right; but how could he justify a pleasure trip when the spies of Pepin harassed at every opportunity?

As if she read his very question, Aeyani said, "Go to the wood and indulge in the hunt. There you shall be reacquainted with your self, and those dispositions and desires that make you unique. Your sagacity, stamina, and passions will be sharpened anew. You will be reborn to continue the battle against the things that vie to destroy us all in this mortal life. For the passions of the gods are conscious and manifest in the mortal if we but choose. It is our duty and our right to embrace these passions. Freyja has rich blessings for you, my chieftain, if you will only let her give them."

Her words piqued him and he mused, "Passions of the gods. Freyja's blessings. May I assume She is not pleased that I act like an abstinent priest of Christ these days?"

Aeyani chuckled. "She knows. But She has more designs for you than abstinence."

"I will remember that," he promised, though he feared he'd forget even this much soon. But he tried to be hopeful; at least it would be reverent to Freyja who had sent this most unexpected order. "Our village is full of desirable women. And who knows, perhaps the daughter of our ally will have me."

Even as he spoke these words he knew the hypocrisy in them. Knowing bemusement glittered in Aeyani's eyes.

"You do not want Vivi for your wife," she rebuffed calmly.

Rulf remembered that morning, and Vivi bringing the stein of freshly drawn water to his table where he always took the first meal of the day. She was lovely, with large brown eyes that twinkled when she smiled and thick waves of brown curls. Vivi had a tiny waist that seemed to beg to be embraced. It was custom for the unmarried women of the tribe to take their turns serving the chieftain's table, though this young woman was not one of their own but rather a guest. That his guest would take it upon herself to follow this custom had impressed Rulf, and the more so for her people did not as strictly adhere to the custom as Rulf's people, which required the maidens to serve divested of all clothing. She was indeed a comely sight, and Rulf could see where any chieftain would be proud to claim her as his own.

But Rulf also suspected it was not completely a sign. Out of respect Vivi had decided to serve in the Chieftain's Hall. For his closest companions also took their meals here, and Rulf's young kinsman, Luxan, was seated at the table nearby. The young woman, while following decorum to pour Rulf's mead first, wasted no time in scampering off to where the leanly attractive, dark-haired Luxan sat.

Vivi was the daughter of Weythur, chieftain of a small tribe that lived in the next valley. A tribe of Sorbs that had crossed the Aller had taken to marauding that tribe's stock, and upon Weythur's request for help Rulf had sent two dozen warriors to help rout the brigands. Now Vivi had shown up with Rulf's returning warriors, sent by her father to thank Rulf for his assistance. Weythur had also sent an offer for Rulf: the offer of his comely daughter as a wife to his ally.

She had arrived nearly a fortnight before. Rulf enjoyed Vivi's company; she was well mannered and sweet natured. But despite these things and her undeniable beauty, Rulf simply wasn't interested in wedding the girl. Besides, he had noticed how her face flushed whenever approached in conversation by Luxan, and likewise how very often Luxan just happened to have business wherever Vivi was. Luxan was the keenest-eyed archer in the village, yet despite his applauded skill and poignant, somber good looks, rather reticent. But something about Vivi had brought out the assertiveness in the young man. It pleased Rulf to see this, and he would not be the man to get between the blossoming romance of any couple.

Rulf decided to ask Luxan his feelings toward the girl that night. And if his suspicions proved correct, Rulf would send a messenger to Weythur telling the old warrior that his daughter had a suitor. Rulf would let Vivi herself decide if she wanted to remain with their people, and depending on her decision Rulf would phrase his upcoming message to Weythur to reflect her wishes. His old friend, while expressive in his gratitude, was one who abided the old ways of their distinctive and ancient shared cultural heritage. Rulf knew that Weythur, despite his gratitude, would not blaspheme the ideals of fated passion as was held sacrosanct by Woten and Freyja.

What was more, Rulf himself could not blaspheme them either by taking to wife a woman he desired but didn't love.

"No," he affirmed to the Vitki, "I do not wish her as a wife."

"Put her out of your mind," Aeyani told him, "put all considerations out of your mind. Prepare for the hunt in the morning and go. Your council will ask no questions. In fact, I am sure they wonder already what has taken you so long to get away from all this for a time."

Rulf felt tired and rubbed his eyes. "A man needs time alone," he agreed. "Very well, Aeyani. I will leave at dawn. Tell your husband I will need him to sit in my place on the council until I've returned."

Aeyani got to her feet and nodded. "Certainly. I bid you good night, Rulf. And Freyja's blessings be upon thee."

Something about her tone made Rulf's skin prickle slightly. And he was suddenly curious without knowing why.

"That waterfall you spoke of," he said, "you know it is supposed to be haunted by the spirits of martyred priestesses?"

Aeyani shrugged. "You are not afraid of spirits, are you?"

He grinned. "Only respectful."

Aeyani spoke, but the timbre of her voice was husky and sweet as the perfume of the flowers sacred to the gods. "As you always have been. This is why I give you this opportunity."

Rulf was puzzled, and the Vitki's words chilled him somehow. But the strange glint in her eyes told him not to ask what this meant. Rulf stood and, kissing her hand, bade her good night. When the Vitki had gone Rulf went to his bed and thought of the upcoming hunt he'd consented to. He knew this respite, as Aeyani termed it, was overdue, and he saw that he'd be doing himself a service, and his people, too, to let himself forget other matters for a while. As he closed his eyes he began to feel a rekindling of the old enthusiasm for the hunt. He'd always enjoyed this sport, and even the feeling of aloneness that came with pursuing the beasts one on one.

And yet, there had always been something missing. A sense of something besides responsibilities to come back to.

Something about Aeyani's words made the loneliness he'd managed to keep buried for so very long chafe. Looking at his own sorrows was not a custom Rulf was either acquainted or comfortable with. And he forced himself to think of ghosts thought to dwell in the waterfall, and the dreadful ponderings on them helped him to forget the loneliness, and at last he drifted off to sleep.

Inga had long past come of age. Sired by a fallen hero, strong and just, Inga was the most tenderhearted daughter of the goddess Freyja. Her loyalty and countless selfless demonstrations had earned her an untold but special place in her mother's heart.

The goddess realized Inga's loneliness; it was her daughter's retiring disposition that made her hide from the attentions of the gods who visited the palace and fields of love in Vanaheim, and as well, the unwed dead heroes. Some of her other daughters called Inga coward, but Freyja knew better. She perceived her daughter's secret ambition to make herself known to a man who could capture her heart. Bravery, Freyja knew, was not always brash and pompous, as it was expressed in her other daughters. The goddess herself was the lady of love and passion as much as bravery, and of all her daughters, knew Inga the most like her. She perceived the passions that stirred with feminine modesty and grace in Inga's veins. And of all her children, she quietly acknowledged this meek daughter, the one who embodied her graces most fully.

Yet there was this matter of Inga's debilitating shyness. The goddess had considered forcing Inga to present herself in the great hall and show her beauty and qualities for all the males to admire. Such a command Inga would doubtless obey. But Freyja knew, too, that her daughter needed to perceive and appreciate her own worth in her own manner if the lesson were to be significant and one that couldn't be forgotten. And thus the goddess asked Tezek, the palace seeress, to help find a way to mend her daughter's self-doubt.

Wise Tezek consulted her runes carved from remnants of the Skein of Life. And when the runes had spoken the seeress told her mistress what had been revealed. And thus the goddess called Inga to her bedchamber.

"My child," Freyja said gently, "in the world of mankind, there is a wood special to me. It was here that I lay with Johat, guardian of the Cup of the Destitute, and after nine moons, gave birth to three nymphs. These daughters, you know, were slaughtered by the priests of the new religion, as was their father, who now resides here. Even though the blasphemers left years ago to crusade elsewhere, the wood was tainted by their heartless act, and the sacred fall sings with the lament of my daughters.

"I wish you to journey to Earth, to the wood I speak of, and there cleanse all within in my name. To do this, you must bathe beneath the shower of the tumbling fall and speak my name to the four elements, and to Spirit, wherein my immortal essence may be perceived and touched by all."

Inga quailed. She had never visited the world of mankind, and had heard rumors of how violent and cruel the race had grown since becoming mortal. Nevertheless, Inga's honor was deeper than her fear.

She bowed her head humbly. "Thy will is my course, Mother."

Thus did Inga put on the plumed gown that was her swan maiden's mantle and left Freyja's palace. Her sisters, who had mocked her, watched in astonishment as Inga flew into the route between Vanaheim and Midgard, the dominion of the goddess Urtha. It was spring in the world of men, and nightfall ruled the skies as Inga descended the heavens. She sailed above wild lands and rivers and grottoes. She also passed over many villages and towns of those pledged to the new god. But the old ways still held to flora and fauna, and Inga used these things as her guides until at last she found the sacred wood.

Lush and fecund it was, but as soon as Inga lit through the canopies, she felt the specter of the murders imprinted on every leaf, stone, and blade of grass. She sailed toward the scent of the waterfall, and the echo of violence resounded in her head. As Inga's webbed feet lit upon the bank of the pool, her nostrils filled with the ghostly smell of the nymphs' blood and the un-washed sweat and perverse pleasure of their killers. Never had Inga known such sadness before concerning her sisters' murders. The knowledge of how far away this wood was from Vanaheim was daunting. For several minutes she listened to the night birds and watched the fireflies mating in the air. Calmed a bit by these vibrant sounds, Inga gathered courage. With a purposeful thought, she cast the pins of the feathers from her pores. The avian hood fell back over her neck, and she let the entire gown fall away to the ground. The dewed grass was cool beneath her bare feet, and her own reflection shone in the placidly rippling water. A petite, lithe young woman stared back. Her black hair was longer than she remembered, the intensity of her black eyes softened by thick dark lashes. Her lips quivered with fear, while the air chilled and hardened the nipples of her small breasts. The moonlight filtering through the branches imparted its luminous quality, so that her pale naked skin glowed like milk and her hair shimmered like cobalt.

Into the pool Inga stepped. The cold water rose no farther than her knees as she approached the fall. The soft roar allayed her last fears as the splaying droplets tingled her skin. As she entered the fall, her breath was momentarily taken away. She wrapped her arms about herself and lowered her face and breathed more easily. The sensation of the cascade over her flesh became a relaxing sensation. She thought of her duty to Freyja, and her thoughts drifted to things sacred and earthly. Gradually she became aware of her own femininity and of how the rhythm of the waterfall seemed to resonate with femininity itself. Her body throbbed with sensation and long-denied desires burgeoned with poignant need. In her mind's eye, she saw her own attractiveness. For the first time, she wondered how she could have viewed herself for so very long as a mere child. Inga was grown and unique in her allure by her mother's grace. As much as any of her sisters she was a swan maiden, a Valkyrie, and more important, feminine. The yearnings she tried so hard to ignore were hers by that right and gender.

Strengthened by these thoughts, Inga turned to her task. She closed her eyes and lifted her chin so that only her face projected through the cascade. She visualized her mother's face and all that she embodied: femininity, fecundity, motherhood, equity, and the everlasting embrace of delight, which transcended death and mortal illusions. As Inga concentrated on each blessed facet, power flowed inside her. It warmed her skin and heated the water and eventually touched the very air and earth all about her. Inga heard Freyja's name in all the forms worshipped by mankind, and even the unspoken name that needed no articulation. It stirred the waters of the pool and rustled the leaves. It kissed the air and fertilized the earth. It cleansed every niche and space inside the wood. Inga felt it banish the leftover anguish of her mistreated sisters and exorcize the last traces of the corruption left behind by the crusaders.

When she was satisfied that the ritual was successful, Inga drew back and, raising her face once more, let the fall wash over her hair and skin. She was herself as always, but she was conscious of herself and enjoyed what she had discovered. She would return home shed of the self-doubt that had clung to her as tightly as the swan's gown. She could hardly wait to walk amongst the Vanaheim courtiers and venture into the places of stolen kisses and sensuous embraces. As her sisters were, she would take her place in Vanaheim as a desirable female, ready to be seen and appreciated by the eyes of the heroes and visiting gods and light elves.

Inga stepped out of the fall and, pulling her hair over one shoulder, she wrung out the excess water. The night air felt even colder on her wet skin but her joy was too exuberant to allow any cares. She looked to the bank where she had left the mantle, and it was then that she saw the stranger. A large figure crouched in the water at the opposite side of the far bank. Terror—wild and almost paralyzing—overcame her. The tree branches shadowed the face but as the stranger began to wade forward, she distinguished the broad shoulders and masculine contours.

He spoke. "You are real."

Inga recognized his Saxon tongue since several of her mother's handmaidens spoke the language. As the warrior advanced, Inga could hardly breathe above her racing heart. In a moment, the man towered over her. The milky moonlight caressed his features and she saw how very striking a face he had. His golden hair tumbled about his shoulders like a lion's mane. His brow was high and his eyes deep-set, which glistened a warm emerald shade in the moonlight.

The warrior acted as one enchanted. His stare daunted Inga but he was so handsome that her fear began to give way to another sensation, one that made her feel vulnerable and prickly hot. She wondered what it would be like to be held captive in his embrace.

He touched her cheek, and she trembled. "Beautiful," he whispered, "as Freyja herself."

Inga quailed. Yet, she could not suppress the joy to hear her mother's name spoken so reverently on such luscious lips.

He fell to his knees in the pool and pressed those very lips to her stomach. Inga felt a fire kindle deep in her thighs. His arms lifted and encircled her hips. He clasped her buttocks as his mouth moved slowly down. He kissed the thatch of hair over her pubis and his tongue darted over the silky folds beneath. Inga's breath quickened and she watched as if entranced as he clasped her possessively. His lips spirited up and down over the seam of her pussy. She swelled with sensation; her clit throbbed and pounded against his hot tongue. Her modesty fled and, gyrating her hips in rhythm to his ministrations, she embraced his neck and lavished kisses upon his golden crown.

"Beautiful, graceful swan maiden!"

The warrior rose to his feet, leaving Inga's pussy throbbing for his mouth. With a greedy smile, he lifted her into his arms. To the bank he carried her and, stepping out, set her to her feet. His clothing was here and, pulling up a fine green cape, he spread this out across the grass. Inga's sex throbbed as she drank in the vision of him. The hair on his powerful arms and legs was fine and golden, and his buttocks firm and supple. When he stood straight again, she admired the golden curls that dusted his chest. Under his lusty gaze she blushed and, lowering her eyes, she saw his proud, erect cock amid those curls.

He lowered to his knees and, taking her hand, ushered her down upon the cape. As his hands cupped her face, she welcomed his kiss. More potent now it was, demanding and tender at once, and as Inga clasped his shoulders, he laid her gently down. His mouth skimmed over her throat and swept over her breasts. He sucked them gently, nursing upon her nipples until they were hard with sensation. His hands slipped to her thighs, and these he parted, tantalizing her pussy with his deft caress.

Through her passion she could not help but worry that she would not please him. "I am a maiden yet," she confessed.

He unfolded her nether lips and rubbed her clit. A stab of intense pleasure rippled through her.

"Will you hate me," he asked, "if I rob you of that claim?"

"No," Inga moaned. She was thoughtless with desire for this beautiful man. Sitting back on his knees again, he lifted her hips. The scorching head of his cock pressed against her fount. Inga's body was alive with desire, and she could not still her undulating hips.

Licking his lips, he asked, "What is your name, little swan maiden?"

"My name is Inga."

"Inga," he repeated silkily.

His hips lunged, and he entered her. Spasms of pain spiraled through her tight pussy. But he draped himself over her carefully, moving his hips gingerly until her pain relinquished and gave way to a sensation quite pleasant.

Inga clutched him, savoring the feel of his hard body as his huge cock drove in and out of her with a now fervent rhythm. He kissed her full on the mouth again, just as she felt him reach her very core. Inga held on to him dearly as he came, relishing the riveting sensation of his orgasm as it coursed into her.

Unquenched, Inga undulated under his hard, spent body and

greedily received his next fierce kiss. She moaned plaintively, "More, I want more of you!"

He rose to his haunches. His golden body was dewed, his blond hair mussed now, lending a brutal aspect to his piercing gaze.

"You shall have more, all in good time. For you are mine now, daughter of Freyja. Mine to treasure and teach the arts of love-making. But you must also accept that as your master I will determine when you are to know pleasure."

The chieftain stood up then and gave her an intense look that sent a hot shiver through her limbs. From his tousled clothes, he picked up a large sack. From this he took a length of fabric, which he went and dipped into the pool. He came back then and knelt beside her.

"Unfold your legs, swan maiden," Rulf said.

Inga saw then the trickle of maiden blood on the insides of her thighs. He washed this away and cleaned her nether mouth as well. The chieftain's touch was so tender, and when he was done, he kissed her again, stood up, and went back to where his clothes lay. Into an inner pocket of his vest he tucked the rag. Lifting the sack, he walked to the other side of the pool. Inga watched as he stooped down and touched something white lying there.

She realized with a shudder that it was her swan gown.

Rulf seized it before she could utter a sound. Standing again, he raised it high, and examined the flawless plumage that burnished like opaline satin in the light of the moon. Inga sat up, her heart thundering with a new terror. He had claimed not just her maidenhood, but now, too, the sacred pelt. It was not hers any longer to wear or even ask for, and attempting to steal it or obtain it by trickery meant her death.

As long as it was in the chieftain's possession then Inga was his property, body and soul.

He put the mantle into the sack and, cinching the drawstrings, laced and tied them. Inga was in tears as he walked back and set the sack on the grass beside his cape. He knelt again and, lifting her chin, kissed her with much tenderness.

"You have nothing to fear, Inga. I asked the goddess to show me if I was worthy . . . and she delivered you. I will honor you for all my days, my precious and beautiful love hostage."

She wanted to be angry, to beat him with her fists and denounce him as a deceiver. Sore was this unexpected loss of her own property, unbelievable the thought that the loyalty to her mother was to be rewarded by enslavement to a mortal man. He was no god, nor was he a fallen hero demonstrated to be worthy of either Valhalla or her mother's hall of pleasures.

Yet Inga had no delusions about her true feelings. She would not have gone back in time and spurned his advances if she could. The chafing passion for him was only more incited by his claim. Even in his humble mortal's apparel he was intimidatingly beautiful.

He now shouldered a wide scabbard that bore a mighty sword, and around his waist he strapped a rawhide belt. From this was sheathed a dagger. A warrior, she realized. As he helped her to stand, she wept for the shameful enjoyment her helplessness brought. Surely, she reprimanded herself, her sisters would not so wantonly have conceded to a man's claim, nor would her mother condone it.

No, an inner voice reproached, *this I cannot claim fairly, as in my cowardice I refused to participate as an adult in the Vanaheim Court. All I knew were the pursuits of a child.*

He kissed her tears away and stroked her hair. "I will honor you, have no doubt."

Inga tried to hide the daunting eagerness his touch incited. "But I know not even who you are."

"Rulf," he said. "Son of Urich and his beloved Hilde. I have served as chieftain to our people since my father's death. But you may call me lord and master."

Inga perceived the mixture of pain and pride in his eyes, emotions that he tried to conceal with an indifferent look. "A warrior king."

Rulf nodded. "And hopefully a just king."

He took the cape and, brushing the dewed grass away, draped it about her shoulders. "I prefer to look upon you as you are, but it is not so warm outside the sacred wood." There was a heavy broach of copper pinned to his belt, shaped like a star, and this he used to fasten the cape at her collarbone.

"You are very gentle for a warrior," she mused softly, "lord and master."

Her words brought a lusty flicker to his green eyes. He touched her nipples and licked his lips.

"Always with women and children."

Inga smiled. His lips grew bold, and it seemed he was as anxious to take her again as she was to have him do so. But he only kissed her brow, took her hand, and guided her out of the wood.

Upon his pale war steed Rulf sat Inga, holding the reins loosely with his left hand while holding her securely in the crook of his right arm. Night was giving way to daybreak as the steed crossed the hilly wilderness. The glint of the dawn bore down in golden shards upon them from the eastern sky.

Their destiny was Rulf's village. Inga was terrified at meeting other mortals. How would they react? What would they do?

"Why, you are trembling," he said. "Are you frightened?"

At Inga's whimper, he said reassuringly, "You are my slave and trophy. No one will dare mock or harm you."

He said it with such faith that Inga was comforted a little.

"Besides, you are a swan maiden. Despite the intimidation that the Franks have used to force us to worship their god, we have renounced the conversion forced during my father's reign. We are, and will continue, avowed to the old gods."

"Forced your tribe?" Inga said. "But why would anyone force another people to worship any god?"

Rulf's mouth hardened. "It is the way of the Christian crusader priests and kings. For the last many years they have invaded numerous tribes in order to force their beliefs. After some battles, entire conquered peoples have been put to the sword for not disavowing their own gods and pledging themselves to their Christ."

"And they did so when your father was alive?"

"Yes, but we renounced the vows. This has caused a tumultuous relationship with their powerful leaders. Fortunately for us, their bloody escapades made sworn foes among some tribes. Foes who are more inclined than my people to seek vengeance. So the crusaders have been busy dealing with that repercussion."

Inga shuddered. "Do you think they will try again to force you?"

"The time will come, have no doubt. The popes of Rome— the most influential of their priests—have recently put their backing to the mayors of the Frankish palace. These mayors are now the true kings of the Franks; the Church has slaughtered or imprisoned most of the descendants of Merovech. The Franks lust for Germanic lands, and therefore have no contention about making vassals of their conquered."

Inga was still concerned. "Yet your people are free from invasion?"

"Yes, but not threats. We must pay tributes to the son of Pepin in order to stave off attack from his allies. The only reason he has not tried again to invade us is that he is under the belief that I possess a great treasure. A treasure that, were I to possess it, would make any attempt to besiege a fool's choice. I will not deny his concerns to his ambassadors or levy masters, of course. The more in the dark they are the better. But the truth is that if this treasure does exist, it is not in my possession."

Inga was touched that he trusted her so well as to reveal this. Shyly, she touched the arm holding the rein. How shrewd and brave he was, she mused, and as golden as the sun.

"Do not worry about these things," he continued. "I sense that one day soon we will have to uproot and find a home elsewhere. Some place hopefully safe from the warrior crusaders. And you will be with me."

How assured of her fate in his hands! As overwhelming as this strange, mortal world was, she was not blind to its beauties. The daylight yawned before them, as the steed came to the crown of a knoll. As it began to descend, Inga saw in the valley below a village of thatch-covered longhouses situated before fecund, rolling countryside, all of which was barricaded by a great palisade of freshly cut oak staves. Tendrils of smoke wafted from a few of the chimneys. Inga heard the baying of a few dogs from inside the fence.

As the horse got closer to the village, Rulf suddenly let go of the reins and brushed her hair behind one shoulder. Hungry little kisses he imparted over her exposed throat, making ripples of sensation crest through her. She whimpered in frustration, and was hard pressed to keep from making some wanton movement right there on the steed.

"The others can wait for a proper introduction," he murmured silkily. "I am going to take you to my room once we get home."

Rulf's face beamed proudly. He shook the reins and made an encouraging clicking sound that sent the steed into a brisk run.

A burly sentinel opened the village gate. The bold look he gave Inga made her blush. Thankfully, other than a quickly exchanged greeting, Rulf did not engage the man in conversation. But as they passed through the gateway and took the avenue that bore left, Inga saw another sentinel peering down from the crow's nest perched atop the palisade. The dirt avenues of the village were wide and clean, and the steed seemed to know without urging exactly where to go. At the entrance of the stable, the animal stopped. Rulf dismounted and lifted Inga off. He took the sack that held her gown and opened the door.

"Handel?" Rulf called in.

In a couple of minutes a youth, no more than thirteen or fourteen years of age, emerged from the dusky stable. He gave Rulf a sleepy-eyed grin.

"Good morning, my lord. How went your hunt?"

"My patience was rewarded," Rulf said, "with a most unexpected quarry."

The boy's gaze traveled down the length of Inga's one exposed leg. Inga gathered the cape about her leg and inched closer to Rulf. She saw the youth's face redden and felt Rulf's soft chuckle. He handed the reins to the youth and told him to remove the animal's saddle and give him water and oats.

Rulf took her northward, down a street flanked by rows of small cottages and longhouses. The path opened upon a little grassy court, with a white-wattle domed well that stood in the center. Behind the court stood a very large, cross-sectioned house. The door they came to was huge, at least eight feet high, and made of rich cedar carved with scenes of warriors battling beasts and animals, while naked maidens looked on from the sidelines. Rulf did not knock, but opened the door and led Inga inside.

The entrance hall was paneled with cedar; from either side hung weapons and skins. Rulf and Inga continued into the great hall situated in the center of the house. Daylight streamed into the room from an ingenious round glass pane set in the apex of the high beams. This glass was stained with the ghostly blue silhouette of a pale wolf. A magnificent round brick fireplace stood in the center of the room. Encircling this like spokes were eight lengthy tables and benches. To either side of the room were arched entranceways leading into the eastern and western hallways of the cross-section. As they walked through,

Inga looked back and saw two great tapestries hanging from the walls that flanked the entrance door. The one to her left was deepest blue, with golden images of a wood clearing where danced nude maidens. The tapestry to the right was woven of crimson cloth, with indigo figures of Freyja and Od locked in a passionate kiss.

There was a dais in the back of the den where another table stood. It was shorter than the others, but more elegant in design, with dragonhead legs and a stunning marbled black slate top. A cushioned bench stood to the foreground of the table and behind it, a throne of pale ash. High on the partition behind the throne hung a gleaming brass shield and below this a formidable battle-ax. At the extreme left of the partition was a door fashioned of richest, unadorned oak. But the handle was an opulent piece of craftsmanship, fashioned from gold in the form of a water nymph.

Their footfalls echoed softly as Rulf led Inga up the dais and to the door. He opened it and, taking her hand, guided her into the corridor behind. It was a narrow hallway, illuminated by torches on the walls. Inga's eyes adjusted, and she saw that there were several entranceways set to either side down the long corridor, each secluded by curtains of costly damask. But it was to the doorway at the very end of the hallway that they preceded, curtained not by damask but a drape fashioned from furs.

Rulf pulled aside the furs and gestured Inga forward. The furs fell softly but early morning light poured golden into the room through windows. Inga watched as Rulf strode to the large bed covered with more furs. He knelt and, placing the sack on the floor, pushed it far beneath the mattress. Inga looked about at the furnishings but she did not have time to take in much. She felt the chieftain's hand on her shoulder. As she turned Rulf swept her into his embrace, kissing her deeply. The virile taste of him intoxicated Inga. He pulled the cape from her shoulders, as his roving caresses enflamed her.

Her thighs were moist and her clit ached for him. Rulf picked her up and carried her to the bed and laid her down. Kneeling over her the chieftain strummed her clit. Poignant sensation roiled through Inga. She moaned, raising and undulating her hips shamelessly. Rulf moaned deeply and, standing, removed his clothing. He was beautiful in the light, his cock hard and erect.

Rulf grasped Inga's thighs and draped over her. With an eager thrust he was inside her. Sore Inga was from their first lovemaking, but his searing manhood felt so good inside her. He fucked her rigorously this time, singing her core with his cock. Lost beneath waves of mounting sensation Inga moaned helplessly. And just as she thought she could take no more of the almost cruel pleasure she climaxed. As her heated nether mouth pulsed Rulf plunged harder and harder. With a low groan he clasped her dearly and she felt the zenith of his own pleasure deep inside her.

"My sweet swan," he moaned against her ear. "No longer a maiden but a love slave. My love slave!"

The words scorched her sweetly. He kissed her and she savored the sweet helplessness his lips bestowed.

Inga was happy to lay beside him in the great bed. Perfectly molded their embraced bodies felt and she loved the feel of his warm breath upon her shoulders.

She wondered if Freyja knew she was happy. She thought of immortal Vanaheim, and of her sisters, the handsome bold eternal guests. Inga did miss the beauty: the soaring parapets of her mother's palace, the fecund hills and streams, and the high, ice-capped mountains that kissed the rosy skies. Rulf's lands were still formidable and strange to her. It would take some time for her to get used to mortals and their ways. And for the first time she understood mortal disquiet, or at least she was beginning to, from just knowing Rulf's heart and the concerns of those around him.

Eventually Inga slept, and her dreams were ripe with delirious images of him.

Some time later, Inga was awakened by a cheerful voice nearby. Opening her eyes, she was startled by the appearance of two young women who stood close to the bed. Rulf was gone, and the afternoon light shone cozily on the buff-stained wallboard and wood furnishings.

"My lady Inga?" one of the young women greeted her. "I am Blichilde, and this is Audavene. We are here to escort you to the bath house."

Inga sat up and looked at them. They were both very attractive, wearing little dresses of light fabric that barely reached their thighs. The bodices were low, granting good exposure of their bosoms, which were apparently cupped and lifted by some device. On their feet they wore little half boots of pale leather. Blichilde was blond, with her hair weaved in two braids that reached her knees, while Audavene had soft brunette hair that fell in waves to her waist. Inga suspected these two must be other slaves of Rulf, and she was overcome with disappointment.

Audavene held up a blue robe. "Your master wished us to take you now, as the feast will begin early this evening, and he is sure you'd wish to wash first."

Inga got out of the bed and let the girl help her on with the robe. They escorted her to a door at the back of the room. It was narrow but high. Outside was a path of stepping-stones that led directly to a small building not a hundred yards behind the longhouse. The building was circular, the exterior walls created by pegged flat cedar timbers and roofed by a crown of beehive-shaped wattle. A heavy curtain concealed the doorway and, as Blichilde drew it aside, Inga saw that the inside served as a private little bath house. The floor they stepped onto was tiled with blue and white stones and at the center stood a magnificent brass tub with dragon-claw feet. Plank board ran the circumference of the interior wall. Although there were several small torches on the walls, these were cold and the light of day poured in through a round aperture in the ceiling.

The tub was already filled, with steam rising lazily from the water. Folded towels were stacked on the plank board, beside which stood stone bottles with cork tops. Inga imagined these were soaps and perfumes, but these trifles did not comfort her. She took off the robe and Blichilde helped her step into the tub.

As she sat down, she turned her face, for her eyes smarted with jealous tears.

Did you really think a man like the chieftain would not have other women?

Inga chided herself for her vanity. But it hurt nonetheless, to imagine having to share him.

The heat of water, which immersed her to the breastbone, relaxed her a bit. She could not help but wonder if they were assessing her, comparing her. Surely they were. Besides their beauty, she deemed they had little to be jealous of except perhaps that she was Freyja's daughter.

Audavene found a clean pail and scooped it full of water. Then she urged Inga to let her head fall back. Audavene poured the water over her hair so that it was wet, while Blichilde brought a bottle.

"It is to clean your hair. Let me show you."

Blichilde poured the thick substance into her palm and applied this to Inga's scalp. She massaged it into a white lather and began to gently scrub Inga's hair.

Inga bristled. She longed to be in Vanaheim, hiding in the gardens or the solitude of her own rooms. Why, before being awakened by these two she had imagined she might be happy with the mortal chieftain. And now, so bitterly clear, was the truth of the ways of his heart.

"Your master has ordered a grand feast," Audavene said, "and asked the Gaul harper to play tonight. Our chieftain is so enamored of his captured love chattel and wishes for everyone to see her."

"Ah," Blichilde remarked dreamily. "I never thought to see the day."

Inga sighed with deliberate force and bore Audavene's ministrations resentfully. Then a question arose in her mind, something piqued by what they had said.

"You say my master? Do you not mean our master?"

Audavene looked amused. But Blichilde, carrying over a pail filled with fresh water said, "Certainly not. I am wife of Rulf's kinsman and best friend and Audavene is a wedded slave."

Inga's joy must have been evident, for Blichilde chuckled. She winked at Inga and said reassuringly, "You have no rivals, my dear."

Inga felt a great relief. Yet she was curious, for surely the chieftain had other women. This question she posed to them as they rinsed the suds from her hair.

"Rulf's wife died some time ago," Blichilde said. "He's taken no woman—neither betrothed nor love chattel—since. Why, I have not even heard of him visiting one of the Vitki priestesses, who are trained in the great pleasures sacred to your mother."

Inga lay back in the tub with her head resting on the edge. Blichilde and Audavene sat on the bench, and now she was glad to have their company.

"How did his wife come to die?"

A rueful shadow came to Blichilde's face. "She killed herself, my lady."

Inga felt the pain in Blichilde's voice. "Why would she do such a thing?"

There was several moments' silence and then Blichilde answered, "My kinswoman, Dauhredei, was mad. Mad by religious fervor. She wanted to be with her god and so let herself waste away."

Inga was stunned. She sat up, gaping incredulously. Madness she had heard of, some mortal imbalance of the mind. But never had she heard of an individual taking such a drastic action to meet her deity. It made no sense to Inga at all; everyone met their god sooner or later.

"I do not understand. Rulf is a handsome and worthy man. Why would any woman give up such a man to hasten the inevitable?"

"Why, it is madness," Blichilde said. "There is no rationale to it. And she abandoned not only her husband, but her little daughter as well."

"Daughter?" Inga said. "He has a child?"

Blichilde shrugged. "I would say so by the most elementary of definitions."

Inga was surprised by the coolness of this statement, especially from a relative of the girl's mother. "What do you mean?"

"That sounded harsh," Blichilde said. "Vanda is a most beautiful child and her father loves her. It is just that she is more like my aunt and uncle, her grandparents, than is healthy."

Audavene raised an eyebrow. "Vanda is not yet twelve years old. She has her father's earthy wisdom to guide her and the influence of her good people here."

"It is possible," Blichilde sighed, "if he would stop spoiling her and letting her dwell in that big melancholy room with those gloomy attendants and her mother's priest."

"I do not think the chieftain spoils her," Audavene countered. "He is concerned that to force her to give up these remnants of her mother will drive her straight into the fanaticism that destroyed the woman."

"It is not the fanaticism that concerns me," said Blichilde. "It is as if she spurns her Saxon heritage and her Merovingian roots as well, from our grandsire's side. I fear she is too much like the Burgundian side of the family—the Nibelungs, with their love of manipulating evil and dictating the lives of others."

Inga thought this must be an exaggeration. "This cannot be. The Nibelungs destroyed my sister Brunhilde and her children. I cannot see a mere child predispositioned for such evil."

"I know Brunhilde's story," Blichilde said. She was thoughtful a moment and continued cautiously, "Nibelung sorcery is not dead, Inga. Dauhredei's parents will not let it die, nor let their children forget their once powerful positions. Now that they have become minions of the Church, their avaricious designs have a strong ally to destroy the pagan world. Let us pray that through your influence, Rulf can indeed spare his daughter from their ways."

Audavene patted Blichilde's hand. "Your outlook, I fear, is overshadowed by this visit from Estheria. As fickle as she is, look for her to gather her courtiers and trot home at any moment."

"Perhaps you are right. I do not want that woman close to Vanda."

Inga was curious. "Who is Estheria?"

Blichilde's lips pursed. "She is Dauhredei's sister, my kinswoman, too. Two weeks ago she arrived without notice. A visit, she claims, to visit her niece. But I am not fooled. Her interest is the chieftain and, more accurately, the treasure that gossip says her sister led him to."

"The Nibelung treasure?"

"Yes. My aunt got it into her head that Dauhredei called upon her dour angels to bring it to him. This is only because their own magic is so convoluted with petty jealousies and greed that they cannot ascertain where their ancestors hid it. Much easier to blame the mad daughter than to admit their own powers have grown too chaotic to control. As for Estheria, she accumulates things of power like some women collect gowns. She is fascinated by any token, small or great, that she can possess."

Audavene sneered. "For all of Estheria's wiles, Rulf recognized what she was before he even wedded Dauhredei. She is as stupid as she is beautiful if she thinks she can blind him now with her glamour."

The two laughed, but the conversation left Inga uncomfortable. She would have pried further into this matter, but she did not want to appear overly nosy. Surely, she considered, in due time, the chieftain would tell her everything he deemed she need know.

"Do you think Vanda will like me?" she asked.

The women both looked at a loss for an answer.

At last Blichilde said, "Does it matter? You are Rulf's chosen and a gift from the goddess. Who knows? It may take a gift from the goddess to help the child shed the influence of her mother's scandal-mongering priests."

Inga tried to take solace in this, but she could not shake the many questions that plagued her. She felt sorry for Vanda and wondered if the chieftain would allow her to attempt a friendship with the girl.

While she dried, they talked about the food the cooks had devised for the feast. She blushed when Audavene told her that it was the chieftain's desire for them to bring her to the great den as naked as when he had found her. She was distressed to hear this. Certainly the handmaidens and slave girls in Vanaheim were not shy about their bodies, but she had always been so modest, even to her mother's exasperation.

Audavene and Blichilde brushed her hair and smoothed scented oil over Inga's skin. She was ready for the feast, whether she liked it or not. But her sunny chieftain would be there, yes, and just the memory of his touch melted her anxiety a little. She was grateful when they gave her a shift to wear back to the main house. It was dyed white with little ruffles at the hem and Audavene said it suited her hair. But Blichilde reminded Inga that she'd have to remove it before the feast.

Upon returning to the chieftain's bedchamber they informed her that Rulf wanted to escort her to the feast himself. Inga was grateful when Audavene brought her some food from the kitchen. It was only a bowl of porridge and bread, but Inga was so hungry that she thought the food could not have tasted better if it had been prepared in the kitchens of Vanaheim.

The women sat with her on the bed and they talked together for a long time, getting to know one another. Inga liked them both, she soon realized, and was glad when they assured her that they would not be very far away from the chieftain's table that night. When Inga asked what to expect at the feast, her companions laughed.

"One never knows," Audavene said. "But Rulf allows no violence in his hall, nor any rude behavior toward the womenfolk. Our tribe is not savage, but constant to the mysteries of Freyja and her husband, Od. Therefore our men are not enamored of battle without cause. The foreign priests and travelers would slander all of Germany as brutal, but this is not the case."

As evening approached, the household began to fill with voices. At last Blichilde told Audavene that they should go and see if their husbands had arrived. Just as they said their farewells the fur drape was pulled aside. Inga was overjoyed to see Rulf, but she felt embarrassed to go running to him as instinct prompted. It did not matter. As soon as he saw her, he strode over and, ignoring her new friends, pulled her from the bedside and into his arms.

"My pretty swan maiden," he murmured. Inga clung to him, savoring his kiss to her throat that made her flesh trill.

Blichilde and Audavene slipped out quietly. Rulf sat beside Inga on the bed and drew her palm to his lips.

"I hope you were not overwhelmed to wake up alone," he said. "I intended to introduce you to Blichilde and Audavene, but my page arrived with news of a rather heated dispute between two of our farmers."

Inga noticed the red velvet drawstring bag that hung from his shoulder. "You must be exhausted, my lord."

"A little exasperated perhaps. I plan to retire early tonight. Were you told about tonight's feast?"

She nodded.

"I wanted to be here to escort you myself." He added with a

smoldering glint, "And I want my people to feast their eyes on you, my little trophy. I will, however, not force you to make an entrance without me."

Inga blushed and her eyes lowered. "I am anxious," she confessed. "I hope they will not hate me."

"I cannot imagine anyone hating you, Inga." Rulf took her face between his hands and kissed her very tenderly. "You are sweetness incarnate."

He took off the bag and loosened the drawstrings. From inside he drew a piece of jewelry made of gleaming brass. He raised it for her to see, a smooth brass torque collar.

"For you," he said. "Turn and lift your hair."

Inga was delighted. He drew the collar about her throat and cinched it just slightly, but she liked the cool feel of it on her skin. When it was latched, she let down her hair and touched the brass.

"Thank you, my lord. It is lovely."

"It is more than that," he said. "It is the undeniable mark that you belong to me."

In her happiness Inga remembered what he had said about no one hating her and the things she had learned from the attendants. She took a hesitant breath. "But I have heard that you are a widower, with in-laws adept in dark sorcery. The Nibelungs."

His smile was sweet. "Dauhredei was my wife, and yes, of the Nibelung family. We married when we were very young. I was far too inexperienced to make a proper husband. But I felt I had no choice, for my father was seeking an alliance with all those who at the time said they wished to form an alliance against the Frankish force. Her father claimed a mutual desire to that end and asked only that one of my father's sons take his eldest daughter, as they wanted the youngest left to offer one of the sons of Pepin. I volunteered. Of course, her father reneged on his assertion and became Pepin's ally, even after Dauhredei's sister decided she would have no Frank for a husband."

Inga felt a stab of pity for Dauhredei. "You did not love her?"

"What can a thirteen-year-old boy know of the intricacies of the human heart? She was comely when she let herself be and five years older than myself. A woman ripe for love and companionship and, even at my tender age, I was not utterly without experience with women. It was apparent to me and everyone else that she needed love. Her parents were arrogant, repugnant folk. They lavished their hopes and ambitions entirely on their other daughter, who was as calculating as they. I believed fully that my affection would fill that void in Dauhredei's life that her parents had created."

"You were faithful," Inga said.

"Of course. But in the end, I failed to give Dauhredei the only thing she truly wanted."

"What was that?"

Sadness furrowed Rulf's brow. "The respect of her mother and father. When she heard they had converted to Christianity, she, too, converted, and strove to be the most Christian woman in the world. In the end, it killed her. I did not glean her expectations. When I sent a herald to tell them that she had died, they sent through him the message that they were entertaining some renowned priest from Britain and could not be bothered to waste their time on the dead."

"What of your daughter? Vanda?"

Rulf stroked her hair, saying, "Blichilde's fears you have heard. Do not fret about my little girl. You are ethereal like the moon, and Vanda's brooding shadows will wilt beneath your light. I am sure that you will help bring Vanda out of this grief for her mother."

Inga was complimented, and knew that for him, she would attempt anything. In his presence she felt close to the best virtues of mortals. Yet, the scope of her new experiences filled Inga with anxiety.

230 / Anya Howard

She confessed ruefully, "Your world is beautiful, yet I sense the cruelty within it!"

Rulf scooped her into his arms. "It is the motives of men and women that count; this is what one must either respect or be wary of. I will not give up easily the faith that one day this mortal world shall be immortal, a world where men are as the gods and women as the goddesses. The two faces of the Eternal. As long as aspiration survives in mankind's consciousness, despite even the darkest and unholy trials, I have no doubt that in time, that day shall come."

Inga smiled hopefully.

"I must go bathe soon in preparation. But before I do, I would like you to meet my daughter. My servants tell me she has taken a rare venture to the garden outside her chambers, for the harper gave her a bolt of fine silver cloth and she took it out in the sunlight to admire the threads. Shall we go speak with her?"

Inga was nervous, but appeasing. "Yes, I would like that."

The garden Rulf spoke of was surrounded by a stone wall that stood to the chieftain's shoulders. Rulf lifted the latch that opened the slender door and, taking Inga's hand, escorted her in. Immediately Inga was struck by a heady fragrance of flowers and blooming shrubs. Rulf led her through a copse of fruit trees that opened upon a small courtyard. Immediately they were faced by a cordon of five women, all garbed in long black hooded gowns. Such a contrast in dress to Audavene and Blichilde these women were, and their pale brows were furrowed angrily.

"What do you here in the lady's courtyard?" one of them demanded.

Rulf looked taken back. But his tone was affable as he corrected the woman. "I am the lady's father, madam. Surely you have not forgotten who gives you hospitality here?"

The one who had spoken pursed her lips. "Ah. Chieftain

Rulf. It has been long since we spoke." She lifted an eyebrow and said pointedly, "It is our custom to ask the purpose of unannounced visitors. Especially in light of the fact we are not allowed to lock the garden door."

Rulf's tone took a cold measure. "There is no reason to lock the exterior door. If vagabonds or any with harmful intentions wish to come in they can easily enough climb the wall itself."

"Ah," the woman replied with a wrinkle of her nose, "as long as the wall is not heightened, I suspect you are correct, chieftain."

The woman's accusation was not lost on Rulf. "Please step aside. I wish to see Vanda."

The women looked at one another dubiously. The first gave Inga a distrusting look. "What of this servant? The lady Vanda has no need of her."

Rulf felt no reason to explain anything to these women. He said in his most brusque tone, "Let us pass."

The women grunted in unison, but they moved aside. And now Rulf saw his daughter sitting on a bench in the center of the court. She was holding a small harp in her lap, and as Rulf and Inga approached she looked up. Her face was unreadable, but Rulf was struck by how lovely she was growing up to be. Her bones and features were delicate like her mother's had been, her cheeks a becoming ruddy, and her deep-set eyes the bluest shade Rulf had ever seen. Vanda's hair, once blond, was turning a deep and faceted shade of brunette and had been set in a thick braid that was wove in a coronet. Rulf thought it made her look regal, but unnaturally so for her age. He had no doubt her pious holy women had encouraged her to wear it this way, as it was so different from the custom among their own pagan women.

"Hello, Vanda," he said, and, smiling, bent down and kissed her forehead. As he kneeled at the bench Vanda gave a wide smile.

"Good afternoon, Father," she greeted him. She scooted over

on the bench and gestured for him to sit. Rulf was overcome
with joy and sat down beside her. He smiled up at Inga as he
did, and was glad of the tenderness shining in the swan
maiden's eyes as she watched the two of them.

"Are you well, daughter?"

Vanda nodded. "Oh yes. And you?"

"Very well," he said. "Vanda, I wish you to meet someone."
Rulf gestured to Inga. "This is Inga. She has come to stay with
us."

Vanda gave Inga a brief glance, but her attention seemed for
her father. "Do you remember this harp, Father?"

"Oh, yes." He smiled and touched the strings of the thing.
Soft chords lilted in the air. "It was your mother's. I always admired the craftsmanship of it. As I was told it was made of a
rare wood from her native land. It is so very pretty, I am glad
you are taking good care of it, Vanda."

Vanda touched the strings so that another riffle of melodies
struck the air. "I do take care of it," she said, but then the child
gave Inga a sidelong look. "But pretty things do not last."

Rulf was shocked by the implication, more so that his own
young daughter could speak so cynically. He glanced at Inga;
noted the distress on her face. And looking over at the group of
women who stood now by the shade trees Rulf knew he must
soon have a talk with these so-called holy women. Such cyni-
cism in a child could only have been taught by someone familiar with it.

For the time being he let it go and gently cuffed Vanda's chin
fondly. "Tell me, how have you been spending your time, Vanda?"

Vanda's eyes took a more innocent light. She told him about
the flowers she'd been planting with her women, and yes, that
she liked the pony he'd had brought to the stable to ride,
though she did not often do such. Still, Vanda told him, she enjoyed talking with the animal and brushing its mane and tail.
She told him she had several companions, children of his friends

and servants, whom she frequently invited to play in the court-yard. This pleased Rulf greatly. Vanda told him how she en-joyed the company of little Alois best, as he'd taught her how to call the birds from the trees and how to make a pipe from willow branches. She evidently had great fondness for Alois, and Rulf listened happily as Vanda laughed and retold a funny story the boy had told her.

But at last Vanda sighed. "But he is not Christian, and so we shall not be together in heaven."

Rulf was troubled. "Ah, my child. None of us know what awaits us after death. I am sure Alois shall know his reward, whether it be in Christ's bosom, Valhalla, or whatever meeting place of the souls he will ascend to. Do not be concerned; if you are to be with him in that faraway day, then doubtless you shall."

Vanda's eyes flashed with distrust. She looked to her women, and she relaxed a little. But her reply was stiff in its politeness. "If you say so, Father."

Rulf felt their glaring eyes pore over him. Deliberately he ig-nored them and, kissing Vanda's cheek, he reminded the child that he would see her at the feast that night.

Vanda ran her fingers across the spine of her harp and yawned. "Yes, Father."

Rulf rose then and watched as she caressed the strings, creat-ing a sweet but sad melody.

"We will talk again very soon," he promised.

Vanda's face raised and gave him a polite smile. There was a quality of poised hollowness in this smile. Rulf's skin turned cold. He bent down and kissed her once again. But he was glad to feel Inga reach for his hand, and he clasped it firmly as they strode toward the women. This time they made way quickly, and he felt those crawling eyes follow him and Inga out the door again.

On the other side of the garden wall he warmed again, and

the air seemed fresher, the atmosphere not hardly so intimidating. He was a man grown, a warrior, but he could not deny the negative vibrations those holy women exuded. He looked at Inga and was heartened by the difference between her and those women. Here was warmth and tenderness; all that his young daughter needed in a guardian.

Rulf cupped Inga's face and whispered, "I am so glad you are here."

Inga was glad she'd met Vanda. What a lovely girl she was, and she could see how much Rulf loved the child. And yet Inga was filled with relief to be away from that courtyard and especially those black-garbed crones that attended the girl. Rulf's tone was merrier now that they'd returned to the bedchamber. Inga wanted very much to forget her faint annoyance about the girl's pointed remark. But the more she thought about it the more her dislike grew for those women. For Inga knew it was their influence that had inspired Vanda to say such a spiteful thing.

So Inga thought about the upcoming feast, and she drank in the sight of Rulf as he removed his vest.

"Now, I shall go bathe for the feast," he told her. "I will dress like a king tonight, so I shall not look like a vagabond and shame my swan maiden."

Inga breathed in his scent and stroked his golden hair. "You could never do that, my lord."

Rulf made a husky murmur and kissed her again. Then he stood up and, with a final, lusty look, went out again. Inga lay down on the bed while he was away. Her body ached with frustrated desire. She hid under the covers and touched the collar. The knowledge that he wanted it known that she was his property made her shiver hotly. Her fingertips swept slowly down to her breasts. The nipples swelled and hardened and as she massaged them and thought of Rulf, her sex fomented. With her own hand she tantalized herself and thought of him deep inside her. How she longed for his thrusting cock. She drew up the shift hem and stroked herself, pinching her clit, and thinking of his lean, driving hips until she felt close to an orgasm.

Suddenly she heard footfalls outside the doorway. She rolled over at once and pretended to be asleep. In a few moments the covers were drawn away and she felt Rulf's fingers glide across her buttocks.

"It is a good thing I forgot my robe," he said. "I see now how very impatient you can be, my swan maiden."

Inga opened her eyes and rolled onto her back. Rulf was sitting beside her, undressed, his mouth set in a disapproving way, and she felt sheepish under his stern eyes.

"I missed you," she crooned.

"You will not do that again unless I instruct you," he said firmly. "You are mine to take pleasure in, mine to stay frustrated until I allow you satisfaction."

Inga reddened with chagrin, while her pussy throbbed painfully under his look. "Yes, my lord and master."

A fond smile came to him now, and his green eyes smoldered with his own lust. He lifted her breasts and rolled her nipples under his thumbs so that they hardened and tingled. Inga's desire rose now: she felt the juices grow thick and hot between her thighs. Rulf lay over her and kissed her throat, so that it tingled and her body shuddered for the need of him.

Rulf suddenly grasped her about the waist and rolled her over. He gave her buttocks a light smack that made her spine sizzle.

"Up to your knees, my little swan maiden," he said.

Inga got to her knees and Rulf directed her to take one of the large bed cushions and place it before her. Then he leaned her forward so that she was bent over the cushion, her bottom raised to his scrutiny. She looked over her shoulder and watched as he reached down and touched her pussy. His fingers glided across her clit and between her buttocks. With his thumb he touched her anus. The touch made Inga feel exposed, and she blushed hard. He patted her here, driving the sensation like a heated poker through her. Embarrassed beyond measure she whimpered, even as, to her mortification, her hips rocked back and forth.

"Do not be embarrassed," he crooned. "Even with this touch your passions can be compelled, little swan maiden. And I enjoy compelling them."

Inga's face smarted. But she tried to relax and accept this pleasure. His hand drifted down now, and he unfolded her tender vulva and pinned her little clit between two fingers. He kneaded it until it was hard and throbbing, and Inga felt her broiling juices trickle down both thighs.

He draped over her now, and kissed the back of her neck, and still he tormented her pussy. "Is it frustrating, to know I may not let you know satisfaction?"

"Yes!"

He murmured proudly. "I may just have to order my blacksmiths to make a special sheath for this hungry nether mouth. We often have these special belts made, just to keep our women from relieving their desires. Made of meshed brass and kept locked with keys only their men possess. But before we put them on our women, can you guess what we do?"

Riveting with desire, Inga could hardly think. "No, my lord," she wept.

He tweaked her pulsing clit. "A very special oil we apply here," he said. "This heightens their desire, and yet it is frustration sublime."

Inga moaned, but he seemed content to ignore her. "Yes," he crooned, "I may have one of these made for my wanton little love slave."

He rose to his knees again and, clasping her hips, asked fiercely, "You are my love slave, yes?"

Inga nodded. "Yes!"

His sizzling rod plunged into her. He fucked her hard, his lean hips pounding against her bottom. She came to a dizzying orgasm. Her blazing depths pulsated as he continued to ravish her. With his own orgasm he gave a deep, contented groan.

A few moments later Rulf lifted Inga up to her knees again and clasped her against his sweat-dewed chest. He pulled her hair aside and suckled her throat tenderly.

"Some love slave are you." He chuckled. "You have enslaved me with this possession of you!"

Inga turned and threw her arms around him, kissing him wantonly, uncaring if he approved or not. "I care for you, my lord. I want nothing more than to belong to you." And with a quickening of sad nostalgia she confessed, "I did not know happiness until you stole my freedom!"

He kissed her lovingly. "I believe you, my swan maiden. And I want you to know that I am humbled to know you feel this way."

Inga smiled, cherishing the happiness that filled her as fiercely and as sweetly as the ecstasy of their lovemaking.

"But now, truly, I must go bathe." He sighed. "And you shall undress while I am gone. We feast with all my companions and dearest folk tonight, pretty one. And I want them to drink in the full measure of you . . . to know how very generous Freyja can be in her gifts."

Inga adored the mischievous glint in his eyes. With a last kiss to her brow, Rulf got up from the bed and found his robe.

The chieftain's great hall was filled with guests. The place was ablaze with light from torches on the walls and candles on the tables. A hale young man tended the venison on a spit that had been raised over the hearth fire, while serving girls, wearing only braids, brought round jugs of mead to fill the cups of the thirsty. A splendid harp was placed under the tapestry of Freyja and Od. The bench nearby was empty at the moment, but plates of food and stone goblets of elderberry wine had been left for the harper.

Beside Rulf's throne a cushioned, four-legged bench of smooth rowan now stood. Rulf lifted Inga up and sat her here, whispering in her ear that it was called The Bride's Bench. Rulf ordered a jug of elderberry wine brought for her in a goblet of finest crystal to match his of gold. He said the mead was too strong for one not accustomed to it. Inga felt honored, complimented. She would have draped her long hair about her, to lend some modesty against the eyes of the guests, but Rulf pulled the weight of it behind her shoulders and told her how proud he was that his warriors could view her.

On the bench across the table sat Blichilde and her husband, Bybaer. A tall warrior this Bybaer, and as Rulf informed her, both his cousin and a berserker priest. The resemblance between the two men was unmistakable.

Despite the richness of Blichilde's black gown, her breasts were naked above the low-cut bodice. Now Inga could see the glint of the uplifting brass breast shield Blichilde wore. Upon her throat was a wide leather collar, from which hung a leather leash. The end of the leash was bound lightly about her husband's arm. To the other side of Blichilde sat another couple, a beautiful woman dressed in a costly gown of silver satin and an elderly warrior. The warrior's once-handsome features were marred by a scar that cleft his mouth and chin. These two, Rulf told Inga, were Aeyani, a great Vitki, and her husband, Thorm. These guests were all very polite and Aeyani commented that it was her honor to be seated near a swan maiden. But the other guests in the hall stared at her; some of the men openly leered.

Just before the venison was served, some of the womenfolk came up and offered Inga flowers and bolts of their finest cloth. Two little girls gave her necklaces of pretty river shells and pieces of amber.

The girls' mother said, "You are a blessing upon our tribe."

Then an elderly skald rose from his seat. He raised his cup and declared, "Hail to wise and equitable Rulf. May he revel between the legs of his beautiful love trophy tonight and, when he dies, may she greet him in Valhalla with her thighs damp and her heart racing!"

Inga was mortified. Never had she heard such crude language in Vanaheim. It was the fields and palace of pleasure, but at least everyone there was well mannered. Inga felt Rulf's arm about her waist, and she was glad when he bade her to sit in his lap.

"I will ask my warriors to practice their compliments," he promised.

It made her feel better and silently she forgave the old man. As the feasting commenced she suspected there could have been many worse things they could have said. She was not one of them; she was not even from Midgard. Yet she felt no malice whatsoever. As new and discomfiting it was to sit here naked beside the chieftain with the brass collar so blatantly exposing her position, most of the women in the hall were either half clad or not clad at all. She knew that the embarrassment she felt was from her own naïveté.

While the others were preoccupied with their feasting Rulf lifted Inga's chin and kissed her mouth. With his left hand he parted her thighs and glided a hand over her sex. He petted her dewy secret flesh and tweaked her clit. He soon had her painfully, needfully stoked. Inga moaned softly and tried to force her hips not to move. But as he continued to torment her in this delicious way, it became impossible not to squirm. Inga, sure now the others saw what he did, blushed terribly and pouted against his broad chest. But he turned her face, forcing her to look at him.

His smile was sweet but knowing.

"You are my little doll," he whispered. "To taunt and love wherever I will."

Rulf turned to address a question from the Vitki, but from

time to time his hand drifted back down to touch her dewy pussy.

But as the night wore on Inga noticed how her warrior looked from time to time toward the archway of the western corridor in the house's cross-section. She guessed that he was looking for his daughter. But she did not arrive, even though there were several other children seated with their mothers and fathers.

Melodious notes filled the room. The guests quieted, and all heads turned toward the harper. He wore a long robe of undyed wool, and his deep russet hair fell in waves to his waist. Inga guessed he could not have been more than fifteen years of age. But his long fingers worked the strings of the harp with an eloquence that almost equaled the musicians of Vanaheim. It was a tender melody he strummed, and as he began to sing, Inga was aroused by the most vibrant images. It was a ballad about a distant, verdant meadow where a dead couple—separated in life by a family feud—dwelt and loved in eternal bliss. No one spoke as the harper played, and Inga was too mesmerized to eat.

When the harper's song was done, the chieftain appeared more relaxed. He embraced Inga lovingly. "Be my companion here and forevermore, my fair swan maiden?"

Inga bowed her face and her voice shook with emotion, "Yes, my lord." She could not help but feel a fast and growing fondness for this man. His desire for her and the pride he took in possessing her was flattering. But more than this, Inga respected Rulf and, despite the fact that he was a tested warrior in a brutal world, she felt utterly safe with him.

Rulf smiled triumphantly. Without a thought to who was looking, he grasped her about the waist and kissed her hard. Blichilde giggled softly beside her husband. But Inga could not care less. The chieftain's taste thrilled her; she could almost feel his hands roaming over her as they did in the privacy of his bedchamber.

Then a hush fell over the room. This time, Inga did not hear the harp's strings, and when Rulf looked up, she saw the passion drain from his face. The other guests were turning to look at the same figure he eyed: a woman standing under the archway of the eastern cross-section. Lofty tall with two thick blond braids that flanked her large bosom and descended to her knees, she wore a gown of blue silk with a bodice cut just low enough to give a peep of her creamy cleavage. There was a broach of knotted design pinned at the bodice, centered with a large diamond encircled by pearls. The glint of the diamond engaged the eyes all the more to her breasts. Inga saw how some of the men looked at her, and she was not blind to the woman's astonishing beauty. Seeing how Rulf stared at the statuesque blonde rendered Inga with the most painful envy and self-doubt.

With graceful strides, the blonde went directly to where the harper sat. Inga could not overhear what she said to him, but the man nodded and began to play a low, sensuous tune. Then her beaming face looked straight to the chieftain's table. Rulf sighed as she approached the dais and his arm stiffened around Inga's waist. Inga glanced at Blichilde, who frowned and nodded. As the woman stepped up to the table and made a flouncy bow, Aeyani grunted loudly.

"Good evening, Rulf," the woman said in a husky voice. Her blue eyes sparkled and her cheeks were a high dusky hue. Her smile broadened her full lips and made deep dimples in her cheeks. Inga saw that her blond hair was not just very long, but rippled with waves even at the crown. She imagined it must look like shimmering waves of starlight when unbound.

Rulf's greeting was chilly. "I hope you can tell me where my daughter is. Her attendants were told to bring her to the feast."

The woman just beamed brighter and gave Inga a passing look. "This must be the swan maiden that your village is agog about."

"Inga," Rulf told her curtly. He said to Inga, "My love, this is Estheria. My daughter's aunt."

Inga felt his dislike for Estheria and knew now that not for an instant was he attracted to the woman. Nodding respectfully, Inga felt Estheria's blue eyes bore straight through her, as if she did not regard Inga as another living entity but as some thing to dissect and study body and soul. The emotions Inga perceived in Estheria were eerie and convoluted, all the more so for they were not shrouded by any typical expression of malice or contempt but managed flawlessly beneath layers of coy frivolity.

Estheria yawned behind her fingertips. There was a wide silver ring on her forefinger, capped with a large dragon figure with tiny glimmering jewel scales.

"Naked as one of your servant girls and collared, too. But so puny," Estheria tut-tutted. "I suppose this is nothing less than what legend promises curious men."

Inga was not ignorant to the woman's insinuations. She sat up straight and raised her face proudly. Although plain compared to this woman, she was Freyja's daughter and chosen by the chieftain.

Aeyani spoke up, "You did not answer Rulf. Can you tell him where Vanda is?"

Estheria ignored her, too, and took a seat beside Blichilde. Rulf gestured to one of the serving girls and told her to bring a plate for his sister-in-law. He reached for the jug of mead and started to fill one of the extra cups on the table for her.

"I wish no mead," she said.

When the serving girl approached, Rulf told her to bring a fresh jug of elderberry wine, too.

As the serving girl turned, he said patiently, "Please be so kind as to explain why my daughter is not here."

"It is my fault," Estheria said. "We went for a walk today and I brought along all the letters my parents sent her. These we read together and we talked for a very long time. Vanda is quite curious about her mother's people." Estheria's mouth pursed attractively. "I think it only fair that she know about all her kinsfolk, do you not agree?"

Rulf looked caught between exasperation and remorse. "Of course. It is only that it is important that she is here tonight. The gods know that I indulge her preference every other night to dine alone with that priest and those bloodless women."

"I am no Christian myself, Rulf. But I am not convinced that forcing Vanda to accept pagan customs or pagan idols"— Estheria cast a hard look at Inga—"is the best way to reach her. She is torn between the ways of Christianity and pagandom. As one who cares, I would like to talk to you about possible ways you can reach Vanda."

Blichilde snorted. "Rulf has been more than patient with Vanda. You hardly know the child yourself, kinswoman."

Estheria sighed softly. "With Rulf's permission, that situation could be remedied."

Rulf was thoughtful a long time. At length he said gruffly, "Very well, Estheria. After the guests have gone, I would hear your thoughts concerning Vanda."

Aeyani's mouth gaped and her husband spit out some expletive undertone. But not even Blichilde voiced an argument. Rulf seemed anxious to forget that Estheria was sitting there now and made a toast to Inga and the fortune that had led him to find her. Then he called the harper to the table and gifted him with the golden goblet.

The night grew old and one by one the guests came to thank the chieftain and pay their farewell regards to Inga. Eventually Aeyani and her husband gave their fond good night, too. Blichilde was yawning when Bybaer said they needed to retire to their own bedchamber. Rulf asked them to escort Inga to his bed on their way. Inga was more than disappointed, for there Estheria still sat, grinning smugly and acting too haughty to speak to anyone except the chieftain. Rulf stood up and lifted Inga down from her seat and told her to go with the couple. Inga felt hot tears brim in her eyes.

"I want to stay!" She threw her arms around him possessively. Spying the contemptuous look Estheria gave from under her long lashes, she knew it was more than mere jealousy she felt. Rulf was guileless and instinct warned that Estheria was anything but that.

But Rulf scolded her, "Do as I bid, Inga. I will join you soon."

Rulf's hall was chilly now, for the night air was cold and the flame in the hearth had nearly died out. The torches threw strange shadows over the tables, though this illumination softened Estheria's features, making her more beautiful than ever. He felt almost guilty to admit this, since Inga was waiting for him. He feared she may have thought his dismissal callous, and he wasn't happy over that. However, Rulf could find no legitimate argument not to hear Estheria out. She was Vanda's aunt, and no caring father could dismiss a relative's sincere concern. But he'd recognized Estheria's deliberate slings aimed at his swan maiden, and he would not give her opportunity to do that again.

One of the handmaidens had left a jug of the best ale at Estheria's request. But at the moment Estheria only toyed with the broach she'd removed from her bodice and laid on the table. She traced her fingers over the glittering stones absently, although Rulf could feel how she waited for him to speak. He looked at her, noting the faint ghost of her unsettling smirk on her succulent lips.

Such a pity, he thought suddenly, for such a tempting mouth to be wasted on this shrew. Rulf drained the dregs of his mead and with a sigh, lowered his cup to the table.

"So tell me," he said, "what do you feel I can do to reach my daughter?"

Estheria mused a moment, then said, "You do realize she has stopped seeing you as her father?"

Rulf felt a sad pang and, coupling this feeling, resentment. "What makes you an authority on her feelings, Estheria? It is true you little know the girl. Occasional correspondence does not make one an expert on the heart of someone we are little acquainted with."

The corner of Estheria's mouth twisted in a tight smile. "Neither does ignoring the child."

"I do not ignore Vanda," Rulf objected. "I have allowed her the comfort of her mother's religion and companions."

"While you have done what?" Estheria countered. "Gone frolicking off to the wilderness and let your guard down for the lust of that alleged daughter of Freyja?"

Rulf felt his hackles rise. "I only brought home the swan maiden this morning. How dare you, Estheria. I thought you wanted to speak to me about Vanda. Instead you sound petty."

"Petty?" she murmured. "Do you imply that I would seek your affections myself?"

"That is not what I meant. But you seem to have some hatred for Inga. And such feelings have no place in this conversation, especially as your reasons to ask for this audience."

Estheria laughed. "Audience? Then I am only a subject while in your household . . . not *family*?"

Rulf was already exasperated. With this affinity for avoiding a direct answer by clawing the intent of someone's words to shreds, Estheria was indeed her parents' daughter, soul and psyche.

"Yes, you are family. You are here, are you not? Surely you can overlook expressions that my position has, unfortunately, accustomed me. But you have avoided my point."

"Ah," she said. "The truth is, chieftain, that I in no way feel threatened by your swan maiden. But I do feel the customs of your people have failed to provide Vanda the pride of family. It is perhaps for this that she would prefer to live in seclusion. But I do have a proposition that might change her heart."

Rulf was still annoyed, but for Vanda he was willing to listen. "Yes? Then tell me. I will consider it."

"Thank you," she said, and then with a blithe smile, "I am thirsty. Will you join me in some of this fine ale while we talk?"

"Certainly," he said and grabbed the jug handle. He uncorked it and poured the golden liquid to the brim of Estheria's glass before filling his stein.

Estheria thanked him and seemed to measure her next words. As she did so she picked up the broach. But it slipped from her fingers and, striking the floor, bounced several feet away.

"Oh!" Estheria exclaimed.

Chivalrous instinct got Rulf to his feet. He walked to where the broach had landed, just under one of the benches at another table. He stooped, retrieving it, and he could not help but admire the lovely piece. With the lightweight spun metal he realized it had been made by adept Burgundian craftsmen. The diamond was magnificent, but it was the pearls that he thought most beautiful. They were an irregular tear-shaped form and hued of luminous pink, which Rulf recognized as the variety that could only be found in the rivers of Estheria's homeland. Dauhredei had had some similar fine pieces with the same unique pearls, necklaces and broaches both. These Rulf had stored away and planned to give to Vanda when she was a little older. He smiled to imagine Vanda grown and wearing them. With her sober beauty she would indeed be stunning as a queen.

Rulf turned and walked to Estheria's side. Handing her the broach he said, "This is stunning. Burgundian jewelers truly have no rivals. I have Dauhredei's pieces stored safely away. These Vanda will inherit, and I look forward to seeing her wear them."

"Thank you," Estheria said. She pinned the broach on again.

With it in place she quickly adjusted the front of her gown so that the bodice lifted her large breasts slightly. It was a functional but very feminine motion; and Rulf chided himself and sat down, deliberately forcing his thoughts from that flawless flesh.

Estheria handed Rulf his stein and lifted her glass. "You are such the gentleman, Rulf."

Rulf smiled uncertainly and raised the stein to his lips. The ale was excellent, but he could not truly savor it. Estheria's mood was detectably changed, and it made him uncomfortable. He wanted to hear her proposition and get this over with.

Taking another swallow of the ale he welcomed the relaxation it imparted. "What is your proposition, Estheria?"

Estheria sipped fastidiously. "I wish to bring Vanda home with me. She doubtless would like to meet her mother's people, and my parents do wish to see their granddaughter. A visit will also put some distance between her and the political instabilities which I know overwhelm your attention these days, Rulf. And I also think that an absence just might give her a chance to reflect on her relationship with you . . . so that she might come to fully appreciate the kind of man her father is."

Rulf was thoughtful. Indeed, what Estheria said made sense. And yes, even if Vanda was too young to comprehend or even name the atmosphere that surrounded the tribe, this shroud of political worry had to affect her.

Estheria added, "Besides, she enjoys my company. I can see that. I would not allow those dark and dour companions to accompany her. She would be free of their influence. And I am sure that seeing my example she will soon enough no longer cling to their influence or even desire their company."

There was no hint of boasting in these words, and Rulf nodded.

"It would give me opportunity to send them packing without Vanda falling into panic," he agreed. Rulf drank some more of the ale and felt a sting of warmth in his throat. For a moment his vision was bleary. *I am more in need of sleep than I thought.* He squeezed his eyes shut a moment; and when they opened again Estheria's face seemed flushed with a pale radiance. He cleared his throat and tried to ignore the heat he felt rise in his chest. "Do you really feel you can accomplish this? To relinquish these specters of her mother's madness will be a formidable task. It is how she clings to her mother's memory; that which, in her heart, confirms her loyalty to Dauhredei. It is sad, but I know it true."

Estheria inhaled deeply, and contemplated him with wide eyes. As Rulf waited for her answer his heart quickened and felt overcome with heat. Estheria's face grew hazy before his eyes. Her features softened and contorted; her very shape and contours transformed. Rulf saw that he no longer sat across from his sister-in-law, but the tender vision of his swan maiden. She was wearing a gown of uncertain design and color, and he felt suddenly irritated that she would cover herself without permission. And yet, he was so glad she was here.

"My Inga," he said. For one fleeting moment he noticed the silver ring on her finger; one he'd not noticed before, with what appeared like a dragon chiseled in the cap. He kissed her hand and forgot the ring. "I thought I told you to go to my chamber!"

She gave him a bold smile and leaning forward, kissed his strong hands in a subservient gesture. "My lord and master, I could not wait to see you!"

Her sensuous silky voice made the lust course violently through his veins. His cock hardened and he was struck with the urgent desire to tear her gown off. He stood and, taking her sweet hands, raised her to her feet.

"You are dressed," he said. "I did not tell you to do that. But I cannot say I won't take delight in removing that gown."

She pressed into him, her lithe body undulating against him. "My lord," she whispered. "Will you not go and bolt the door?"

Rulf grinned. "Why should I?"

Her voice was timid. "Please?" And then her tongue flicked ever so tellingly over her lips. Rulf's lust surged. He nodded and strode quickly to the hall doors. He shut them and drew the heavy oak bar between the handles of the doors, thereby shutting anyone from entering. He returned to her and, clasping her face between his palms, kissed her mouth.

Her lips were cool and not so passionate as before. She felt hesitant in his arms; her kiss wary even as it was welcoming. But even this unexpected impression was no obstacle. He knew now that he'd never loved anyone as he did Inga. It was more than passion, more than love; rather the divine marriage of both. The gods had brought him his feminine counterpart. He had not known how lonesome had been his existence until they had been brought together. And he had no intention of existing without her again.

His lips parted from her mouth and, regarding her proudly, he stripped the gown from her shoulders and let the fabric fall to the floor. She stood exposed before him, her pale flesh so misted with radiance that his eyes watered.

"What have you done to me, swan maiden?" he growled and, lifting her by the waist, sat her upon one of the cleared tables. She gave a small laugh and unfolded her thighs. Her sex was glistening white, the little seam dripping wet. She suckled her fingers and tweaked the plump folds. With a forefinger she drove into her nether mouth and, her hips rocking, she made a plaintive moan.

"Take me, Chieftain Rulf! Take me now!"

Rulf untied the cords of his breeches. His cock was scarlet with readiness.

"You are the most divine of women!" he growled. Clasping her thighs, he pulled her to the edge of the table and plunged into the enticing sex. Her legs wound about his waist as he pumped her. Something was different, not so familiar or perfect the feel of her. But he could not stop now. Rulf's hips rocked, drilling her to the hilt. His orgasm was strong, and as his seed poured into her he could feel a part of himself drain away.

The smile on her face was icy, and for one potent, frightening moment he saw beyond the deception. She'd put something in his drink when he went to retrieve the broach. It was not Inga whom he had made love to, but Estheria! And he was aware of a devastating lack of fortitude. She had not just deceived him with her magic tricks, but also had stolen away his very resolve.

He was repulsed, and wished nothing more than to order her from his sight and home, never to return. But his body and voice were beyond compliance of will. She clenched the ends of his long hair and pulled him forward. Her tongue flicked over his mouth, and she quaked with delight as she tasted the dew of sweat upon his lips.

"Dress yourself, chieftain," she ordered.

To Rulf's dismay he found himself obeying.

"Now extend your arm."

It was as if his body were not his own, but a thing machinated by Estheria's command. As he offered an arm Estheria took it and got off the table to her feet. She ordered him then to retrieve her gown and help her re-dress. Rulf was disgusted with himself, but as hard as he attempted, he could not resist her.

And there she stood, richly dressed and adjusting the long, flowing braids over her shoulders. Estheria looked as regal as she was evil, and Rulf was seized with panic. What did the sorceress intend? And more important what were her intentions toward Vanda and his people?

Estheria drew close to him again, and folded her hands over his cheeks. Her gaze was cool even as the familiar wicked smile pinched the corners of her mouth. "You are so handsome," she said, "so virile. Is it any surprise I hate you so?"

He did not understand, and when he attempted to inquire,

the words came out in an incoherent mumble. She laughed softly and, kissing his mouth, said, "I understood why my father offered my older sister to the pagan chieftain's youngest—the strongest, the most resilient of all his sons. I was too young to protest that alliance, and my father never failed to let me know that he intended me for the most favorable union when such time was ripe. All the same, I loved you, Rulf. I loved you since the first day I beheld you through the eyes of a girl as young as Vanda. You were young, too; but that virility and resilience was so strong, so dignified that it showed in your every modest word, your every casual move or gesture. Unlike other men of such caliber you felt no need to flaunt these traits. This self-possession made them even stronger, more formidable.

"While I understood that your marriage to my sister was only a political alliance—at least in the eyes of the matchmakers—my passion for you never quailed. We all knew of her madness, and unlike our parents I understood their part in its conception. So I waited and I dreamt and I waited even longer. And soon after I came of age did I hear the wondrous news that the pitiful wretch indeed took her life. Since then I have frequently visited, each time sure that after your years with Dauhredei you could now appreciate an intelligent and warm-blooded woman. I am everything that piously mad Dauhredei was not. With my every visit I was sure, yes, that you would ask me to be your wife. Ask me to share your life and bed, your future. But you have remained aloof, even I dare say hostile at times? Despite all that I have—all the qualities that stay my father's hand in wait for the richest and most powerful offer—you have deliberately spurned me.

"But this visit is my last. For here I am, what to find? News that you have laid claim to a swan maiden. Ah, and then I saw her: all fair and shrinking, obedient and naked. Not like my pious sister, not at all. And nothing, nothing like what I can offer you! A love slave, weakling and compliant? How dare you, Chieftain Rulf! What pathetic choices; the choices of a man not fit to be extended my admiration. You betrayed that admiration; you mocked my love. And out of passion for this weak, wretched love slave you dare betray me!"

The smile disappeared from Estheria's mouth. Rulf felt her fingernails dig into his cheeks. His flesh seared and he felt blood trickling down the sides of his face.

Estheria's eyes flared, and for a moment her face glowed with madness just as had destroyed Dauhredei. But he knew instinctively that Estheria's madness would not be used against herself. Instead it would drive her to punish all those she believed had offended her.

"How dare you, Rulf!" she roared. "How dare you spurn all that I offer for that compliant, frivolous creature!"

She kissed Rulf roughly, and bit his bottom lip until it was also bleeding. "A daughter of some silly Norse goddess," she whispered hotly, "when you had a goddess of flesh and blood waiting right before your foolish eyes!"

Anger panged in his heart, and he struggled to speak. At length a single labored sentence he uttered. "What do you plan?"

Estheria struck him across the face. "A man of few words as always," she mocked him. "What do I plan, Rulf? Your swan maiden won't be as easily commanded as a mortal man. For her I must employ other means." She admired the dragon-engraved silver ring and gave it a kiss. "You will take me to where you keep the swan mantle. And if anyone asks you will say nothing. And then, dear chieftain, I will take you to where my gift to you and your beloved swan maiden is to be presented."

Dark rage filled Rulf. Yet her magic forced his body to betray him so that when next she ordered him to lead her on to where the swan mantle was his feet strode against his will to lead her.

Rulf's chamber was silent as Estheria pulled back the furs.

He entered and, like a puppet driven by strings, proceeded to the bed. Inga was sound asleep, the milky moon haloed around her peaceful face. His heart raged that he could not rouse her and warn her of what was happening. The back of his head seared with Estheria's urging. He gave her a baleful glance, and then his knees fell of her accord. He knelt on the floor and stretched his arm far under the bed. Feeling the fabric of the sack, he grasped it.

As the chieftain got to his feet he heard Estheria's muffled, triumphant giggle.

The chieftain's bed had felt huge and empty without him. It had taken Inga long to fall asleep. When she finally had, discouraging visions haunted her dreams. She saw Freyja reclining on her throne, terribly distressed and weeping. Inga tried to run forward and give comfort to her mother, but her legs would not move.

As the swan maiden awoke the first glint of dawn splintered through the windows. She was still alone in this room, and her heart weighed heavily with a medley of jealous and worrisome feelings. It was not proper, she knew, to question her Saxon master. But she could not forget Estheria with her flawless beauty and her biting snobbery. Of all the women Rulf could have whiled the hours away with, why did it have to be her?

She tried to remember the way Rulf had spoken to Estheria. His concern was for Vanda, surely, and his reasoning for talking with Estheria was only out of that concern.

Over this thought, Inga heard her name spoken. She opened her eyes but saw no one, not even movement behind the furs.

Inga, come.

The voice, she knew now, sounded only in her head. It was not Freyja who called her, nor any of her Valkyrie sisters. It was recognizable, though Inga could not place it.

Come now, swan maiden!

Inga was seized with the compulsion to rise from the bed. She yielded to it but when next she felt driven to run out the narrow back door she was alarmed. She tried to start back to bed when her head jarred with pain. Further resistance constricted her breathing, as if invisible hands were choking her. Inga's heart skipped several beats and she felt the blood flow slacken in her veins.

Come, Inga.

Inga knew her mortal power depended on obeying so she followed the urge that led her through the door to the outside. Her naked body shivered in the brisk early morning air, but she could not turn back. Compulsion directed her to run down the path here. She skirted past the bathing house and through the garden enclosure behind it. There was an earthen street that ran parallel here, and this she dashed across, sprinting between the two cottages on the other side. Into the village pastureland she came. A few pregnant mares and colts grazed in the tall grass. But they ignored Inga as she sped across the grass for their attention was on the small knoll between them and the oak stave palisade that encircled the village lands. Fire burned at the very top, contained in a perfect ring and so hot that Inga heard the breeze sing against the spiraling flames. A figure wearing a hooded vermillion robe stood gazing at the blaze. Inga's eyes saw at once that it held something in its arms. She squinted, and she perceived against the horizon the soft, familiar shape of the thing, the silvery white texture. It was her swan maiden's gown. As shocked as Inga was she had no time to worry over this; all she could think about was the flames she was running headlong toward.

Just before she plunged in, her legs came to a halt. She fell breathless to her knees. The heat singed her skin. She heard the shouts of men behind her and, looking back, saw at least two dozen running from the village main with pails of water. Out of the corner of her vision, Inga saw the robed figure advance. It cast a fist toward the sky, and as the hood of its robe fell back, Inga saw the glow of the flames burnish two long blond braids.

Estheria's Burgundian incantation impregnated the breeze. The breeze whipped up now and sped toward the rescuers. As it reached them, their feet stopped in their tracks. One by one the men fell prostrate to the ground.

Inga glared at the sorceress. "What have you done, woman?"

Estheria replied in a very satisfied tone. "The legends are true: He who possesses the mantle enslaves the swan maiden . . . even if he is a woman, I see."

Inga was seized with anger. "How did you come to possess it? What have you done to the chieftain?"

"Rulf was persuaded to give me your precious mantle, Inga," Estheria said smugly. "And easily enough."

Estheria snuggled a cheek against the feathers and murmured. She mocked Inga, "Wings of the swan, regal mantle of the forbidding princesses of Vanir. Ah, so holy to pagan women, so coveted by men. And yet, here it is mine, naked Valkyrie. Property of a mortal woman who holds no alliance to any gods. A woman who trembles not on bowed knee before your Freyja. And given to me by no less than he who you thought devoted."

Inga was appalled, and yet she detected some half-truths behind Estheria's jeering revelation. She tried to get to her feet but Estheria's will held her kneeling to the earth. "Very well. You hold my gown now. What are your intentions?"

"Anything I wish." Estheria stroked the white plumes with the long, sharp nails of her fingers. Her lovely features were hard as ice. "But what you can offer, swan maiden, is nothing I seek. You may be a goddess's child, but you know no useful magic. It is the possession that is of consequence. And more than this: a just compensation for all the disrespect shown my family by your precious Saxon."

Inga looked down to the rescuers. More people had come out of the village and clamored around the fallen. Some of these pointed to the knoll, and Inga saw confusion and dread in the faces of all.

"Do not concern yourself with the Saxons," Estheria said. "They only sleep and will continue to sleep, as does Rulf. I will leave this day and return to my own land with this compensation to take."

"What makes you think the tribe will allow you to leave?"

Estheria's malevolence swelled the air like the presages before a thunderstorm. Bitterness punctuated her every word. "I am no naked love slave. I will leave for I have power that makes these fools cringe. Not even their Vitki's seith powers or the berserker's mysteries know how to battle Nibelung magic and win. Not on the mortal plane. Thus shall I leave and take my niece with me. You, on the other hand, will return to Vanaheim . . . the hard way."

Inga knew the woman could order her to kill herself and there was naught she could do. But something disturbed Inga even more.

"Where is Rulf?"

A cruel smile lit Estheria's face. "Just where I left him after he made love to me."

Inga's breast panged at the sorceress's words. She could hardly believe that her greatest fear had been realized. Whatever the truth, Inga's feelings did not change. She loved Rulf.

"Now you may go to him," Estheria said. With her power over the mantle, she forced Inga to rise. They regarded one another for several seconds as Estheria's eyes glittered. "I have changed my mind. I will not force you to go to him. But if you do—of your own free will—I promise not to let the fire consume him. How is that for a trade, naked slut?"

Inga felt an anxious knot in her stomach. "Where is he?"

Estheria glanced at the towers of flames. "He is in there. Asleep just as the lord of the Asgard host put your sister Brunhilde to sleep as punishment. As Brunhilde, he will not awaken unless he is kissed by one brave enough to cross the fire."

Inga understood this woman completely now. She was proud, jealous, and without moderation in revenge. The heat of the fire was already parching Inga's skin. She envisioned Rulf being burned alive by the descent of the raging flames, his skin scorched and eaten away in its wrath. The columns looked impenetrable to life. How was she going to reach him without losing her own mortal shell? A spirit only then in the eyes of Midgard? And the pain . . . it was unimaginable. . . .

"You shudder," Estheria jeered. "I imagine that courage is not a virtue for those who let themselves be pampered and worshipped in the name of lust."

Inga was afraid to the depths of her soul but she loved Rulf more than she feared the pain. Even if the attempt proved fatal, she was determined to stay by the sleeping man's side. He would not be alone as this jealous sorceress suspected.

Her glare snapped toward the sorceress. "Swear upon your Nibelung heritage that if I enter the ring you will not let the fire consume him."

Estheria looked wary. "Why go in? Even if you enter, you will die. Neither rain nor even the water carried by those pathetic villagers can douse this fire. And most certainly the lips of a dead Valkyrie hath not power."

"This shouldn't concern you," Inga countered. "Or is it that you're only afraid of the rules of your own game?"

Estheria's eyes blazed. She squeezed the gown as if she could throttle the thing. "Strike yourself for that insolence!"

Inga's hand lifted and she slapped her own face.

"Again and again!" Estheria seethed. With both hands, Inga slapped the sides of her face, until her cheeks were swollen and stinging and the sorceress cackled with laughter.

"Enough," Estheria said at last. Inga's eyes bore into her as she said, "I hate passive whores like you. But if indeed you have the courage to brave the flames, I will enchant the fire so it does not harm your Rulf. I would have you remember one thing in turn."

"What is that, Estheria?"

"That after Rulf made love to me, he declared that I am the most divine of women. This, too, I swear by my Nibelung heritage."

Estheria was smiling triumphantly and Inga was tempted with wrath. But it only lasted a moment. For in her heart Inga sensed that this revelation was only the perverse boast of some twisted grain of the truth.

Assured, Inga stepped back several feet. Estheria was smirking. She did not believe that Inga would rush into the conflagration. For Inga to back down would be the crowning touch of the sorceress' vindictive triumph. But the swan maiden was not about to let her savor victory or allow Rulf to remain alone.

Inga regarded the fearsome inferno once more and fought the panic that vied to paralyze her. Without another glance at Estheria, she closed her eyes and ran forward. The heat snatched her breath even before she plunged into the raging ring. Her flying hair at once began to crackle and her skin seared immeasurably. She could not contain the screams as she ran madly on. The moments were tormenting hours but at length she felt fresh air on her face and grass below her scorched soles.

She fell upon the ground and rolled until the flames were extinguished. Her eyes could hardly open and every inch of flesh was vibrant with pain. Lying on her stomach, she could see Rulf lying on one side in the center of the meridian. The ground had been recently dug up just beside him, and an empty chest stood in the uncovered earth with its lid opened. She crawled to him and rejoiced to find that he was breathing. He looked to be dreaming fitfully, and she raised her hand to his shoulder.

Then she began to wonder how long they would remain here. If she awoke him, he would only try to fight to get them out of the ring. This, she was sure, would be fatal to a mortal man. She had inherited certain strength from Freyja, but her mortal half was hardly invulnerable. She was aware of how hard it was to breathe now. Her lungs felt scorched from the inside. As her mind began to fatigue and her denuded eyes closed, she remembered the decision made earlier, one that she did not regret. She would stay by Rulf's side even if her physical body succumbed. The life force was draining rapidly from her body, and this seemed the best she could give him now.

Inga! Kiss him now before it is too late!

The voice Inga heard was unmistakably familiar. It came from her mother, Freyja.

Open your eyes and kiss your beloved if you will save him!

With great effort, Inga opened her eyes again. She gathered the last reserve of strength in her limbs and, sitting up, turned Rulf's shoulders so that his head lay in her lap. His face was tranquil now, so handsome and dear to her eyes that her weakened heart fluttered. She almost hated the thought of him awakening and seeing her burnt and mutilated. But her mother's presence gave her courage and she bowed and kissed his lips.

Rulf's eyes opened, and as his eyes drank in the sight of her, the horror showed on his face.

"Inga . . ."

A scream penetrated the ring. It was a forsaken blare of sound. The second issue was with a bestial ferocity that brought Rulf to his knees.

"Estheria!" he seethed and drew Inga into his protective arms.

Then an amazing thing happened. The fire began to wane in height and intensity. In a matter of minutes, the columns coiled downward into the earth. The flames smoldered and then spurted out completely. Estheria's inferno was nothing more than a black halo of smoking grass.

Outside the halo lay a horrible sight. It looked like a great bird with feathers reddened and soaked by its own blood. The legs were indistinguishable. Inga knew the other limbs were a ghoulish commixture of wings and arms. The creature's face was turned toward the couple, and they both listened to the last rasping breath it drew. The face that stared at them was a twisted caricature of bird and woman. As Inga tried to imagine what it was, she saw the last of the creature's life extinguish in its disbelieving blue eyes.

These eyes were the last things Inga saw before slipping into timeless darkness.

Inga awoke in a bed in a tidy little room, lit cozily by lantern light from the table that stood below the window. The stars were peering through the velvety sky beyond the opened shutters. Inga smelled the scrumptious fragrance of lavender from the clean sheets and was aware that she no longer hurt. She felt her scalp and found her hair had grown back, thick and long as ever. Her skin was likewise undamaged. She trembled with happiness and had started to call out Rulf's name when she saw her swan gown lying at the foot of the mattress. In that moment she was aware, too, that the torque collar had been taken from her throat. She did not see it on the bed or anywhere in the room.

"You are awake."

Blichilde and Audavene stood in the doorway. They came and stood by the bed. Both were smiling tenderly.

"You were so brave, Inga," Audavene said. "You saved our chieftain from Estheria's baneful magic."

Inga sat up and stroked the gown's silky plumes. "Is everyone all right? I feared the menfolk were dead."

Audavene said, "Just as your kiss awoke Rulf, so did their wives' and lovers' kisses awaken them."

Inga remembered then how afraid she had been to do just that. The fear of Rulf remaining in that baneful ring of fire had been unthinkable, as unthinkable as the possibility of him dying trying to battle through it. Then Freyja had urged her to awaken him and then the ring diminished. Together, she and Rulf had watched that pitiful creature die.

She was still fearful. "Where is Estheria?"

"Do you not know?" Blichilde asked. "In her unbound lust for power she dressed herself in your gown. The attempt killed her."

A chilly tingle of blended relief and horror passed over Inga. Now she understood what the horrible creature had been—or rather, who it had been. And she knew well why the foolish Estheria had failed. The answer was in the magic of the swan maiden gown.

"One may enslave the swan maiden," she uttered. "But no one except one of her own blood daughters may wear it and live."

"It is our fortune that the greedy fool did not know that part of the ban," replied Audavene. "And once Rulf placed the mantle near you, its power healed your wounds."

Inga wanted to see Rulf at once. But she remembered Estheria's boast about the two of them.

"The chieftain . . . is he all right?"

Blichilde sat beside Inga and smoothed her hair. "Yes," Blichilde answered slowly. "He sent us to bring his apology. He is ashamed for the wrong he did to you, by not suspecting Estheria's potion."

"Potion?"

"In the form of a powder," Blichilde explained. "The powder carried in the dragon ring Estheria wore. Its effect was potent. She gave it to the chieftain when they were alone in the great hall. He told me that under its influence, he thought that Estheria was you."

Tears of joy sprang to Inga's eyes. "And so she convinced him to give her my gown?"

"Yes. He led her to the little hill where he planned to bury it. It was the powder. In his right mind, he would have remembered that no true swan maiden could ask for their mantle back."

Inga pulled the covers aside and got out of the bed. She was excited as she said, "I will go at once to him, give my assurance that I do not blame him. Where is he?"

Blichilde and Audavene exchanged worried looks. "You cannot," Blichilde finally said, "as he's forbidden it. You must take your gown and leave."

Inga stared at her incredulously. "I cannot believe this! Of course I will go to him. I belong to him."

"No more, Inga," Audavene said. "It is his wish that you take what is yours and return to Vanaheim. He is quite adamant."

Inga could not believe what she heard. The women bowed to her now, and Blichilde gestured to the sacred gown. "The village champion waits in the hall, along with a retinue of maidens. They will escort you to the sacred wood or wherever else you wish to go."

Audavene bowed her head. "Go in peace, Lady Inga. And take our gratitude for gracing our village for a time with your company."

"I do not want to go!" Inga protested.

But now both handmaidens retreated from the room. Inga felt as if her returned life force had suffered a blow as potent as death itself. Tears of disbelief poured over her cheeks. Fate was crueler than Estheria! She had come to love Rulf more than life itself, and now she was to be released from a slavery she did not wish to be unshackled from.

Inga wiped the tears away. She took the gown in her hands. She reflected on the days and moments spent on Earth; of the love and rapture she'd known with Rulf. She understood that just as she adored his fortitude and loyalty, Rulf treasured her meekness and tenderness. It was these very things he treasured above any right in possessing her. And in his mind the chieftain believed that he needed to shield her. But Inga wanted to be with him in this life and the next, to meet his challenges alongside him, to share his joys, and yes, kneel in adoration until the end of her days.

There was only one argument that might sway the good Rulf not to throw away the gift Freyja had given them both.

Inga pulled the dainty fabric over her arms and head, letting it drift down her torso and legs. At once the material clung to her as if that of a second skin. Her hair snaked down into the cloth, and obeying her desire, the long collar sheathed her throat and the hood tautly capped her head. The mystery of the dress saturated Inga body and soul. For the first time, she felt the potent determination of Valkyrie passion burning hot and unyielding through her veins.

More important, her countenance was burnished with the regalia of Freyja and all that she represented.

Inga drew aside the curtain at the door and stepped out. It was a part of the Chieftain's Hall she had never been in. Bybaer was waiting here. He was dressed in the verdant green breeches and shirt of a pagan champion, with a hunter's cap pinned with an eagle's feather to one side. Seeing Inga, his eyes widened and his mouth moved as if he would speak. But awe stifled the words. A line of little girls stood waiting behind him, all attired in gowns of solid white and coronets of flowers. Their faces betrayed their own awe. A very young one amongst them pointed.

"The swan maiden!"

Bybaer knelt to one knee. "We are your humble escorts, lady. Voice your destiny and it is ours to go."

Inga touched his head in blessing. "You are a good man, Bybaer."

Adoration made his voice quiver, "Thank you, lady."

Inga looked over the line of sweet faces, saw how they beamed in reverence. "These little girls are to go and pick all the flowers they can carry and litter them over the hill where Estheria lit her evil fire. Thus it will be consecrated in my mother's name. And you, dear champion, will take me to your chieftain."

The girls squealed as one and dispersed with laughter. Bybaer got to his feet, but while his eyes remained lowered, his voice betrayed reluctance.

"My lady, the chieftain has commanded that you are to leave."

In a voice as resolute as any chieftain's command, she said, "This is not a request, champion."

The knock at the doorframe brought a gruff response from the chieftain.

"I said that no one is to disturb me."

Inga gestured to Bybaer. He was obviously tense, but inclined his head silently and pulled the furs aside.

A small candle on a table gave light to the otherwise dark room. Rulf sat in a backless wooden chair beside it. His attention was focused idly on a piece of wood he was carving with a small, bone-handled knife. He did not look up as Inga entered and let the furs fall behind her.

"I did not know one of my servants had suddenly gone deaf," he said.

Inga spoke strongly, "What did you do with my collar, chieftain?"

Rulf looked up at once. His eyes shone fiercely, but she saw how his hands trembled ever so slightly as he laid the knife and wood on the table. The quiet that suffused the room was heady with unspoken emotions.

At last Rulf announced, "You are no longer love chattel, lady swan maiden. Your property is returned, your freedom restored."

"By whose decision?"

Rulf frowned slightly. "By mine."

Inga directed the full countenance of her powers to radiate through her. She glowed—blood, sinew, bone, and flesh—with the holy radiance of a true daughter of the goddess. Rulf shuddered and fell to his knees. Like a slave, he bowed his own head.

"I deserve banishment for not seeing the enemy I welcomed into my own village and home," he declared. "No man of wisdom would have let such a malevolent creature near his tribe or child. Yet I placed you in grave danger, lady. I am not worthy to claim and possess a daughter of Freyja."

Inga felt the chafing remorse that passed through his psyche. It grieved her to the core but she knew that pity would not impress him.

"The Nibelung sorceress chose to betray the trust you gave out of sheer love for your daughter. You saved my mortal semblance by quick thinking when you placed the gown near me. If nimble action is not a sign of a man's worth, and love is no token of his most devout motives, then I have been misled. It is the motives of men and women that count; this is what one must either respect or be wary of."

Rulf was crestfallen. "You shame me with my own words."

"You do not believe those words, chieftain?"

"Oh, yes. I believe them." His jaw hardened and a tear welled in his eye. "But your love is better spent upon a wiser man than the one who kneels before you."

The love Inga felt for him was painful in its intensity. Her own hands shook with emotion as she laid them upon the crown of his head. The vestige of power undulated wildly through her, blinding Rulf in radiance and filling the room with the glorious light of Vanaheim.

The power of the Valkyrie thundered in Inga's reproach, "Then do not kneel, chieftain!"

Inga released her power with a luxurious exhale. The power of it pealed through the room, rippling Rulf's hair and caressing the furs at the door and the covers upon the bed. She bade the gown farewell, and the light of Vanaheim danced in ecstasy and seeped back into the pelted fabric. Then as the garment fell from her body, the weight of care slipped away altogether. No longer was she the Valkyrie bound to power but the swan maiden at peace with love. Attired in flesh and desire and nothing more, she smiled and knelt to the floor and, taking her sacred vestment, lifted it to him in offering.

"My love is yours already," she said, "and my respect, always, if you will possess this until the day of my mortal death."

The heavenly illumination faded. Again they faced one another in the soft candlelight. The brooding disappeared from Rulf's face, while the resolve she had come to adore returned. Rising to his feet, he carried the gown to the bed and laid it at the foot. He captured Inga's hand and swept her into a fevered embrace.

The lips of Inga's golden chieftain ravished her throat, imparting kisses that drove her at once into throes of sensation.

"Never again shall I kneel to you," he said huskily in her ear, "but adore you with my claim!"

Rulf lifted her suddenly, throwing her over a shoulder, and carried her to the bed. Gently he lowered her upon the glossy honey weave quilt. He pinned her down and, kneeling on the floor, he grasped her about the hips and pulled her to the mattress edge. He unfolded her legs and pressed his warm mouth against her sex. He licked the tender seam and, parting her tender nether lips, lapped at her clit. It swelled with sensation, and he dipped a finger deep into her slit. Inga's body fomented with desire. As he fucked her this way his tongue made circles over her aching clit. Inga's hips undulated with pleasure and, grasping the covers, she could not help but rock in motion with his skilled tongue. Inga moaned, her sex drenched and musky. She was on the brink of ecstasy when Rulf gave a command.

"Kneel on the cushions, my beauty."

Inga obeyed as quickly as possible, crawling across the silken fabric and settling herself between the heavy posts. Rulf took off his vest and, his skin burnished gold in the candlelight, made her pussy swell.

"Turn toward the wall, Inga, and raise that delectable little backside where I can see it."

Inga would have rather soaked in the sight of him undressing. But when she was reluctant to move, he gave her a stern look that made her move quickly. On all fours she knelt, staring at the wall as she listened to him undress, very aware of how moist and anxious her sex was becoming. In a few moments she felt him get onto the mattress.

He came up behind her, straddling her calves with his knees. Rulf's hands skimmed over her buttocks. He massaged and plumped them. So strong, so manly were his hands. Inga could not keep her ass from rising high. She felt his loins against her thighs.

Rulf pinched her nether lips. The little pain made her hips rotate decadently. He slapped her fount, producing a wet sound that shocked Inga. Her cheeks burnt and, when he then tweaked her clit, a desperate, decadent moan issued from deep inside her.

He lifted her up to her own knees then and swept her hair away from her throat. His lips braised over the tender skin here. His slow, fervent kisses exacerbated her passion to a violent frenzy.

His masterful whisper was delightful music to her ears. "This evening in the feasting hall, you will be naked and bound with a chain to my seat!"

"Lord and master," she wailed.

Rulf's hands clamped over her breasts, pulling her back so that she felt his hard cock poised against her buttocks. He pinched her nipples between thumbs and forefingers, making them pain deliriously. Inga undulated without concern for decorum, blind to everything but this pleasure. The next moment his hands drifted to her hips. Rulf raised her up and thrust her down, skewering her pussy with his steely manhood.

Up and down he bounced her. The head of his cock spanked her utmost depths. Inga felt the momentum of pleasure escalate. As Rulf's hips ground she was rocked by countless spasms of pleasure. Rulf pounded more urgently, and when his embrace tightened, she felt his body shudder from his own orgasm.

Inga's head fell back upon his strong shoulder. She was breathless and felt small, captive, and utterly helpless in his robust embrace.

"I love you, Inga," he said. "I want you as my love hostage and pray, humbly, that you will consent to be my bride."

Inga turned her head and kissed his moist lips. "Oh yes! For I love you, my honorable Saxon, and will accept no other as my master or life's companion."

A fleeting image of the splendid halls in Vanaheim flashed before Inga's eyes. She could see the silvery walls and golden trappings; for a moment she even smelled the lavish fragrance of flowers that wafted eternally through the windows over the gardens. As Rulf pulled her down onto the mattress and kissed her waiting lips, she caught in the gleam of his golden hair the weeping eyes of Freyja.

They were tears of joy. Inga knew that her mother could not be more approving of any man than the Saxon who had made her daughter his love hostage.

During the day the caress of the sun's light laid bare the spectacular flora of the ancient grove. Birds sang in the trees and the sacred pool glinted green and gold beneath the heavy boughs. Rulf's steed stood on the emerald bank and, as the chieftain dismounted eagerly, it lowered its head and nibbled eagerly at the lush blades of grass. Rulf inhaled deeply of the clean, sweet air and eyed the waterfall. The cascading waters were jeweled white foam; the resonance a melody that seeped into his soul. Formidable was the reassurance of that sound; of ancient power that poured forth from the womb of the earth itself, something that would survive even if the pool waters were to be dammed and the great trees felled.

Around his neck Rulf wore a leather cord, which held a small leather pouch against his chest. He touched the cord thoughtlessly and stepped down the bank and into the pool. Wading into the water he thought of that vision of Inga that first time he'd seen her. A vision bathed in milky moonlight and clothed only in the sacredness of Freyja's femininity. He had been enchanted from the first moment, and now he was as much slave to her as she was to him. He loved her like none other and felt boundlessly fortunate to know she returned that love.

But the chieftain also knew that the day was approaching quickly when once again he'd have to uproot his tribe and family. The inevitable spoke through the Vitki runes and from portents in the animals and flora. Even Freyja herself gave warning to Inga through dreams. The time of the pagans in mortal Midgard was coming to an end; the old rites, cultures, and ways would someday only be history. The gods promised salvation in the fabled lands if the mortals were worthy and wise enough to find them. The prophecies spoke of a time of reckoning and justice to be dealt to the persecutors. This time was in an uncertain future, however, and for now the pagans had no recourse but to either kneel before the warrior servants of Rome, or to take refuge in those lands not yet claimed by the Christian conquerors. There were still free lands north and northeast and Rulf had decided that he would send scouts out on the morrow. These men would find the most sensible new locale while the rest of the tribe readied for the move.

But for now Rulf allowed himself not to be overburdened by these considerations. He reached the waterfall and stood before it. The sunlight bore down full and golden here upon his head, while beads of water splayed like tiny darts over his face and arms.

Rulf removed the cord from his neck and opened the pouch. From this he took out a loaf of bread. It was good barley bread he had made, rolled and baked with his own hands, and filled with the first honey from the tribe's bee hives. Only the second loaf of bread he'd ever baked in his life; and he smiled to think the reason for both had been the same reason.

He now held the loaf over his palms and bowed his head. Gratitude and reverence filled his heart. He thanked Freyja for sending him Inga, and for delivering the tribe from Estheria's plot. He asked the goddess to watch over them all and help him make the wisest decisions in regard to the tribe. And when his prayers were all said he opened his eyes and kissed the loaf. Into the bubbling fountain at the bottom of the waterfall he dropped the loaf. He watched the water claim the loaf and pull it beneath the cascade. The fragrance of roses filled his senses and for a moment he felt like he was being watched.

It was only a feeling, and if more, he had neither reason nor desire to discover why. The chieftain smiled and waded back toward the bank.

Join Crystal Jordan
ON THE PROWL!

On sale soon from Aphrodisia!

Antonio watched the men circle his mate from atop a building far above the alley they'd cornered her in. A few nimble leaps brought him to the end of the shadowed corridor. He jerked his clothes off and dropped them as he ran, shifted into his Panther form to let his black fur blend into the night, and stalked the men as they had stalked her.

The predators became the prey.

He ran his tongue down a long fang, anticipation and rage boiling hot in his veins. They would pay for scaring her. God and all the saints couldn't save them if they harmed her.

It had taken two days to track her scent after he'd sensed her in the city. And now he'd found her. Nothing compared to the ice that froze the blood in his veins when he heard her first scream, the terror of seeing men hunt her. Yes, these men would beg for his mercy before the night was through. A growl rumbled from his chest as he moved down the alley, his claws clicking on the pavement.

When one of the men grabbed for her, a roar ripped from his throat. Everyone froze, turning in slow motion to stare at the newcomer. A Panther. He bared his teeth and watched the man closest to him turn ghostly pale. He could smell their fear, taste the tang of it on his tongue, and he took a small amount of satisfaction in that.

This close, even his rage couldn't cloud the fact that the men weren't human. They were Panthers, like him. Worse, they were from his Pride. The Ruiz brothers—Marcos, Juan, and Roberto. His own people, under his rule. Why would they hunt a Panther female? If she belonged to another Pride and was visiting his territory, then her Pride leader would hold him responsible for any harm his people caused her. Not to mention she was his mate and he would shred them alive for hunting her in the first place.

She screamed, and the frozen tableau broke into chaos. Antonio lunged forward, slicing his claws into Roberto's calf. He went down with a spray of blood and saliva, squealing and clutching his leg.

Antonio leaped over the fallen man to sprint forward, intent on reaching his mate. Juan shifted to Panther form, hissing a warning, but it meant nothing to Antonio. They were past the point of warnings. A single leap forward and the two of them clashed midair, claws and fangs tearing into each other. Antonio slashed across the young Panther's face and he rolled away with a whimper, his black fur matted with dark crimson blood.

Antonio's tail whipped around as he sprang for Marcos. The man tried to climb the wall, but he had no more chance of escape than Antonio's mate had. Antonio dragged him down to the ground, his fangs digging into the man's jeans. Both front paws planted on the younger man's chest, making him wheeze, and Antonio shoved his face into Marco's. A growl vibrated his vocal cords, and what little blood was left in the man's face fled. His bloodshot eyes went wide with horror.

His mate's soft cry reached Antonio's ears, jerking him back from the edge of feral. He shuddered, fighting the instincts of his Panther nature. He turned toward her, wanting to comfort her and soothe her fear.

But she wasn't looking at him—she snarled at Juan, bracing her back against the wall as she hissed deep in her throat. A purr rumbled in his chest at her courage.

Marcos took the opportunity to speak. "Please, sir. Listen to me. She doesn't deserve protection. She's a—"

A roar ripped free from Antonio's throat as he transformed into his human form. He hoisted the shorter man up by his T-shirt until they were nose to nose. "*Silence!* The three of you will be in my study when I return to the mansion. Is that clear?"

"But how long until—"

"Obey me. You won't enjoy the consequences if you don't. But I will." He dropped Marcos to his feet. The younger man scrambled away and ran. His brothers had already disappeared.

He turned back to his mate. "Are you all right?"

"Yes. You?" She shoved her dark hair out of her face, her fingers sifting through the streaks of blond that shot through the long strands. He soaked in the details of her, taking in every curve of her face and body. Her chocolate-brown eyes searched him and they went wide when she saw the straining erection jutting between his thighs. Shifting back had left him naked. A wry smile pulled at his lips. He was going to have to figure out where he'd dropped his clothes and hope some vagrant didn't steal them before he got there. For the moment, he focused on his mate.

She sucked in a quick breath when he took a step toward her. Swaying on her feet, she stared at him for long moments. The silence stretched to a fine breaking point. She shook her head, pressing the heel of her hand to her forehead. "It can't be."

She'd finally sensed it—that they were mates.

"Oh, but it can be. It is." Stalking forward, he backed her up against the brick wall. His nostrils flared to catch her sweet scent, the one he would become addicted to. He had no doubt she had the same adrenaline humming through her as he did, and it morphed into something hotter, more carnal. Anger and fear still pumped through his system. His shaking fingers fisted at his sides. His eyes narrowed at her and a dart of excitement flashed through her gaze. The delicate smell of her wetness filled his nostrils. It was heady. She swallowed, her lids dropping to half-mast.

She released a breathy laugh, and naked want shone in her gaze. "I don't believe it. We can't be mates."

"Let me prove it to you," he growled. His hands wrapped around her waist, lifting her against the rough brick. Her legs curved around his flanks, she arched against him, and made him snarl with his need. She drove him wild. Jerking her dress up, he found her naked underneath. Perfect. He pushed forward, his hips fitting into the cradle of hers. The blunt tip of his cock rubbed over her slick folds. Her gaze flashed with the same desire that burned in his veins. "Your name. Tell me your name."

Her little pink tongue darted out to slide along her lips. "Solana."

She whimpered, tightening her legs about him. He groaned, but held back from plunging his dick into the snug fit of her damp pussy. Barely. "Yes or no, Solana?"

Her hands reached for him, fingers burying into his hair. Choking on a breath, she arched her hips toward the press of his cock. "Yes."

He thrust hard and deep. She screamed, the slick muscles of her pussy clenching around his dick. He groaned, hammering his hips forward. Her back arched, and she shuddered around him. He held on to his control by the tips of his fingers as her orgasm fisted her sex around his cock again and again. She was so responsive, so amazing. He kept pushing into her until her moans caressed his ears and she moved with him toward another orgasm. A tear leaked down her cheek and she hissed softly. Her head rolled against the brick wall, and her eyes slid closed. He wanted her gaze on him, wanted to see her come apart in his arms. "Look at me, Solana."

She moaned, but didn't obey him, so he seated himself as deep as he possibly could, and stopped moving. Her brown eyes flared open. "Don't stop."

"I won't." He withdrew halfway and plunged back in, starting a slow, hard rhythm. She whimpered, clamping her knees on his hips, but she kept her gaze locked with his. Passion flushed her face, made her dark chocolate eyes shine. She was so beautiful—the most beautiful woman he'd ever seen. His mate. A grin curved his lips. "Tell me you want me."

A deep blush raced up her cheeks, her fingers tightening in his hair. She glanced away. "I'm doing it with you in an alley. Do you really have any doubts?"

He smiled down at her. "Ah, but I want to hear you say it."

Clamping her pussy around his cock, she pulled a groan from him. A hot, purely female smile flashed across her face as she locked her gaze with his. "I want you. I want you to fuck me hard and fast."

He choked on a breath and gave her what she asked for. The scent of her, the damp feel of her around his thrusting cock drove him right to the edge of his control. His fangs extended and he knew his eyes had turned the deep gold of a Panther's as he held himself back from shifting. The sound of her demanding he fuck her harder made his head feel as though it were going to explode. And if he was lucky, he might get fifty more years of this with her. A purr tangled with a groan in his throat. "You make me crazy."

"*I* make *you* crazy? Do I need to mention we're in an *alley* again?" She laughed, and it made the soft skin of her belly quiver against his. His breath hissed out.

He rotated his hips against her, and she shivered. The urge to finish the mating swamped him. To bite her. To make her his forever. Mate.

"No mating. No biting." She pressed her lips to his before he could take what he wanted. Her tongue twined with his, and their kiss was as harsh and demanding as their coupling had been.

He drove into her soft, willing body until she strained against him, until all he could think about was the orgasm just beyond his grasp. Fire crawled over his skin, settling deep inside him. The muscles in his belly tightened as the need to come overtook him. When she pulled her mouth free, her cries of passion rang in his ears, spurring him on. She twisted in his arms, sobbing as her pussy milked the length of his cock. A harsh groan burst from his throat as he froze, every muscle in his body locking as he jetted deep inside her.

They clung to each other in the aftermath of orgasm, their breathing nothing more than rasps of air. The instinct to finish the mating still clawed at him, but he forced himself to ignore it, to savor the feel of her in his arms. His mate. Unclaimed, but his.

She stirred against him, pushing at his shoulders. They both groaned when he pulled out of her. Her muscles clenched around his dick in one last spasm, and he fought the urge to shove back into her, to thrust his cock deep and sink his fangs in her flesh until she knew she could never be parted from him.

Dropping her feet to the ground, she slid out of his embrace and stepped away from him. She smoothed her dress down around her thighs, not looking at him. "I don't even know your name."

"Antonio." He stepped in front of her, silently demanding she acknowledge him, what they had experienced together this wild night. "I am Antonio Cruz."

"Cruz?" The color leeched from her lovely face. "Esteban Cruz's heir?"

Arching a brow at her reaction to his name, he shook his head. "Not heir. My father died last month."

"Ah." Her shoulders drew into a tense line. Obviously, his father had made no friend with this woman. "I'm afraid I don't keep up with Pride politics."

"You weren't at the loyalty ceremony. I would have remembered you." He might not have been able to resist taking her then and there. His cock swelled again.

Her arms folded protectively around her waist. "I'm not a member of your Pride."

"Which one, then?" Once they were mated, she would have to leave her current Pride to join his. Unless she was a Pride leader herself. Then, well, things would get complicated. But the only Pride in the world with a female leader right now was in Australia . . . and she was well into her fifties. Definitely not his mate.

"None of them." She lifted one shoulder and let it drop.

"No Panther is without a Pride." It just wasn't done. They found strength in numbers. Without the Prides, they had to hide who they were from everyone, and in cat form were the prey to any human with a gun.

"This one is." She turned away, ghosting down the alley.

"Wait." He took a step after her, confusion flooding him at this new turn of events. "Why?"

She didn't turn around, just paused for the briefest of moments. "Why no Pride? I was part of your father's Pride, but I left when I came of age." Bitterness edged her soft voice. "Or I was invited to leave."

He had no doubts about his father's ruthlessness and need to control everything and everyone around him—including his heir—but the more members a Pride had, the more prestige for the Pride. Bigger was better. "My father wouldn't do that."

"Even to a non-shifter?"

His mouth opened and then snapped closed as shock rocked through him. He watched her slip away, disappearing into the cool mist of the San Francisco night.

"*Dios mio.*" Nausea fisted his gut. A non-shifter. A Panther shifter unable to change forms. They were second-class citizens in the Prides, treated as nothing. Less than nothing, depending on the Pride leader's attitude toward them. So much of what made a Panther a Panther remained a mystery, including what made a non-shifter unable to change forms. Some of the older, more superstitious Panthers thought non-shifters were a curse upon a Pride.

Scientists believed that panthers were any large cat that was black, usually a genetic mutation of a leopard or jaguar. The average human thought panthers were a separate species all to themselves. The average human was much closer to the truth than they knew. While leopards and jaguars *could* be all black, a true Panther was a shapeshifter able to transform between animal and human forms. Some thought it was a demonic curse, others thought it was a blessing from a benevolent god. The truth of their magic had been lost long ago. Now it didn't matter why—they just needed to survive.

Contrary to popular legend, a wereanimal's bite wouldn't turn someone into a shapeshifter. If only it were so simple to keep the population alive. Panthers had to breed in their animal form, and humans couldn't be turned into Panthers. Survival was a constant struggle. It might be easier if they could breed without being mated, but they couldn't. Panther children were rare and highly prized. That the Cruz family had *four* children was almost unheard of among the Prides. If anything, one or two was much more normal.

The Ruiz family was another with exceptionally high breeding rates—and the Ruiz boys' actions toward his mate made sudden, sickening sense. She must have come and gone in his

Pride while he'd been fostering in South America. With his very conservative father as a Pride leader, he didn't even want to imagine what she must have been through. And what more would she have to go through now that he had discovered what she was to him?

He swallowed. His mate couldn't shift, couldn't have children. And he was the Pride leader. God help him.

What the hell was he going to do?